HOMICIDE IS HAVING
A FIELD DAY.

Business is picking up for Lt. Mendoza and his men in the Robbery and Homicide Division, L.A.P.D. A diplomat's daughter is missing. An old woman is brutally murdered. And a shocking double suicide follows as a chaser. A stash of drugs is uncovered. A cop is shot without a motive. An anonymous tip points to an impending killing. As the bodies of homicide victims pile up all over town, Lt. Mendoza and his men sharpen their crime-solving skills on the razor-edge of danger.

FELONY AT RANDOM

DELL SHANNON

*This low-priced Bantam Book
has been completely reset in a type face
designed for easy reading and was printed
from new plates. It contains the complete
text of the original hard-cover edition.*
NOT ONE WORD HAS BEEN OMITTED.

FELONY AT RANDOM
*A Bantam Book / published by arrangement with
William Morrow and Company, Inc.*

PRINTING HISTORY
*William Morrow edition published April 1979
Mystery Guild edition June 1979
Bantam edition / July 1980*

ISBN 0-553-13954-1

Published simultaneously in the United States and Canada

Bantam Books are published by Bantam Books, Inc. Its trademark, consisting of the words "Bantam Books" and the por-
trayal of a bantam, is Registered in U.S. Patent and Trademark
Office and in other countries. Marca Registrada. Bantam
Books, Inc., 666 Fifth Avenue, New York, New York 10019.

PRINTED IN THE UNITED STATES OF AMERICA

0 9 8 7 6 5 4 3 2 1

For Mary Allison
Old Friends Gold,
New Friends Silver
All Much Worth Having

Human reason is like a drunken man on horseback; set it up on one side, and it tumbles over on the other.

—MARTIN LUTHER

1

URBANELY, THE PROSECUTING ATTORNEY STOOD UP for brief cross-examination. He was a spare middle-aged man with an unexpectedly musical voice. "When this oral confession to the crime was made, Sergeant Palliser, you were alone with the defendant?"

"Yes, sir," said Palliser.

"But the confession was repeated in your presence and that of another officer?"

"Yes, sir, before Detective Landers and myself."

"How much later?"

"Approximately ten minutes."

"I see. And you then informed the defendant of his rights before formally arresting him?"

"Yes, sir."

"Thank you." The prosecuting attorney sat down. The judge looked at the clock and then at the attorney for the defense.

"Mr. Gilbert, is it your intention to call any other witnesses?"

The defense attorney half rose courteously. "No, your honor."

"Then I think we will adjourn for the day, and begin to take the closing presentations tomorrow. Court stands adjourned."

Palliser left the stand and went down the aisle to rejoin Mendoza in the second row of wooden chairs. There was a little stir as the judge disappeared into his chambers; a bailiff approached the defendant, who was slouched at the table beside his attorney. The defendant was a tall, thin medium-black man, seemingly uninterested in the proceedings.

"And that," said Palliser disgustedly, "will drag it

on until next week, for God's sake. Tomorrow being Friday, there's not a chance it'll go to the jury until Monday at least, and how long the jury might take on it—"

"*Tenga paciencia*," said Mendoza, cynically amused. "And nice if we could all work a five-hour day, John." It was barely four o'clock. He stood up; at this hour there was a blue shadow of beard showing on his long jaw, but the silver-gray Dacron suit, snowy shirt and discreet dark tie were as impeccable as usual. "After seven months, what's another few days?"

Palliser growled. "Taxpayers' money. Still two hours to the end of our shift, I suppose we'd better go back and see what's happening."

Mendoza's eyes followed the defendant being shepherded jailward by the bailiff. He was looking amused and annoyed at once. "Yes," he said. "The mills of the gods have nothing on our courts." They started up for the double doors.

It had been seven months since Steve Smith had been arrested and charged with the rape and murder of Sandra Mosely. The D.A.'s office hadn't gone for a plea bargain, evidently wanting to see a dangerous killer get more than token punishment. At the first trial, four months ago, one of the jurors had had a slight heart attack, nullifying all the proceedings up to then. This trial had got under way last Friday, and with the judge not convening court until eleven A.M. two days this week, now it was bound to go over at least to next Monday before going to the jury.

Palliser was still muttering as they got into his car and started back the few blocks to Parker Center. Mendoza sat back and lit a philosophic cigarette. It was the last day of July, and as usual in Los Angeles very hot; with daylight saving, really only the middle of the afternoon, the heat seemed to shimmer visibly off the concrete below and above and on all sides.

At the tall bulk of the police headquarters building they went gratefully back into chill central air conditioning, and rode the elevator up to the Robbery-Homicide office. Sergeant Lake was slouched at the switchboard in the anteroom reading a paperback;

2

only Jason Grace was in, hunched over his typewriter in the communal office.

"What's going on?" he echoed Mendoza's query. "What ever does go on but the same routine? There's a new body—man dropped dead in front of the Greyhound bus station. Probably heatstroke or heart attack. Tom went out to break the news to his wife—there was I.D. on him. George and Nick picked up one of the possible heisters, talking to him now. I don't know where Glasser and Conway are." He yawned and brought out a cigarette; his straight-featured chocolate-brown face, with its line of moustache as precise as Mendoza's, looked morose. "Thank God, only three weeks more and I go off on vacation."

Palliser sat down at his desk; there was a report centered on the blotter. He scanned it rapidly and said, "Well, there you are—another handful of nothing. That market clerk came in to make a statement— here's Tom's report—and he gives us just what the other three victims did. Male Caucasian, in the twenties, five ten to six feet, and the same M.O. Handwritten note, *Give me all your money*. And a gun. Nobody can say what kind or even how big. Just a gun. What the hell are we supposed to do with that?"

"We are so often asked to make bricks without straw," said Mendoza. He sat down at Hackett's desk —this was Hackett's day off—and contemplated the desk calendar idly. The doctor had said, and Alison had said, the last week of July; but as of this morning Alison had still been bulging uncomfortably with James-or-Luisa, and very volubly tired of it. In the last month, she'd been bulging sufficiently that she couldn't fit behind the wheel of the car to drive, and all the running around and overseeing the work on remodeling her old *estancia* had come to a halt—probably, he reflected with a grin, to the relief of the various workmen involved.

George Higgins and Nick Galeano emerged from one of the interrogation rooms down the hall with a shambling, big black fellow. He shambled right on out, and Higgins and Galeano came into the office looking disgruntled. "Up in the air?" asked Palliser.

"As usual," said Higgins sourly. The note-wielding heister wasn't the only one they were looking for; they had vague descriptions on three others, and at the usual legwork, in the merciless heat, were hunting the possible suspects out of Records and leaning on them, without result up to now. "No alibi, but no evidence either."

Tom Landers came trailing in, looking very hot and tired; his perennially youthful face was drawn, his tie pulled loose, and he was shedding his jacket as he came in. "Why anybody lives in this climate— That poor devil was in the sixties, and too fat—should've had better sense than to walk eight blocks to a market in the middle of the day. When I finally got hold of his wife, I thought she was going to have a heart attack too. I ended up calling the paramedics for her. What a life! And now I've got to write a report on it."

"Oh, there you are," said Lake to Mendoza, looking in. "I buzzed your office awhile. Carey's on the way up to see you."

"*Caray*," said Mendoza, mildly annoyed. Lieutenant Carey of Missing Persons had in the past handed them some difficult problems. But he might have expected something of the sort; aside from the various heisters, and unusually for midsummer, business had been slow the last couple of weeks, and they were overdue for new problems. He went down the hall to his office and swiveled the desk chair around to the familiar view over the Hollywood hills; today there was smog and heat haze obscuring them grayly.

A minute later Carey bustled in looking harassed. "We don't know that this is anything for you at all, Mendoza, but I thought you'd better hear about it in case it turns out to be. It's—"

"You're always so thorough," said Mendoza. "Sit down and relax. Who haven't you got now?"

Carey sat down but his restless energy kept him fidgeting in his chair. His blunt bulldog face wore a reproachful look. "It's nothing to joke about, damn it. I mean, an eight-year-old kid—a girl—and the probability is it's a snatch, the Feds think so, but it could be something else. We've been scouring the area since

4

noon, and nothing's showed, but it could be some nut got her into a car and took her right out of the area. If that's what happened, she ought to show up somewhere, sometime—all too likely dead. I just thought—but the Feds just came in, and they think it's a snatch."

"So let's wait and see."

"I just thought I'd brief you," said Carey. "I've got a feeling about it—no snatch. I just don't see how anybody could have pulled one. I think it was just some freak—um—seizing the opportunity, if you get me. Because the County Museum—a bunch of kids from a Catholic school, couple of nuns leading 'em around—and only a few people knew this McCauley kid was going with them—"

"The County Museum?" said Mendoza, faintly intrigued.

"That's right. They—"

"But school is out. Public or parochial."

"This is a boarding school—I gather pretty swank and expensive—place called St. Odile's. Brentwood Estates. Evidently—I haven't got the details on that, it didn't enter in—some of the girls stay there all summer. The McCauley girl's father lives here—Bel Air—he's something to do with an oil company—"

"Money."

"Oh, very definitely, by the look of him—he's been out all day helping us hunt, all broken up. Anyway, the girl was living at home for the summer, but she wanted to go on this trip to the museum, so he drove her up to the school this morning. There were about fifteen kids with the two nuns. And the hell of it is, nobody can say exactly where she disappeared from—just somewhere in the Museum of Natural History, and you know that place—oh, well, there are five or six big halls, not all that well lighted. The kids were supposed to stay together, but they straggled. When the nuns counted heads outside the building—that was about eleven-thirty—Joyce McCauley was missing. They hunted for her for a while before they finally called McCauley, and he called us."

"And now, going by the rules, you bring the Feds

in, and they're telling you to wait and see if a ransom note shows up."

"That's just what. And I don't know, Mendoza, but I've got the feeling—just some nut spotting her, trailing after the other kids, and grabbing her. She's a pretty little kid, blonde."

"In a public building? She's eight? She'd have fought him, made some noise. A thing like that'd have been noticed."

"You think so? That damned place is like a morgue," said Carey. "No, like a church in the middle of the week. Hardly anybody there—great big rooms and dim lights—and echoes. There's an attendant at the entrance to confiscate cameras, but he doesn't pay any attention to people leaving. And whether she was grabbed by a pervert or somebody thinking of ransom, the same thing applies. I don't know, Mendoza—" Carey shrugged and got up. "We've beaten the grounds all afternoon, she's not there. But if she turns up somewhere raped and dead it'll be your baby."

"So I can hope the ransom note shows up instead?" Mendoza grimaced. Inevitably his mind slid back to that time when they'd waited for a ransom note, the twins missing; he spared a moment's sympathy for the McCauleys. "You'll let me know."

"One way or other," nodded Carey, and went out.

Mendoza contemplated the hazy hills and yawned. Why did anybody stay in this climate? Quite a lot of people had jobs here they couldn't leave; but he could. They could leave everything and go north quite a long way, to somewhere where it never got over sixty degrees. Only there was Alison's grand old Spanish mansion getting refurbished, and the ten-thousand-dollar fence around the four and a half acres, and the projected ponies for the twins, and Alison's lately acquired new retainers, Ken and Kate Kearney, who would live on the premises and look after the livestock and help with the house. Involved was the word, thought Mendoza; before he knew it, his red-haired Scots-Irish girl would have him master of a feudal household; God knew what she'd find to do next.

He heard the other men talking back and forth out

6

there, languidly discussing the heisters, the latest body. It was half past five. He got up, picked up his hat, and went out. Tomorrow would also be a day.

Three minutes after he'd left, Sergeant Lake hurried down the hall. "Boss gone?"

"Just now, why?" asked Higgins.

"Damn—I'll see if the desk can catch him—" But the desk sergeant downstairs said Lieutenant Mendoza had left a couple of minutes ago. "Well," said Lake resignedly, "I suppose he'll find out about it when he gets home."

Mendoza turned the Ferrari onto Rayo Grande Avenue off Laurel Canyon at quarter past six, and swung into the drive, automatically watching for cats. Alison's Facel-Vega was missing from the garage, but Máiri MacTaggart had been driving it occasionally to keep the battery up. However, at this time of day—

"Lieutenant Mendoza! I've been watching for you— They just left! Just half an hour ago! Mrs. MacTaggart—"

"Daddy, Daddy, *Mamacíta's* gone to get James-or-Luisa!" "Daddy, when are we gonna get James-or-Luisa? Mama said—"

Three excited people came running across the lawn from the house next door, Mrs. Fletcher the neighbor on that side, and the twins. The twins, who would turn five in another month, easily outdistanced fat, red-faced Mrs. Fletcher.

"Daddy, *when* are we gonna get—" "Daddy, where's James-or-Luisa comin' from? How long—"

"Quiet, *niños*—*¡vaya despacio!* They—"

"Just left, half an hour ago," panted Mrs. Fletcher, nodding excitedly. "The pains were seven minutes apart and Mrs. MacTaggart said they were going to the hospital and no waiting around for the doctor, he was out of his office. And I'm only too glad to look after Johnny and Terry, and oh, I do hope Mrs. Mendoza will be all right—you'll want to get there as soon as—"

"Yes, thanks very much." Mendoza squatted before the twins. "Now, *niños,* you be good. Máiri'll be home soon to get your supper—I don't know when Mama'll

7

be home, Terry—" He dived back into the Ferrari and slid down the drive; in the street, away from possible cats, he stepped on the accelerator and, turning onto Laurel Canyon Boulevard, reached to switch on the siren.

At the Hollywood Hospital, up in Obstetrics, he found Máiri MacTaggart sitting composedly in a comfortable waiting room, every silver curl in place, while a distracted-looking man paced the floor and another sat opposite, head in hands. "There you are then," she said cheerfully. "I did call your office after I found that misbegotten doctor wasn't in. But it'll not be long to wait, this one has a mind of its own."

"How do you make that out?" asked Mendoza. "I suppose there's a doctor with her now?"

"I would suppose so," said Máiri, "though I'm not that confident of hospitals myself, I'd put more trust in that old war-horse of a nurse got her settled in bed. Why, the way it's acted so obstinate all along—it should have come last week—and then making up its mind to come so sudden. Up to half past three she was fine, only complaining something fierce about being short of breath and feeling like the fat lady in a circus, and I give you my solemn word she'd only just said to me, 'I don't think it'll ever come,' when the bairn kicked her a good one and the pains started right off. Seven minutes apart in less than an hour, and I wasn't about to dither around trying to get that doctor. We're going to have a lively time with this one, it'll be obstinate and contrary as its mother."

Mendoza burst out laughing. "All the same, I'd like to know what's going on."

"You'd best tell them at the nurses' desk that you're here, so they'll let you know. And I'd best be getting home to the twins." She stood up and cocked her head at him fondly. "Don't fret about Alison—she'll be fine. You call me as soon as it gets here."

He promised, and went out with her to tell somebody whose husband he was. "Oh, yes, the new one in nine-eleven," said a blonde nurse brightly. Mendoza didn't think much more of hospitals than Máiri did. He

8

went back to the waiting room, where the two distract-
ed young men were muttering at each other; it appeared that this was a first-time round for both of
them. "She's been in there since eight this morning,"
said one of them. "It can't be much longer, can it?"

"I don't know—I've been here since noon," said the
other one; his eyes looked wild.

Mendoza lit a cigarette and hope Máiri was right.
This one had been a good deal more trouble than the
twins, what with the unexpected morning sickness;
having exhibited the obstinacy in refusing to arrive on
time, it might now decide to cause more trouble. Half
an hour later he went out in search of somebody to
answer questions, but nobody seemed to know anything. The only reading matter in the waiting room was
a stack of old *National Geographic*s. He lit another
cigarette from the stub of his latest one and tried to do
some constructive thinking on the note-wielding heist
man. That was the fourth job he'd pulled, and it was
just a little offbeat; nobody had heard him say one
word yet.

There weren't any unsolved homicides on hand,
which was very unusual for the middle of a heat wave.
Bodies: but just natural deaths, suicides, overdoses,
or simple homicides with the X's known: just paper
work to do. The calm before the storm, very likely; it
wouldn't go on like this. The heat wave would be with
them for another two months at least, and normally the
homicide rate climbed as the temperature climbed.

He lit another cigarette and looked at his watch: five
of eight. He realized he was starving. He thought about
that damned trial; speedy justice, hah. This was the
second time those witnesses had had to be brought all
the way from Fresno, and of course seven months after
the murder the victim had faded into limbo. Juries
could be funny. It was all very straightforward evidence; but, of course, even if he got life, he'd be
eligible for parole in seven years. Only the people of
California had voted in a return to the death penalty;
the politicians were still managing to stall on that.

He had just looked at his watch again to find that it

was nearly half past eight when a grim-faced nurse looked in and said, "Mr. Mendoza?"

"Yes." He got up.

"You have a little girl and your wife's fine. You may see her in just a few minutes."

One of the other men let out an anguished howl. "That's not fair!"

"He just got here!" said the other one aggrievedly.

"Well, when you finally decided to do it, at least you didn't waste any time, *amada.*"

Alison looked tired but very self-satisfied; she peered down her length in the hospital bed and said, "Thank God, I can see my feet again. I had the most awful premonition, Luis—just getting bigger and bigger the last month—that it was another set of twins—"

"*¡Dios me libre!*"

"Exactly," said Alison. "At least we've been spared that. Did they let you see her?"

"*¡Cómo no!*" said Mendoza. "Don't worry about it, *cara*—doubtless she'll improve in looks. I suppose she'll grow hair sometime."

"Just because the twins were born with hair—" Alison squinted up at him indignantly. "She's a beautiful baby. Only it strikes me as very odd that she weighed only six and a half pounds, the size I was." The door opened and she sat up looking pleased. "Food —I'm starving to death. And I'll bet you are too—you go home and let Máiri feed you, darling."

After he'd had something to eat he called Hackett, and then Piggott and Bob Schenke sitting on night watch. Hackett, of course, called Higgins, who called Mendoza to hear the details. Higgins was belatedly interested in babies; since taking on Bert Dwyer's widow and two kids, he and Mary had had one of their own, his darling Margaret Emily. "I'll bet she's a cute one," he said to Mendoza. "Luisa what?"

"Luisa Mary. She's bald as an egg and the way she was yelling I'd take a bet she's got the hell of a temper."

"Now, Luis," said Higgins, amused.

"And I was just talking to Matt. I knew it was too good to be true—they'd just got a call to a new homicide. Three bodies. I don't know any details."

"So here we go again," said Higgins.

On Friday morning, with Henry Glasser off, they took a preliminary look at the new homicide: Piggott had left a first report on Mendoza's desk. Palliser and Landers drifted in late and offered congratulations on the new arrival; Jason Grace, down the hall at the coffee machine, said indignantly, "Nobody told me— the baby's here? Which? When? Ah, that's good news —glad to hear it." If his tone was a little wistful, nobody commented; he and Virginia had another application in at the County Adoption Service, hadn't heard anything yet.

Conway and Galeano had gone out on the heisters before anybody else came in, and their policewoman Wanda Larsen was off on vacation.

The new homicide just looked messy. It was at an old apartment on Benton, in the Westlake area: reported by a Miss Betty Bernard, and they hadn't been able to question her much. She said she'd come to see her sister, that was how she found the bodies, the door was unlocked. Her sister was one of the corpses, a Mrs. Tammy Coburn. The second one was Mrs. Coburn's three-year-old, and the third she identified as Jerry Lambert. That was about all Schenke and Piggott had got. They'd brought a lab team out for pictures, called the morgue wagon, and left it for the day watch. All three corpses apparently had been beaten to death, but the autopsies would say definitely.

"I suppose," said Hackett, "we'd better go and poke around at it." He'd been reading Piggott's report; he took off his glasses and folded them away—he was used to them now. Higgins stood up with him, the two big men looming over Mendoza, and they started out reluctantly; at an old apartment on Benton there wouldn't be any air conditioning. As they went, Higgins was asking Hackett, "Angel found anything yet? Well, neither has Mary. The prices—"

"And the taxes," said Hackett. They were both, of

11

reluctantly admitted necessity, hunting new residences. Highland Park, where the Hacketts lived, and the Silver Lake area where the Higginses lived, had suffered a drastic upswing in the crime rate—both a little too close to the inner city. No place these days, said Higgins, to raise an innocent child; Margaret Emily was nearly two. And the Hacketts had suffered vandalism to yard and house, but when Hackett's Barracuda had been hot-wired out of its own garage in the middle of the afternoon, Hackett had had enough. It had turned up three days later, a total loss, down toward Long Beach, and Hackett was driving his wife's old Cadillac until the insurance came through. These days Angel and Mary were house hunting for something farther out of town, hopefully, where prices and taxes might be slightly less. And if it would mean extra miles of driving to work, that was how it would have to be.

Conway and Galeano came in at nine-thirty with one of the possible suspects, and Grace told them about Luisa Mary; they left the suspect waiting to look in and congratulate Mendoza. "Give either of you old bachelors the incentive to find a nice girl?" asked Mendoza.

Conway's cynical gray eyes twinkled. "Who're you miscalling? I'm only thirty-two. And Nick's found one, only he hasn't persuaded her yet."

"Give me time," said Galeano mildly. Mendoza wondered how he was doing with that prickly German girl, out of that queer homicide case just after Christmas. Looking at stocky, dark Galeano, he reflected it was about the unlikeliest match he could think of: a good man, Galeano, but no movie star. The girl was ten years younger. But the unlikeliest people did take to each other. He grinned suddenly and muttered to himslf, *"Eso se sobrentiende."* A lot of people might think the Mendozas were an unlikely pair too.

"This Fernandez looks very possible for the pharmacy heist," said Conway. "The right pedigree, and he matches the description, such as it was. We're arguing if we've got enough cause for a search warrant—if we could locate the gun, he took a shot at the clerk and we've got the slug to match up."

"Have a try for it—a judge can only turn you down." Mendoza leaned back in his swiveled-around chair and reflected that he ought to buy Alison a present for producing Luisa Mary—even a bald, yelling Luisa Mary. He was debating the merits of an emerald ring—but she had three—as against, maybe, a diamond-accented watch— But they didn't really go out socially all that much, and she'd probably prefer something to add to her new old *estancia*. She'd said something about statuary—something unusual, for the square courtyard in front. He had only a vague idea where he might find such a thing. There were art galleries out on Sunset—somebody there might know where statuary was available.

The phone buzzed at him and he picked it up. "Yes, Jimmy."

"You've got a new homicide," said Lake. "Geneva Street. The squad just called."

"O.K.," said Mendoza, and got up, yanking down his cuffs. In the outer office, Grace sat alone over a report; Conway and Galeano would have the suspect in an interrogation room. "Business picking up, Jase. Come on." Grace got up with alacrity.

"We might as well shove all these heists in Pending, you know. There's no smell of a lead on any of them."

They took the Ferrari. The address was across the inner city; it was, when they came to it, a little backwater. A short block, no more than six houses on each side. This had been a quiet, even a pretty little block years ago. The houses were all neat frame houses except for one small stucco at the end of the block. They sat on standard city lots, fifty-foot frontages. By the vestiges left, you could see that once front yards had been tended carefully, watered and maintained; old grown-up shrubbery climbed up housefronts and in side yards. But while front lawns were mostly shorn, they were browning now: the water bills too high to allow for lawn water. And perhaps as former owners, who took pride in the little houses, had died or moved away, bushes had gone untrimmed, weeds unpulled; as the prices for all products and services had climbed, houses had gone unpainted, cracked windows unfixed. It was now a block of down-at-heel houses, forlorn and shabby houses; and with the inner city all around, main thoroughfares only a few blocks away, it was still a quiet backwater.

The black and white was sitting in front of a house on the left side about the middle of the block, and the uniformed officer was talking with a civilian on the sidewalk. Mendoza parked at the curb opposite and they walked across the narrow street. There were people out here and there, staring curiously at the squad car: a short fat woman in yellow shorts in the front yard next door, a couple of other women on the other side of the street.

"Here are the detectives, Mr. Purdy." Patrolman Morales nodded at them. "Looks like a break-in, Lieutenant. Sometime last night. This is Mr. Ronald Purdy, he called in on it. Lieutenant Mendoza, Detective Grace, Mr. Purdy."

The civilian nodded docilely. He was an elderly man, middling tall and spare of frame, with thin gray hair carefully combed over a narrow skull. He was neatly dressed in a very shabby gray suit of a cut long out of fashion, and though the temperature must be in the nineties, he wore a white shirt buttoned up and a narrow dark tie. He had a thin, intelligent face with rather sunken, dark eyes, a high-bridged nose. He said in a quiet voice, "I saw the door was open, you see. Pearl wasn't an early riser, and even if she was up she wouldn't leave the door open—the screen door fell to pieces last year and she couldn't afford a new one."

Mendoza glanced at Morales, who spread his hands and said, *"Muerta."*

"You knew the woman here?"

Purdy nodded. He looked suddenly very old and tired. "Excuse me, could I sit down? I'm afraid this has —" Morales eased him into the front seat of the squad car. "Thank you. Yes, she was Mrs. Pearl Davidson. There are some of us left here who've lived along here for many years—my wife and I, of course Meg's been gone for five years. I live in the stucco house up there. We'd lived here since just before the second war. And the Burdines up the block, Guy and June—oh, they'll feel this very much, a terrible thing —and Mrs. Fogel, Martha Fogel— We all know each other well—all moved here at about the same time. Pearl was a close friend of my wife's. Well, we are all all friends."

"Mrs. Davidson lived alone?"

"Oh, yes. Dick died nearly ten years ago. Pearl was nearly eighty, and a little deaf, of course. I—you see, it's a habit of mine to get up early, and when it's so hot it's the only time really to do any yard work. I have a little garden in back. And about an hour ago, I suppose, I went up to the drugstore on Virgil for a newspaper. It was when I was walking back I noticed Pearl's door open, and—went to look. When she didn't answer me—" He stopped abruptly. The hand he raised to his forehead was shaking. He was older than Mendoza had judged at first glance; he couldn't be far off eighty himself.

"Take it easy, sir," said Morales gently.

"Of course it was a shock," said Purdy. "Someone I'd known so long. How time slides by, you know— one day you realize— Never much change along here, oh, some, of course, but— The Davidsons, and Meg and I, and the Fogels, and the Burdines, and the Millets, and the Hallams, we all bought our hourses at around the same time—over forty years ago, it is now. Knowing each other that long—neighbors, friends. Of course it was a shock."

They left him sitting in the squad car and climbed the sagging steps to the front porch. The house had been painted yellow with white trim a long time ago; on the narrow porch were two rickety old wicker chairs. This would have been a block where people sat on front porches on quiet summer evenings. There wasn't a screen door. The wooden front door was wide open; it had been forced, apparently; there were a

15

couple of gouges on the jamb. But it was an old door, and warped; it wouldn't have taken much force to break in.

Beyond the door was a rather small living room, long and narrow. It was in a little mess: the drawer of a table pulled out, chair cushions on the floor. Somebody had ransacked here for any little loot easily found. The furniture was old, the upholstery shabby and worn: conventional furniture dating from the thirties, but once solid and good.

They passed through a small square dining room to a narrow hall, and on the right to an even smaller square kitchen. She was there, on the floor. She had been a thin, scraggly old lady, with sparse gray hair and no eyebrows. She was wearing an old cotton housecoat, originally a gay, blue-and-pink print, zipped modestly up the front; but as she had fallen it had pulled up over her knees, and beneath it she had on a white cotton nightdress. There was an old felt slipper on one foot; the other had fallen off and lay beside her. She was wearing a hearing aid. And she had been garroted: what looked like a thin tough cord was around her throat, partly embedded in the flesh. Her eyes were wide open, giving her an expression of astonishment—that might, of course, have been her last emotion.

The kitchen was clean and neat: an old gas stove, an old refrigerator, worn linoleum on the floor. There were two tumblers standing on one counter, clean and dry. There was a little service porch beyond the kitchen, a solid wood back door locked, with a chain up: probably a screen door beyond that, but they didn't look, pending the lab men's meticulous investigation.

"She was out here," said Grace, "getting a drink of water or something, when he broke in—and Purdy says she was deaf, even with the hearing aid maybe she never heard him. Just a little funny he tried the front door instead of the back?"

"*Pues si,*" said Mendoza. "The back door looks a good deal tougher to force. And there's only a couple of streetlights out there, Jase. Funny place to break in,

16

you'd think anybody'd realize not much loot to be had here. But we're never dealing with the cunning master criminals out of fiction, are we? It's always these little poor people in the high-crime areas who get it."

They went from the kitchen across the dining room to two small bedrooms on the other side of the house, a bathroom between. The dressers in both bedrooms had the drawers pulled out, contents scattered; the threadbare rug in the front bedroom had been turned back. "A halfway pro," said Grace. "He knew that's a favorite place for silly people to hide cash." A couple of pictures had been yanked off the wall: another favorite place. The little bathroom looked untouched. Mendoza used his pen to hook open the medicine chest, and it was all but bare: aspirin, antacid, non-prescriptive vitamins.

"See what the lab turns," said Grace. "But, you know—" he sniffed and rubbed his moustache back and forth.

"Oh, yes," said Mendoza. "Yes, indeed, Jase. The garrote. He broke in just looking for whatever there was—and I somehow doubt, in this neighborhood, that the rumor had got around that Pearl Davidson was a miser sitting on a fortune in cash. Though you never know. And he evidently didn't care whether anyone was at home or not. Maybe he knew who lived here, maybe not—maybe if he did he thought she wouldn't hear him, being deaf—but he didn't hesitate to use the garrote. Did he bring it with him just in case? She couldn't have put up much of a fight."

"Not just," said Grace, "the run-of-the-mill breaker-in. Turn the lab loose and see what shows."

They went back to the squad car and Mendoza asked Purdy whether there had been any rumor about Mrs. Davidson having anything of value in the house. "Old people living alone, sometimes the talk goes round, usually based on nothing, I know."

Purdy looked astonished. "Oh, no," he said flatly. "She had nothing. The Social Security—what's that? In inflated dollars, not much. Dick had a little pension from the railroad. She'd have had about four hundred a month to live on, all told. But less than that to spend, because the taxes have gone up so much. All of us have to save all year to pay those. But the house was paid for, you see. She never kept much cash in the house. And after she'd bought just the necessary groceries, there wouldn't have been much left."

They called up the lab team, and took Purdy back to headquarters to make a formal statement. Hopefully the lab would give them something useful, either known latent prints or something on the rope used as a garrote.

At twelve-thirty Mendoza turned the Ferrari into the drive of the house on Rayo Grande Avenue, and Máiri MacTaggart looked at him in surprise as he came into the kitchen.

"And what in the name of guidness are you doing here at this time of day?"

"I can't think what to get her," said Mendoza. "I suppose I ought to get her something, Máiri. Has she said anything to you—anything she wants specially?"

"Well, I'd have to think. I don't know that she has."

"She said something about statuary for the yard."

"Och, yes. A statue of Saint Francis she wants. On account of the animals."

"Well, I'll have a look around." Animals you could say: three of the cats, Bast, Sheba and Nefertite, were crunching Friskies on the service porch, El Señor the unpredictable was brooding on top of the refrigerator, and Cedric the Old English sheepdog was in the backyard, barking loudly at the nesting mockingbirds in the elm tree.

The twins, belatedly discovering his arrival, came bursting in. "Daddy, when's Mama comin' home with James-or-Luisa?"

"Luisa Mary, niña. Next week."

"I wanta see James-or-Luisa!" demanded Johnny.

"The baby is just Luisa, lamb," said Máiri. "A sweet little girl, Terry."

"But you kept sayin' the baby's James-or-Luisa,"

said Johnny, bewildered. "That's its name. You *said*."

"Just Luisa, lamb. A little girl."

Terry looked equally bewildered. "But everybody said it's James-or-Luisa—"

Mendoza and Máiri eyed each other and burst out laughing.

2

THE BENTON STREET ADDRESS WAS A FOUR-UNIT APART-ment building, old and run-down. Hackett and Higgins had a casual glance at the apartment where the bodies had been; Scarne and a couple of other lab men were still there dusting for prints and looking at bloodstains. Tammy Coburn had not, by the evidence, been the world's neatest housekeeper: there were piles of dirty dishes all over the kitchen, the few cheap pieces of furniture were dusty, the double bed unmade with grimy sheets in a tangle.

"By the way," said Scarne, "we found about three ounces of pot in one of the kitchen canisters."

"Interesting," said Hackett.

The owner of the place lived in the other ground-floor unit, Mrs. Sherwood, fiftyish and fat and largely uninterested in the murder. "I had the TV on," she told them, "I didn't hear a thing till that girl come screeching at the door. I don't know nothing about them, the Coburn girl or the fellow. As long as they paid the rent—" she shrugged. "I don't pay attention to tenants much, why should I? This place needs about everything done to it, but taxes like they are I can't afford to fix it up—people take it or leave it, and I leave them be. All I could tell you, they'd been living here about six months."

There was another apartment house at one side,

19

where they drew a blank, and a duplex on the other. There, an elderly woman told them that just as she'd shut the TV off at nine o'clock last night, a car had made an awful noise driving away out in front. "Just like one of them race cars," she said.

The call had gone down at 9:51, and Piggott's report had said that the bodies were still warm. The noisy car might have been X taking off, or not.

They went to find Betty Bernard at an address on Bridge Street in Boyle Heights, and found out a little more about Tammy Coburn. "Nobody had any reason, want to hurt Tammy! Honest, I nearly died! I nearly passed out, see them lying there like that—poor little Teddy—it must've been some real fiend, you know?" She was vapidly pretty, dark and plump; she fell easily into sobs, blew her nose. "Listen, there was just the two of us since Mom got killed in the accident—it was just awful, see Tammy like that. I don't know who'd want to do that to them."

"Was she divorced from the boy's father?" asked Hackett.

"Oh, him. Yeah, a long time back—they got married when they were just kids, and he walked out and she divorced him, I guess. But Teddy wasn't his kid, that was that guy she picked up with awhile after that, Joe something—a real nice guy, only it turned out he was kind of a lush, you know? She finally got fed up, the welfare money for Teddy wasn't all that great she could feed somebody else's habit, she kicked him out."

"What about this Jerry Lambert?" asked Higgins.

"Oh, he was a real nice guy. They'd been together about six months, I guess. Listen, I never had such a shock—nobody'd have any reason to do a thing like that to Tammy or Jerry! What? Oh, he didn't have any folks here, I think he hitched from back east someplace, I don't know where. Iowa or Ohio or someplace like that. Oh, yeah, he had a part-time job at a Shell station on Vermont, I guess it was. See, I been outta work—I just went over to ask if she could let me have ten bucks till I started at Woolworth's next week, and I walk in on that—"

20

"Did you know that either or both of them was using marijuana?"

She stared and shrugged. "What's the matter with pot? A lot of people use a little grass sometimes." Which was unfortunately true. She denied that either of them would have been on the hard stuff or known a dealer. "That stuff costs." She gave them some names. "Bob Blanchard, he was about Jerry's best pal, I guess. And Bernie and Jan Fuller—" Girl friends of Tammy's. She was vague on addresses; probably Tammy had had a telephone pad with their numbers. "But, listen, nobody knew them would do a thing like that! I nearly died when I walked in there—"

"Can we do any speculating, George?" asked Hackett, back in the car.

"I don't feel much like it in this heat," said Higgins. "Small loss. Though a pity about the innocent kid. Wait for the autopsy—it may provide a lead. Meanwhile, I suppose we've got to find some of these people and ask if Tammy or Jerry had given somebody a reason to hold a grudge."

Neither of them was much interested in it, but they were paid to do a job. They started for the Shell station to ask questions about Lambert; maybe after that the lab men would be out of the apartment and they could take a look at Tammy's phone index.

Disappointingly, it turned out that the suspect Fernandez had a solid alibi for that heist—he'd been in the drunk tank on Wednesday night from eight o'clock on. That was the way the ball bounced; they let him go. On Friday morning the pharmacy clerk was coming in at ten-thirty to look at mug shots; the slug had just grazed him, he'd spent the night in the receiving hospital. Galeano waited in for him while Conway went out on the legwork again. There was still a list of possibles from Records.

The clerk, a weedy young fellow, was still mad. "There just wasn't any sense to it!" he kept saying. "I did what he said, I never made a move at him. Am I gonna argue with a gun? 'Open the register,' he says, 'and give me the money,' and that's just what I did, and then he turns around and shoots at me—there just wasn't any sense in it! Why the hell did he do it, anyway?"

There wasn't much use in wondering, of course. Galeano found cute, blonde Phil Landers at her desk in R. and I., and she brought out some books of mug shots. The clerk commenced to look at them, and time passed before he said, "I think that's him. Yeah, that ugly mug I remember—cauliflower ear and crooked nose—that's him all right."

"You're sure?" asked Galeano.

"Sure as I'd ever be of anything."

"So, thanks very much." The mug shot was that of Arthur Banks, a small pedigree of B. and E., one count of armed robbery. He'd be off parole now, by the dates on his record, and the latest address they had listed was Strange Street in east L.A.

The clerk went away and Galeano, finding the office empty, decided to go out to lunch before doing anything about Banks. He drove up Wilshire Boulevard to the place where Marta Fleming worked. It was crowded at that hour, and she was busy, but she flashed him a quick smile as he sat down. She was easier with him now, friendlier; they went out somewhere at least once a week. But the great thing was that he'd finally got her to meet his mother, and the two of them had got thick as thieves. Covertly admiring Marta's tawny-blonde hair and neat curves as she took an order at the next table, Galeano thought that even if he never convinced her to marry a stodgy, unromantic cop, at least his mother had provided her with a kind of substitute family here—her own mother still in Germany.

She came to him at last. "I am sorry, Nick, we are busy."

"So I see. You can bring me the roast beef sandwich and a chocolate malt."

She looked down at him seriously. "Perhaps iced coffee. The malted milk is too rich—you should lose some weight."

22

"Well, you'd think I would, doing the legwork in this heat. All right, iced coffee," said Galeano. He supposed it was a good sign, that she took that much interest in his health.

When Mendoza sauntered into the office at one-thirty, he found it empty except for Hackett and Higgins bent over Hackett's desk studying something.

"*¿Qué occurre, compadres?*"

"Oh, hell, " said Hackett. "I suppose you'll have to see it. And if I know you—a crackpot anonymous letter is all, Luis, not worth wasting time on. Don't build a story on it."

"Funny, but there probably isn't anything in it," agreed Higgins. "We've got enough on our hands to work without reaching for any more, and anything so damned vague—"

"Show!" Mendoza held out is hand.

"The mail room just sent it up. It's nothing. We've been around some on this Coburn girl, and what shows —which isn't much—says that anybody could have done it. She wasn't overburdened with morals or manners, she and the new boyfriend could have taken up with any riffraff, and—Oh, for God's sake, why did we mention it to him, George? He always likes the offbeat things. Not that there's anything to it." Hackett surveyed Mendoza with annoyance.

"But how pretty—I like it," said Mendoza. He smoothed his moustache with one thumbnail absently, while studying the letter.

It was complete with envelope; both were typed. It looked like an old machine; a couple of letters were permanently out of alignment, the ribbon was old and faint. But whoever had typed it had knowledge of spelling and punctuation. The envelope was a cheap one, five-and-dime stationery, but paper and envelope matched. The envelope was just addressed, *L.A. Police Department,* at the correct address. The letter was short and intriguing.

Police: You had better ask questions at the Wilmont drugstore about a girl named Ruth used to work there.

23

*It looks like murder has been done before and now
somebody tried to kill Bill Loring and maybe the girl
too.*

"How very interesting," said Mendoza. "Now, who's
supposed to have been murdered? Ruth? And another
girl—not to mention Bill Loring. I like this."

"Yes, I knew you would," said Hackett. "All the
humdrum, monotonous damned things we get shoved
at us, anything slightly offbeat you always go for. Give
me that thing. Even if there was anything to it, nowhere to go on it. Do you want to hear chapter and
verse on Coburn?"

"Not particularly. Oh, there are places to look on
this. Ruth. *¡Ca!*" Mendoza reread the letter.

"More immediate cases to work," said Hackett.
"Jase was mentioning the new one—the old lady."

"We won't get anything from the lab on that before
tomorrow, if then," said Mendoza absently.

"I don't mind doing the report on Coburn," said
Higgins, and Hackett regarded him bitterly.

"No, of course not. Stay here in the nice air conditioning while I go out again hunting up every piece of
flotsam and jetsam who ever crossed the path of that
amateur hooker or the boyfriend. I don't give a damn
who took them off. Nobody we talked to would admit
seeing them in the last week, and it's all up in the air.
For God's sake, Luis, stop brooding over that thing."

"Mmh, yes, places to ask question," said Mendoza.
He folded the letter and put it back in the envelope,
glanced at his watch. "Forget about Coburn awhile—
something may show from the lab report. So all right,
George, you do the paper work. Art and I will have a
first cast around for Ruth."

Hackett uttered an outraged wail. "There's nothing
in it, Luis! And we've got these heisters—your old
lady—and Saturday night coming up, with the temperature over a hundred—new ones coming along. Why
you have to—"

"*No metan tanta bulla,*" said Mendoza. "Not so
much noise, Arturo. Let's just take a quick look and
see what shows. I've got one stop to make here, and
then we'll see." He took Hackett's arm persuasively.

At Lake's desk, he dropped off the anonymous letter. "Send that down to Questioned Documents, Jimmy. Anything they can tell us about it." Down the hall, they got into the elevator and he pushed the button for the second floor.

"And where are we bound for here?" asked Hackett as the elevator landed.

"Me, feeling sentimental about Luisa Mary maybe," said Mendoza. "I'd just like to hear what might have turned up on Joyce."

"Joyce?"

They went into the anteroom of the Missing Persons office. The switchboard sergeant opened his mouth to greet them, but the inner door to Carey's office was open and he'd seen them come in; he came out to them. "Mendoza—I'm glad to see you. Come in, I'd like you to hear this."

"What?"

"These two nuns are here to make a statement. I still don't like the idea of a snatch." Carey rubbed his jaw. "These damn Feds so single-minded—all they can see."

"No ransom note? It's twenty-four hours."

"That's right. The Feds have got McCauley sitting on a bugged phone at home waiting for the snatcher to call and name a price. And I've still got the gut feeling." He turned abruptly and went back into his office; they followed him.

There was an FBI man sitting on one side of Carey's desk, a tall cadaverous man named Zachary whom Mendoza knew, didn't particularly like. The two nuns sat side-by-side in twin vinyl-upholstered chairs in front of the desk. A silent policewoman sat unobtrusively to one side, pencil poised over a notebook. Mendoza and Hackett stood just inside the door.

"Excuse me, ladies," said Carey. "I'd like these other officers to hear what you have to say. This is Sister Mary Katharine, Sister Mary Constance. Lieutenant Mendoza, Sergeant Hackett." He didn't spook them by adding, Homicide. "We were talking about your school. This St. Odile's. You say it's an old one."

The two nuns, Mendoza observed with pleasure, were wearing the traditional flowing black habits, starched white headdresses. At first glance they might look like twins, both about the same age, in their early forties; but Sister Mary Katharine had a dimple and blue eyes, Sister Mary Constance dark eyes and a crooked eyetooth.

"St. Odile's Convent School was founded nearly sixty years ago," said Sister Mary Constance. "Though what that has to do with Joyce McCauley—I simply cannot take in all this talk about kidnapping. There has never been the slightest hint of such—"

"What I was getting at," said Carey deferentially, "it must be, well, rather expensive, as boarding schools go."

"Yes, indeed," agreed Sister Mary Katharine readily. "We never take over forty or fifty girls, and every care is provided—it's their second home. Most of the girls who come to us go right through, up through high school. We maintain high standards, but aside from that we are *in loco parentis,* as it were, Lieutenant. A good many of our girls come from families with specialized problems."

"Problem kids?" interjected Zachary.

They looked at him, gently surprised. "No, I didn't mean that at all. For example, several of our present girls have fathers in the diplomatic service, who are abroad a good part of the year. Others are from families whose responsibilities require them to travel a good deal. We have three girls now sent to us from abroad to perfect their English. And some from broken homes, where family difficulties—"

"Which is the case with Joyce," said Sister Mary Constance impatiently. "I really don't see how all this applies."

"Well," said Carey hastily, "at any rate, your girls are mostly from wealthy families?" They nodded. "Hasn't the fear of kidnapping ever come up before? I should think at least some of the parents would have been nervous, insisted on security—"

"Oh, but we have," Sister Mary Katharine assured him, "perfect security. Not that any threat has ever

26

arisen, but of course it's only sensible to take precautions. The grounds comprise three acres, and there's a seven-foot wall all around. The gates are locked at sundown every night, and there are two night watchmen."

"All this talk!" said Sister Mary Constance impatiently. "It's Joyce we have to think about! What are you doing to find her? There must be something you can do—" She gripped one wrist tightly with the other hand, bit her lip. "Forgive me—I don't mean to be rude, but—you see, we've had her since she was four, we are all—very fond of the child."

"We don't as a rule take girls that young," explained Sister Mary Katharine, "but Mr. McCauley was desperate, understandably. His wife died when Joyce was born, and all the money in the world can't conjure up paid servants willing or fit to act as substitute parents. He has to travel a great deal for his company, and he hasn't any relatives at all. He knew St. Odile's because his wife had been one of our girls. Before either of us was there, of course—and he simply begged Mother Superior, and finally—"

"Oh, what does it matter now?" said Sister Mary Constance. "What can we do to help find her, Lieutenant? You asked us to come, to make a statement—anything we can do—"

"Yes, well, I'd like to get it clearer in my mind," said Carey, "just exactly in what order things happened yesterday. Now, the school year is over, but you still have some boarders staying on?"

"Yes, and there are summer classes—arts and crafts, and a remedial class for any girls behind in academic work, though most of our girls—they have such a thorough foundation in the basics— Yes. And some of the girls' families live in the area, of course. Yes, four of the senior girls, their fathers are in diplomatic positions in certain places where it would be unsuitable or even dangerous—"

Carey and Zachary looked uncomprehending, and Sister Mary Constance said laconically, "West Africa. Palestine. What is so worrying is that Joyce has always been a delicate child. She has always been asthmatic—

27

she picks up colds so easily. I knew we nearly lost her when she had the whooping cough—and what's happening to her—what could have happened—"

"She wasn't still living at the school?"

"No, no, she nearly always went home to her father on weekends, unless he was away. She'd been living at home since school was out—it's the first summer she had been. We felt now she was older and Mr. McCauley had found a most reliable housekeeper—"

"She knew about the trip to the museum, it was planned before classes ended. She wanted to go. She'd been there several times, we usually take each class at some time during the year, and Joyce loves it. Her father drove her to the convent yesterday morning so she could go with the others. Several of the girls who live here were driven back so they could go too."

"All right." The policewoman had begun to take shorthand notes at Carey's nod. "How many were in the group?"

"Fourteen," said Sister Mary Katharine.

"Fifteen," said Sister Mary Constance. "Paula."

"Oh, yes, of course."

"Paula?"

"One of the older girls—she helps at the school. Odds and ends," said Sister Mary Katharine. "She's so good with the little ones."

"Were all these girls about the same age?"

"Oh, no. As I say, Joyce wasn't the only one who came from home to go with us. Seven little ones—six-and seven-year-olds whose families live here—had come back. The five girls who are staying the summer with us, and they range from nine to thirteen. Then ourselves and Paula."

"I see. Well, when did you get to the museum?"

"It was ten o'clock exactly. Sister Mary Constance is such an expert driver in traffic—we have a very large station wagon, of course. The museum opens at ten, and we had to wait a minute or two. We went into the Museum of Natural History first. The hall with the Indian artifacts and general archaeology exhibits. Then into the next hall with the exhibits of weaving and pottery. We—"

"Excuse me," said Carey, "wouldn't all that be a little over the heads of the six-year-olds?"

"Oh, no, Lieutenant. It's a question of a thorough founding in basics, and awakening the child's natural curiosity. You'd be surprised what intelligent questions they ask. But I know Joyce was with us in both those halls, and definitely in the hall of wildlife. That's always the highlight of a visit to the museum, the children simply love it and they'd stay for hours. I saw Joyce there, with Paula and Dorothy Austin and Peggy Gavin. We had to round them all up—it's the largest room of all—to coax them out of there, we still had to visit the geological exhibits and the rose gardens, and be back at the convent for one o'clock lunch."

"When was the first time you definitely missed her?"

"When we came out of the building to go to the rose gardens. It was a little after eleven-thirty. Naturally we thought she'd strayed back into one of the rooms we'd been in—we looked—Paula looked—everywhere, and she was just gone. She's a responsible child, she knew she was supposed to stay with the group." Sister Mary Katharine's voice was trembling a little. "There was hardly anyone else in the place, on a weekday morning. We couldn't have missed her if she'd been in the building. She wouldn't have got lost—she wouldn't have left the building alone anyway—"

"Shy," said Sister Mary Constance. "Always shy. Little mouse of a child—but very loving and warmhearted. And she had a doctor's appointment at three o'clock. Mr. McCauley was to pick her up at two—another asthma attack last week, and they were going to try some new shots— It's simply silly to talk about kidnapping!"

"I was about to ask you, who knew Joyce was going on the trip to the museum?"

"All of us at the convent. Well, when I say all, I don't suppose Mother Superior knew exactly. It was just a little summer outing. We knew, and the other girls. Mr. McCauley, I suppose whatever servants he has in the house—"

"We'll be talking to that housekeeper," said Zachary, sounding rather sinister.

29

Carey sat silent, and Mendoza seized the chance to get away, standing up. "You'll be in touch," he said to Carey. "I think I'll agree with you, as far as all that goes."

"Wait for it," said Zachary. "Could be they're building suspense before they get in touch."

"Time will probably tell," said Mendoza. But in the corridor, he added to Hackett, "Only will it? If she did get grabbed by the nut and taken right away—but, damn it, Art, how could anybody have smuggled her out of the building without being noticed?"

"Have you ever been there?" asked Hackett.

"Now that I think of it, no. Alison takes the twins, sometimes. There are some stuffed animals they're crazy about."

"The wildlife hall. On a weekday morning it'd be pretty empty. There's only one official entrance, but I seem to remember a couple of exit doors going one way. He could have grabbed her, tapped her on the head to shut her up, picked her up and walked out easy as one-two-three. Even if he passed somebody on the way to his car, who's going to look twice at a father carrying a tired little kid?"

"Not nice," said Mendoza. "But I don't see a kidnapping planned that way. It'd be the hell of a lot too chancy."

"No, it's likelier it was the nut. Just by chance wandering into the museum at the same time—or spotting all the kids in the parking lot and following them in."

"Mmh, yes. Yes, I could see that."

"And if it happened that way, God knows where that poor kid is now. Or if she'll ever turn up. Are you still set on looking at this very wild goose?"

"Just a little look, Art."

There was, at least, a Wilmont Pharmacy, just down from Wilshire on Vermont. It was an independent pharmacy, and rather a classy place, with a line of giftware and expensive cosmetics. There was just one clerk there, a very pretty girl about eighteen, her white

30

uniform showing a lusciously curved figure. She blinked at Mendoza's question.

"A Ruth ever worked here? I wouldn't know. Mr. Snyder would, I guess, but he's out. He had to go to the bank, he just said to have anybody leave prescriptions to pick up later. I'm new, I only started working this week. But I tell you, you might ask at the deli two doors down. It's about the only place to eat on this block, a lot of people who work along here go there."

At the delicatessen, a bright clean little place, the younger of two uniformed females spoke up promptly. "Would that be Ruth Byrd you mean? That's funny— yeah, she used to work at the pharmacy about three years ago. The first time she came in here, we both did a double take, because see, we lived in the same apartment building then, recognized each other from there. Then I got married and moved, I don't know if she still lives there. I guess she quit the pharmacy, I haven't seen her in here in more than two years." She looked at them curiously. "Well, it was the Winterhaven Apartments on Mariposa. Why're you asking about her?"

"Internal Revenue," said Mendoza at random, and they both turned suddenly stony faces on the two men and shut up.

"Couldn't you have thought up a better excuse?" asked Hackett outside. "After all, Luis, it's only a few of the citizenry that hates cops. Nobody likes the revenuers. Where now?"

At the Winterhaven Apartments there was a door marked *Manageress,* but nobody answered the bell. "She probably couldn't tell you anything anyway," said Hackett. None of the name slots above the bank of mailboxes listed a Ruth Byrd. "And do you have any notion how many William Lorings there might be among six million people? Chase down every one and ask if somebody's tried to kill him lately? The letter's from a nut, Luis."

"*Posible,*" said Mendoza. He sounded dissatisfied.

He was sitting at his desk skimming the autopsy report on that teenage O.D. from last week when Duke

31

came in. "I just thought I'd let you know, I don't think we'll give you much on that break-in. We picked up three good latents, not the old lady's, but they're not in our records—I just got the word on that. I've sent 'em on to the Feds, maybe they'll make them. Apart from that, damn all."

"What about the rope used as a garrote?"

"What about it? We could spend time analyzing it, pin down the brand and maker, but why? It's the kind of thin rope used for clothesline, and you can buy any brand of it in ten thousand places. Unless those prints are on file someplace, what it looks to me is the amateur B. and E., the old lady surprised him and he just used too much force. For all you know, he picked the rope up right there—she had the same kind on her clotheslines in the backyard."

"Oh," said Mendoza. "But it was cut to the right length for a garrote, Duke."

"There is that. You're the detective."

Mendoza said, "Thanks for nothing." But when Duke had left, he sat there staring into space for a long moment, thinking back to that little old house, to the kitchen where the corpse of the old woman had lain on the floor. There was something, some little point, nagging at the back of his mind about that scene—he shook his head; it wouldn't come to him.

And it was after five. He picked up his light-gray Homburg and hoped absently that Máiri had managed to straighten out the twins on the baby's name. The twins were the only babies he had ever had anything to do with, and they had arrived as quite reasonably good-looking babies, equipped with thick black hair. The sight of a nakedly bald, red-faced, screaming infant supposedly his responsibility had been a little shock. He had wondered if the hospital had made a mistake, but that kind of thing surely didn't happen. Or did it? It was a big hospital.

But of course it wasn't Alison's fault. Driving homeward up Hollywood Boulevard, he caught the light at Highland and happened to notice a discreet *Sale* sign on a little specialty boutique past the corner. Purely on impulse he found a parking slot and walked back. The atmosphere of ladies' shops never disconcerted him, and he usually knew what he wanted. Within five minutes he had found Alison a handsome new house robe, pure silk and the color of a tawny, ripe peach. It was not, however, on sale.

Later on Alison regarded it with rapture. "You are," she said, "a very satisfactory husband, *amado*. You always think of everything. Now if I'd been nursing her—and it's a nuisance I can't, but there it is—this would be impossible, the cleaning bills—but as it is it's exactly what I need to feel like a reasonably attractive human female again. Did you get a look at her before they let you in?"

"Mmh, no," said Mendoza.

"Oh, well, never mind, we'll be home on Monday and we can have her all to ourselves."

"Johnny and Terry are slightly confused about names." She was highly amused at that. "Our own fault, I suppose. Children seem to be so literal."

On his way out, the grim-faced nurse intercepted him and led him down to the nursery to look again at the bald, red-faced, squirming bundle. "You've got a live wire there," she said gaily. It wasn't exactly the phrase Mendoza would have chosen.

Angel met Hackett as he came in the back door. "The insurance check came. At last."

"Thank God," said Hackett, bending to kiss her.

"Amen. So I can have my car back. What a nuisance it's been—I always manage to forget things at the market, and shopping once a week isn't enough. Art," her hazel eyes were a little anxious. "Would Sunland be too far?"

"You've found a place?"

"Well, I must say the real-estate people are obliging, driving me all around. It's possible," said Angel. "On a dead-end street—"

Mark and Sheila, discovering that Daddy was home, came running and yelling.

"Daddy, Boy caught a bird and it was all bluggy and Mama—" Mark.

"Three bedrooms and a den, and it's Spanish stucco—"

"All bluggy, and Mama said bad Boy and tooked it away—" Sheila.

"A red tile roof, and of course I asked about the taxes—"

"Boy was mad—"

"He went growl, growl—"

"Twelve hundred. The lot's a hundred and sixty feet deep. They're asking eighty-seven five. I want you to look at it anyway."

"All right," said Hackett. "What about the bird?"

"Oh, it was more scared than hurt, I think. I brought Boy in and after a while it flew off."

The great gray-silver Persian had not, however, forgotten the bird. He was still sulking, crouched on top of Hackett's *Herald* in the largest armchair.

On Saturday morning Mendoza and Grace went out in ninety-seven degrees to do a little legwork on Pearl Davidson. The quiet backwater was baking in the heat, looking deserted; but people were at home. There were twelve houses on the little street, and six of them were owned by the old people who had lived there so long, knew each other from so many years ago. Asking the obvious questions—did you notice anything, anybody? had Mrs. Davidson expressed any fear of anyone, complained of prowlers? was there any character around the neighborhood who might be suspected?— inevitably, they had wasted time on the irrelevances.

Guy and June Burdine lived diagonally across the street from Mrs. Davidson's house, in a white frame bungalow with a little brown grass in front, a weedy flower bed. Their house was next door to Mr. Purdy's stucco place. They were tremulous, shocked, grieved over Mrs. Davidson. Everybody had to die sometime, but to think of an old friend getting killed like that— the crime rate up, everybody knew, but you just didn't expect a thing like this. Forty years, they said, they'd known her forty years. And her husband, before he died of a stroke.

"No, we never saw or heard a thing, Officer," said

34

Burdine mournfully. "We was sitting out in the back-yard till about ten-thirty. A little bit better out there, after dark. No, Pearl never was a fearful woman, she hadn't said anything about any prowler or anything."

"We saw her just that morning," said Mrs. Burdine. She had a round face, but it was drawn and haggard now; she'd been crying. "One of the best friends I ever had, Pearl was. We was going up to the market—thank the Lord both of us still pretty good at getting around if we got other things wrong with us—and Pearl had the arthritis so terrible, it was getting worse, hard for her to go shopping, we used to get things for her when we went. I got her some tea and a package of rice and what else, oh, soda crackers, like she asked—she said she was feeling better, the heat good for the arthritis." She began to cry again, gently. "Getting taken like that—it's wicked."

They said she hadn't any jewelry, except her wedding ring. They looked at each other and Burdine said, "I don't suppose it matters telling now. The little jewelry she had, some things of hers and her family's, she sold it last year to make up the taxes. She was short about sixty dollars—the taxes were seven hundred, and that's wicked too. She'd been saying she didn't know what she'd do this year." He shook his head. "Getting awful hard to get along at all."

He had been in construction work, he said, worked hard all his life; you'd think honest people ought to be allowed a peaceful old age.

On one side of the Davidson house lived a Mrs. Babcock, but she hadn't been home since Thursday; she was up in Arcadia staying with her daughter who'd just had a baby. On the other side of the Davidson house lived a fairly young couple, the Gibbons. "They wouldn't know anything," said James Millet scornfully. "Out most nights dancing and drinking, by all accounts. Only lived here about six months, renting." The Millets were only in the mid-seventies, and their living room was crowded with photographs of five grown-up children and nine grandchildren. They lived three houses down from the Davidson house. "The poor thing, they never had any children," said Mrs.

Millet. "She was all alone, and her arthritis getting so bad— We hadn't seen her in a few days, this awful heat, we'd been sticking pretty close to home."

Millet had had his own service station, sold the franchise when he retired. He had the Social Security, and they'd invested in an annuity years back, but even so things were tight.

Martha Fogel lived across the street from Ronald Purdy's house in another little frame bungalow. She was a tall angular woman with brooding dark eyes; she limped with a cane. They heard the same things from her, and a little grudging praise for good neighbors— the Burdines usually asked if they could get things at the market for Pearl, and for her too, two old crocks not able to get about much. And Mr. Purdy—about the spryest of all of them along here, and probably the one with the most money too. He'd been an accountant with that big department store, Bullocks'. "The sooner all of us old folks are out of it the better," she said bitterly. "But to have Pearl go like that—always the cheerful one, she was, always the one to see a joke— I thought more of Pearl than my own sisters, God rest their souls. And I can't even afford to send flowers to her funeral, though who's to arrange that I don't know. Some of us live too long, that's a fact. It's pain and trouble and grief, whether you call it the Lord's will or whatever. Never sick a day in my life, and here I am with the bad heart trouble come on so sudden, I suppose liable to go off any minute, and I'd be just as satisfied—nobody to miss me, neither chick nor child. And Pearl, that was such a one for dancing and fun— she and Dick belonged to a square-dance club for years, never missed a Saturday night—coming down with arthritis. Some days it was all she could do to get around the house, fix a meal. And nobody to care but us old friends that couldn't help much. Since I took that fall off the porch my knee's right stiff and sore." She told them there wouldn't have been anything of value in the house; but nobody they'd talked to could be sure of knowing that anything was missing. There hadn't been a television in the Davidson house, but they'd heard at once from Purdy that she hadn't had

36

one. She used to go to the Burdines', the Hallams', to watch TV with them.

The Hallams lived at the other end of the block from Purdy. They were in their late seventies, fairly hale and hearty. Like the Millets', their living room was festooned with photographs of children and grandchildren. They had lived here for thirty-five years, knew Pearl Davidson well. They hadn't seen or heard a thing. Such a hot night, and the electric rates up so high they couldn't afford to run a fan, they'd been sitting in the backyard, a bit cooler out there.

The other four houses on the block were occupied by renters, working couples; if anybody was going to talk to them, it would be the night watch. It was doubtful that they'd be helpful.

"A big, fat waste of time," said Grace, getting into the Ferrari.

"I don't know, Jase. Exercise in empathy," said Mendoza vaguely. He looked at the steering wheel soberly, lighting a cigarette. "What Purdy said. Time sliding by. All those old people—the lame and the halt and the blind—"

"Yes, I see what you mean. Just hasn't caught up to us yet," said Grace. "It won't for a while. And I'm hungry. Let's go have lunch."

Angel dropped Hackett off at the Dodge agency on Figueroa at eight-thirty. "I can just as well go with you. I've got the baby-sitter for all day anyway, and I don't have to be at the realtors' until ten."

"No, no," said Hackett.

"Well, I'm not sure I trust you to be sensible, that's all. At the time, that scarlet Barracuda looked like something from outer space."

"I'll be sensible," said Hackett. "What else, at the prices now?" The insurance check would cover the major portion of a new car, but not all: there would be payments.

"Well—" said Angel. She gave him a doubtful look and swung the old Caddy out into traffic.

He looked at the Dodge models and heard some prices and wasn't enthusiastic. He wandered half a

37

block up Figueroa to a Ford agency and looked some more, wandered out again. It was a good time to buy a car, the new models about to come out; but he didn't want to order one with specific options and wait a couple of months for it. And, good time or not, it also meant that the dealers were low on stock.

At the Chevy agency, a block down, the salesman accepted him as manna from heaven and instantly offered him a terrific bargain. "The boss figures on taking a total loss on it, the new ones just due. You couldn't do any better—he was just saying yesterday, if we could break even on it he'd go for a deal."

Hackett heard about it and rather agreed that it sounded like a bargain. It had been a special order, a deluxe Monte Carlo coupe. Real leather upholstery, a special paint job, power all over. The customer had been somebody in TV, the salesman, producer, director, whatever, who'd dropped dead of a heart attack before the car came in, and his wife didn't want it.

"Well, I'll take a look at it," said Hackett.

He was led out to the back lot. "Of course, this special paint job—we couldn't throw in new paint, if you don't like it you could always have it sprayed."

It hit Hackett in the eye, blinding in the bright sunlight. After the first startled moment, he decided that, damn it, he did sort of like it. The handsomely streamlined Monte Carlo was painted a screaming iridescent lime-green with a metallic saffron-colored top and racing stripes. Hackett could hear what Angel would say—and the boys downtown. But it was a good deal.

At least, it was going to be very easy to locate in big public parking lots.

3

YESTERDAY AFTERNOON, LOOKING FOR ARTHUR BANKS, who'd been tagged as the heister at a drugstore last Wednesday night, Galeano and Conway had found he'd moved from the east L.A. address. They had sent a query up to the D.M.V. in Sacramento and got the make on what he was driving, an old Chevy sedan. They had put out an A.P.B. on him, and had gone back to look for other possibles out of Records.

Just after they got back from lunch on Saturday, a call came in from the Hollywood precinct. One of their squad cars had just spotted Banks's car in a public lot off Highland; the patrolman had a look around and came across him in a nearby bar, and picked him up. He was waiting for the downtown boys in the Wilcox Street jail.

"Progress," said Galeano. "We'd better go get him." When he and Conway got there, the patrolman had waited for them, Ramon Gonzales. He had a bruise on one side of his jaw.

"The front office said I'd better brief you. He tried to put up a fight, and naturally I went over him. He had this on him." Gonzales proffered an S. and W. .32 revolver.

"Oh, very nice," said Conway, pleased. "If that's the equalizer he pulled the stickup with, we've got a slug to match."

If anything, Banks's mug shot was flattering; he looked just like what he was, an ugly lout without much brain. He said what he thought about cops and then shut up on the ride downtown.

In an interrogation room back at the office they went at him patiently. "The heist at the drugstore Wednesday night, that was you," said Galeano. "The clerk picked out your mug shot. It was pretty stupid to take a shot at him."

"I don't know what you're talkin' about. I ain't done nothing since I got out."

"Oh, come on, Arthur," said Conway. "We don't have to talk to you at all, we know you pulled that. You were a damn fool to put up a fight with the Hollywood cop—now we can prove it, you know."

"Hah? What the hell you mean? He tries to collar me, I'm clean, why shouldn't I—what you mean?"

"Way the law reads, Arthur—you put up any resistance, we can commandeer anything on you for evidence, see?" Conway grinned at him cheerfully. "And we've got the slug out of the wall where you took a shot at that clerk, so now we can prove it's out of the gun on you, can't we?"

Banks stared at them, mouth slightly open. "Just why did you take a shot at him?" asked Galeano. "He hadn't put up a fight. But anyway, we've got you for it."

"Oh, hell," said Banks. "Oh, hell. Is that right? I should've got shut of that gun. I never knew that."

"Why did you?" asked Galeano just out of curiosity. "He went along, gave you no trouble."

Banks's brow furrowed in painful thought. "Yeah, yeah, I guess he did. But—I dunno—" he licked his lips. "He got under my skin. Wise guy. He looked at me. I mean, like I was dirty. And he had that ring on."

"A ring?"

"From one of them college clubs, frat something. My best girl she went off with a guy belonged to one of them frat things. He just—that guy in the store—got under my skin."

In the corridor, Conway said, "The lowlifes we do deal with. At least one off the books. You can send in for the warrant, I'll take him down and book him." The little irony was, of course, that if he hadn't admitted the job, they couldn't legally have examined that gun: not expecting the evidence to stick in court.

"O.K.," said Galeano. "He'll get a one-to-three and be out in nine months." And next time he fired an impulsive shot it might do more damage.

Conway took Banks out. Galeano started the machinery on the warrant, packaged up the gun and dispatched it down to the lab for the ballistics examination, and went back to his desk to write a final report. Higgins, Grace and Palliser had just come in from somewhere; Higgins was stripping off his jacket, swearing about the heat. Galeano rolled a report form and carbon into his typewriter, and the phone buzzed on Higgins' desk. A minute later Higgins was on his feet.

"We'd all better roll on this, boys—sergeant shot dead." He grabbed up his jacket; Palliser and Grace loped out after him, met Hackett just coming in and gathered him up with them.

Galeano would hear about that sometime. Somebody had to mind the store, and reports had to get written.

"Oh, now, that was a terrible thing," said Mrs. Georgia Goodman. "I hadn't thought of that in ages, until you said the name. Poor thing, she was so young. Why are you asking about her now?"

Mendoza had landed at the Winterhaven Apartments, again at two o'clock, having dropped Grace off at headquarters. This time he found the manageress in. "It's a long time ago," she said. "I hadn't thought of it since. What are you asking for?"

Mendoza said easily. "There's an insurance refund due Miss Byrd. We've been trying to locate her."

"Well, if that doesn't beat all. This long after. I know, insurance companies can be slower than molasses in January. When Mr. Goodman died— But two years and more—and the poor girl dead."

"Miss Ruth Byrd. She did live here?"

"Why, yes." She stood in the open door of her apartment, a short plump woman curiously top-shaped, with a generous bosom and hips tapering to surprisingly slim legs, visible below a short nylon housecoat. "Lived here about a year, she did. Seemed like a nice girl, the little I saw of her. Pretty too. It was quite an upset, that night."

"What happened?"

41

"Well, I don't rightly know. I mean, what she died of. Appendicitis, I should think it was, rupturing you know. She was only about twenty-two, and pretty. It was along one evening, eight or nine o'clock, her brother come asking me to let him in her apartment. It seems she'd called him when she was took sick, and when he came she was too sick to open the door. I let him in with my key, and she was just like a dead thing, white as a ghost and dead to the world. He got an ambulance, and I never laid eyes on her again. He came back the next day, or maybe the day after, and told me she'd died, and him and his wife cleaned out her apartment. That's all I could tell you."

"Where was she working then, do you know? And when was this?"

"Some drugstore downtown, I think. Oh, Lordy, I'd have to think back. It was more than two years ago—it'd be about two years ago last March. Oh, I wouldn't know about her brother, don't even know his name—he didn't live right around here. I couldn't say where."

Mendoza thanked her. He headed the Ferrari back down Wilshire, ruminating. *Murder done before;* and here was Ruth Byrd dead, if not murderously. It was just a funny little thing, and Mendoza was always interested in queernesses. He found a space in a public lot on Vermont and walked back to the independent pharmacy.

The pretty clerk recognized him, gave him a provocative smile. "Oh, yes. Mr. Snyder's here now. In the back." She went obligingly to get him. By the time she came back two women had come in, were leaning on the cosmetic counter, and she made for them reluctantly.

"Yes, sir, and what can I do for you?" Snyder was an untidy, big lump of a fellow in his fifties, paunchy, pasty-faced, with a curiously shaped bald head and an unctuous voice. "Helena wasn't sure just what you wanted." He gave Mendoza a small leer, obviously anticipating a request for some private masculine requirement.

"Ruth Byrd," said Mendoza. "I believe she used to work here?" He added the insurance excuse vaguely.

Snyder looked much taken aback. "Oh," he said. "Oh, yes. She did work here, some good while back. Quite a while back. Two, three years. I'm afraid I couldn't help you at all, I haven't any idea where she is now."

"Was she a satisfactory employee?"

"Oh, yes. A nice girl so far as I recall, very efficient. She left," said Snyder. "I seem to remember she intended to move to another area."

"Would you know anything about her family? There's a brother."

"Oh, I'm afraid not. Not a thing, sorry. After all, she was just an employee," said Snyder. "If you'll excuse me, I have a good many prescriptions to make up."

Mendoza walked back to the Ferrari, automatically switched on the air conditioning and ruminated as he waited for a chance to slide out into traffic. An ambulance. She'd have landed at the Receiving hospital on Wilcox, but he wouldn't take any bets that they'd still have any records on her. Two years ago last March. On the other hand, corpses had to be tidied away. Somebody would have arranged a funeral, and she'd have been buried or cremated somewhere. Cemeteries usually had quite good records.

At Parker Center he rode up in the elevator and came into the office; Lake was off today, Sergeant Farrell sitting on the switchboard, but he wasn't at his desk. Mendoza went into his office, noting Nick Galeano alone in the communal office typing a report, sat down at his desk and got out the six phone books. The brother not living right around, which meant Hollywood or Los Angeles, he assumed—that left choices: the valley, the beach; and probably the funeral would have been in his general vicinity, not Ruth's former one. But there weren't all that many cemeteries.

As he began to make a list, his mind switched briefly to the missing Joyce McCauley. If there had been a ransom demand, Carey would have let him know.

Forty-eight hours now. He thought of the time the twins had vanished, and his mouth tightened a little. That was an offbeat thing too, Joyce.

He decided that the logical first cast was Forest Lawn. About the first cemetery anybody would think of here. He picked up the phone.

"When did you get back?" asked Farrell at the door.

"While you were off the switchboard."

"Well, I was in the rest room. There's a new call down, practically everybody went out on it. A sergeant shot, somewhere around the Silver Lake area. It was a sergeant from Hollenbeck called in, a Sergeant Hoffman—I don't know what Hollenbeck's doing in it. Anyway, there's enough manpower on it."

"Evidently," said Mendoza. "I suppose we'll hear all about it sooner or later."

They had gone out on it expecting to find the sudden, violent gunplay: attempted heist, a sniper. It was sudden and violent all right, but nothing like that.

The address was on a hillside street above Silver Lake. Once this had been a solidly good, upper-middle-class area; in the last few years, elements from the central city creeping in while taxes and inflation rose, the crime rate was up and the streets looked shabbier. But on this curving street the houses were fairly well maintained; the ones on the upper side would have a nice view of the Silver Lake reservoir. The address they wanted was a comfortable-looking white stucco house with green trim, a steep terrace of ivy in front and steps curving to a small front porch.

They'd come in Higgins' Pontiac and Palliser's Dodge. As the two cars pulled up in front and the men started up the steps, the front door opened and a man waited there for them. He was a big solid man in his early forties, in a brown suit and white shirt, tie loose; and they knew he was another cop as they came up to him. He was looking grim and unhappy.

"Hoffman, Hollenbeck," he said. "I'm the one called. No sense call in to the desk, waste time. It's your baby."

"Hackett," said Hackett automatically, "Higgins, Palliser, Grace. What've we got?"

"I don't know, damn it," said Hoffman. "I'll tell you as quick as I can, and then you can get on it. It's Walt Robsen. Also sergeant at Hollenbeck. Longtime partners, Walt and me. A good cop—a solid guy." He was talking abruptly in little jerks of words, covering deep emotion. "The thing's just crazy—nobody with any reason to— There isn't the hell of a lot to tell. It's his day off. His wife—Cathy—was out with the two kids. Left him sitting in the den. She—they—came back about forty minutes ago, I suppose, and found him shot. He's dead. One slug in the head. Cathy's been a cop's wife a long time, she kept her head. Called me—lucky I was at the station. I came up, and called you. That's it. Except that it's crazy—not anything that could happen."

They went into the small entry, big men crowded together. At the far end of a living room to the left a woman was sitting upright on a couch with a teenager on either side of her, a boy and a girl. "I hope you won't have to bother her much," said Hoffman, "right now. She's a good girl, but—they were married eighteen years, they— Oh, hell, hell and damnation! How the hell could this happen—why?"

"We'd better take a look at it," said Hackett. Hoffman turned and led them down a long hall.

"My wife'll come over later, stay with her or— We were all friends a long time. There's nothing any of us could tell you anyway—it's just impossible. Crazy." He stopped at an open door and stood back.

It was a little, maculine-looking den with an old walnut desk, a bookcase on one wall, a recliner chair, a floor lamp. Sergeant Walt Robsen had been sitting in the recliner when he'd been shot, and was still sitting in it. He had laid down the book he was reading, face down on the arm of the chair, and his head had fallen straight back on the chair; he stared at the top of the opposite wall remotely with wide-open eyes. There was a small blackened hole in the middle of his forehead. He had been a good-looking man, with black hair, regular features, thick eyebrows.

45

"We'll want the lab," said Hackett. "Contact wound —powder burns. He wasn't alarmed or on guard."

"And you can ask," said Hoffman, "but there's a lot of shrubbery around the house and the air conditioning's on—I don't suppose anybody heard the shot. Neighbors aren't that close. There's an extension phone in the kitchen, I don't suppose you want to touch this one."

"Not until the lab's been here," said Hackett. "You know we'll have to talk to her." Hoffman nodded silently. "Simple questions. He hadn't got across anybody lately? No threats—trouble of any kind?"

"Oh, for God's sake," said Hoffman. "This is real life and we're real cops, not on TV. It's not that exciting a job, is it? Of course not. How many times do you put the collar on some punk and he says 'I'll get you, pig,' and even if he says it how many punks ever do anything about it?"

"We do have to ask," said Palliser gently. Hoffman looked at him. Hoffman and Hackett—and Higgins, who came to lean on the door—were the same kind of men physically: crowded close in the little room and hall, they might as well have worn badges pinned to the plain clothes. Hoffman looked at tall, slim, dark Palliser, who looked more like a bond salesman, and his eyes were expressionless. "Also about anything in his private life," said Palliser.

"Don't fuss the man, John," said Higgins dryly. "Later."

"Oh, what the hell?" said Hoffman wearily. "There's nothing to tell you about that either. They were an ordinary, respectable couple. Mostly cops and their wives are, aren't they? No trouble. No outside affairs. That's just silly. Wrapped up in the kids—you've got kids, they take time and money, and we don't get much of either, do we? And wouldn't I know? We'd worked together eleven years—made sergeant about the same time. Muriel and I live four blocks from here—we've been pretty close with Cathy and Walt over the years. He was an ordinary guy in love with his wife, she with him—interested in their kids."

"The lab's on the way," said Higgins.

"O.K.," said Hackett. He turned and went down the hall, the rest following. In the living room he sat down on a chair opposite the couch.

Hoffman said, "Cathy, they've got to talk to you. Just some. You take it easy. Muriel's coming over pretty soon."

She was a pretty woman, bright brown hair in a neat cut, an upturned nose, bright brown eyes, a wide mouth. She might be in her late thirties. "I'm all right, Bill," she said. "Honestly. Right now, I'm all right. It hasn't—hasn't got to me yet, I don't think. Of course they want to ask questions." She took a deep breath, looking at Hackett. The two teenagers were quiet as mice. The girl looked about thirteen, and she was going to look like her mother; the boy was older, dark and thin-faced.

"What time did you leave home, Mrs. Robsen?"

"About eleven-thirty. We had an early lunch—nobody wanted much, it's so hot. I dropped Tommy off at the high school, he was going swimming, and Sally and I went on to do some shopping. She needed —that doesn't matter." Her voice was steady. "I'd told Tommy I'd pick him up at two, and he was out in front waiting. I suppose we got home about two-fifteen, there wasn't much traffic."

"Your husband hadn't expected anybody here, far as you know?"

She shook her head. "It was his day off. Too hot to do any work in the yard. We'd mentioned—maybe— asking Bill and Muriel over this evening, but I hadn't called Muriel yet. No, he wasn't expecting anybody, hadn't any plans—he was just sitting there reading. I thought—he'd fallen asleep over his book at first—" And now her voice was shaking. She had an arm around each of the children, and tightened her grip convulsively.

Hackett exchanged a glance with Hoffman, and stood up. "Thanks," he said. "That's all, right now."

The mobile lab truck arrived, with Marx and Scarne on it. The Homicide men stood around watching them get to work, talking with Hoffman, hearing the same things over again.

47

Muriel Hoffman, who was a smart-looking blonde, arrived presently to take Mrs. Robsen and the two teenagers home with her. Mrs. Robsen fumbled in her purse and thrust a ring of keys at Hoffman. "You can lock up the house—when they're finished. I don't know about—Walt's keys—"

"I'll take care of it, Cathy." She was gone when the morgue wagon came. By then the lab team was finished with the corpse, and Hoffman went through the pockets, came up with a set of keys, odds and ends—a crumpled handkerchief, a ball-point pen.

"Well, let's go talk to some neighbors," said Higgins.

They didn't quit work on it until nearly six o'clock, and then drove back downtown to separate and go home. They hoped the lab would turn something useful. The initial report could get written up tomorrow.

In the lot, the space reserved for Mendoza's Ferrari was empty; the boss had already left. Hackett got out of the Pontiac and said, "Oh, I meant to tell you, George—the insurance came through and I've got wheels again. Reason I was late in."

"What'd you get? It's a good time of year to buy, anyway."

"It's up here. It was a buy all right, somebody reneging on a special order and the dealer was stuck." They walked up the lot together.

"Good," said Higgins absently. "It's going to be one hell of a job to move, if Mary ever finds a place, but that whole area's running down, you couldn't help noticing it again today, just walking around— Good God almighty, Art! That's it? What the hell are you up to, going in for the Indy or what?" He gaped at the screaming colors of the Monte Carlo.

"Well, look," said Hackett, "I can always have it painted." And he could hear what Angel was going to say. But damn it, he still liked it. It was a cheerful-looking car.

Mendoza felt lonely in the dining room, and Máiri consented to feed him at the kitchen table while she put together a cake. The cats were wandering around

48

uneasily and getting underfoot; there weren't enough laps to accommodate them the last three days. When Cedric came in as Mendoza was drinking his coffee, he left large, muddy footprints all over the floor, and Máiri let out a shriek of vexation. "Och, that great idiot of a creature, he's been in the twins' wading pool again— Come here, now, while I wipe your feet before you get on the carpets—och, such a household—" The twins were demanding to be read to before bed. "Now, your father's away to see Mama and the new wee sister—you'll need to put up with me, my lambs."

Mendoza left them to it and got to the hospital just as visiting hours began. Alison was sitting up in bed looking energetic; she'd imported a hairdresser and her fiery hair was back to its usual wavy gamin cut. She pounced at him as soon as he came in. "I nearly called the office, and then I realized it could wait. I woke up in the middle of the night and remembered it. Luis, you've got to go up to the house and decide which side of the bathroom you want."

"*¿Para qué es esto?* I'll have all sides of the bathroom, how do you split up—"

"You can't. *Estúpido,* now listen. When we were up there on Thursday, Mr. Hardpenny pointed it out—the contractor, you know. There are two nice big Pullman washstands in our bathroom—marble counters, real marble, you know—"

"Yes, I'm aware that you're sparing no expense."

"One on the east wall and one on the west. And it doesn't make any difference to me which I have. But for yours, there'll be an outlet for your razor right there, and they've got to know where to put it. I should think you'd want the east window for the morning light, but you'd better go and look, and tell Mr. Hardpenny. They'll be back to work on Monday. You haven't been up to see it in ages, anyway, and it really is coming along."

"I'll try to make it."

"You won't try, you'll go—they have to know." Alison sighed. "And at least that was one thing I accomplished that very day. I didn't have a chance to tell you about it, come to think— I ordered the gates.

Máiri and I were up there that morning, and I suddenly thought of it—because they'll take ages, of course—and I got Mr. Hardpenny to write down the dimensions. They're going to be eight feet wide and six feet high to match the fence. And then we went down to Olvera Street, you know that old ironwork shop—he really does beautiful work. I knew it was the place to go to get just what I wanted. He's a darling man, Luis, his name's Ricardo Rodriguez and he's terribly shy, but you should see his muscles. I drew a sketch for him and he said he'd start working on them right away. It'll be months, I suppose—but the fence is only half up anyway." She stretched and sighed.

"You do go so fast, *mi corazón*. I wish to God you were nursing this one—keep you tied down for a while, anyhow."

"Oh, I'll take it easy for a while. Still a lot to do, but there's plenty of time— I don't suppose it'll all be finished much before Christmas." Alison took the offered cigarette. "Máiri said the Kearneys are coming to see me tomorrow. And Angel dropped in this afternoon. Art's insurance check finally came. She thinks she's found a possible house in Sunland."

"So what they save in taxes will go for air conditioning eight months a year," said Mendoza.

"So I told her, and she began to think twice about it. But it was funny, how Art went up in the air and had a fit when she first wanted to move, and then all the vandalism and his car getting stolen made him realize how the neighborhood's running down. Oh, Lord, here's that nurse—" she handed him her cigarette hastily—"I'll get a lecture if she finds me smoking." The grim-faced nurse came in with a glass of orange juice, and Mendoza stood up and tried to look unconscious of a cigarette in each hand. "Heaven," said Alison when she had gone, "I'm babbling—I think I'm stir crazy. It seems years I've been here, and I can't wait to get home."

On Sunday morning Hackett, Higgins and Palliser briefed Mendoza on Walt Robsen. "Let's just hope to hell the lab turns up a lead," said Higgins. "Nothing shows at first glance. The neighbors who were home didn't hear a thing, see anybody coming or going. The people on one side weren't home when we went asking, we ought to go back there again. But there's a lot of trees and shrubbery around that house. But what Hoffman gives us, why the hell should anybody deliberately shoot him? Ordinary hardworking cop, no enemies, no trouble."

"The doors were unlocked, of course," contributed Hackett. "Broad daylight, and he was right there—expecting her home. Anybody could have walked in. But it looked a little funny. He was just sitting in the chair when somebody put a gun to his head. It didn't look as if he'd made a move to defend himself. And if it had been the casual burglar—"

"Extraño," said Mendoza. "You said the air conditioning was on. Enough background noise to cover anybody coming in quietly. And if he was interested in his book— Mmh. Chair facing the door?"

"No—sideways."

"Mmh," said Mendoza.

"You seeing something in your crystal ball?"

Mendoza folded his long hands into a steeple. "You're looking for a new place to move, George—out of that area. You told us why. Same as Art."

"The crime rate—kind of people moving in— You think it was a daylight burglar?"

"Why should a burglar kill him? Tiptoe out again when he found somebody home. They're shy birds as a rule. No, but conceivably—just off the top of my mind—there could be people around there who hate the fuzz, especially as a close neighbor."

"Well, it's a thought of a sort," said Higgins doubtfully. "John and I are going over to Hollenbeck, talk to the boys he worked with. And there seem to be a couple of new ones down to work." Piggott and Schenke had had a busy Saturday night.

Mendoza looked at the night-watch report on his desk and agreed. Three new heists, and a man shot dead in a car on Rampart Boulevard. There had been witnesses to that, to a man running away, and the dead man had I.D. on him.

"It's supposed to go to a hundred and one today," said Palliser. "Well, at least Hollenbeck's air-conditioned too."

Mendoza crooked a finger at Hackett. *"Un momento* while I make a phone call, and we'll see if we're going to hear some more about Ruth."

"That," said Hackett. While Mendoza was on the phone he rang Carey's office. There hadn't been any ransom demand, any development in the McCauley thing at all. He had agreed with Mendoza and Carey on that: not a snatch. But what the hell had happened to the poor kid?

Mendoza came out hat in hand and said, "I found out yesterday that Ruth is dead. We've now located her brother, who is, I hope, going to tell us how. He lives in South Pasadena."

"Wild goose. How'd you find him?"

"Jase's simple mind sets us examples. I called cemeteries and found out where she's buried. Rose Hills. They told me who arranged it—the Thompson Funeral Home. They told me who paid for it. He's still at the same address in the phone book, and I talked to him just now. I understand you finally got the insurance—have you got a car yet?"

"Yesterday. Reason I was late in. I'll give you a ride in her," offered Hackett as they emerged from the elevator and passed through the double doors into the parking lot. "She's a very smooth girl—I like her. And I got a damn good buy on her too." He got out his keys.

"Well, for once I'll take a chance." Mendoza did not like to be driven. "At least I'm not wasting official time, this is supposed to be my day off— *¡Qué demonio!* Is this—this circus wagon—"

"Damn it, I like it," said Hackett.

"¡Santa María y todos angeles!" said Mendoza. But he condescended to get into the passenger seat. "I won't ask what your wife said."

"Actually," said Hackett, "it was such a good buy— I got the thing practically at wholesale—that she didn't say much. What with thinking about another house, and moving costs and all, she's getting miserly these days." He switched on the air conditioning.

The address in South Pasadena was Buena Vista Street. It was a modest stucco house with a neatly landscaped yard. The man who opened the door to them was about thirty, with a round, nondescript face, thinning brown hair, freckles: a stocky, middle-sized man. He looked at them, and at the badges, and said, "What the hell is all this about? Yes, I'm Don Byrd. You're the one who called? Something about Ruth."

"That's right. If we could come in——"

He shrugged and stepped back. They went into a living room only slightly cooler than the ninety degrees outside. No central air conditioning here, only a big evaporative water cooler in a corner. A rather pretty blonde was shooing a couple of small children out a door to an enclosed patio beyond a small dining room. She came to stand beside Byrd, and Mendoza introduced himself and Hackett.

"Police. What's it all about?"

"An anonymous letter, Mr. Byrd." Mendoza was watching him, but he only looked bewildered. "It looked like this." The actual letter was still at Questioned Documents, but he had typed out a copy. Byrd looked at it, sat down on the couch beside his wife, and shook his head.

"What's it supposed to mean? Murder. Ruth wasn't murdered, anyway. I guess you'd better sit down."

"We're just looking into it," said Mendoza vaguely. "We'd like to hear more about your sister—how she died."

The Byrds exchanged a look. "I don't know anything about this," said Byrd slowly. "Who's Bill Loring? I can tell you all I know about Ruth. And maybe I should have tried to do something then—damn it, there was something funny about it—but just then we had Cindy down with rheumatic fever, we were worried sick, and the bills too—it was just one more thing, and——" He sat back looking worried.

"There wasn't much we could have done," said his

wife. "We didn't know enough about what happened. And she was—gone."

"No," he agreed. "Well, what do you want to know?"

"How did she die?"

Don Byrd sighed. "Ever since you called, we've been going over it. And I've been feeling kind of guilty all over again. It's no use, Myra, we should've done more. Seen her oftener anyway. Things go along, you get into habits, just don't think. Now the police, for God's sake—so maybe there was something wrong." He passed a hand over his face. "Look," he said to them. "I drive for the bus company—moonlight playing with a combo, night spots. I'm busy—you got to hustle to earn enough these days. I mean, Ruthie and I were the only family left, after Mom and Dad got killed in the accident, it wasn't as if—as if we didn't care what happened to each other, see what I mean. But she was living in Hollywood, and she didn't have a car then, about six months before that old clunker conked out on her. It wasn't too often we could get together—had the time. The last time we saw her was on my birthday, that was two weeks before, March third. I went and got her and brought her here for dinner. She was—just the same as usual."

"Before what?" asked Mendoza.

"Well—what happened. It was a Friday night. There was a phone call about eight o'clock. A man. Stranger to me, I'd never heard the voice before. He asked if I was Ruth's brother and I said yes, and he said she was pretty sick and I'd better see she was taken care of. Just like that. Naturally I called Ruth, nobody answered, and she usually stayed home Friday nights to wash her hair, so I thought I'd better go and see. And I couldn't get her to answer the door, so I went to the manageress and she had a key. And there was Ruthie on the floor in a sort of coma—scared the pants off me. I called an ambulance—I was wild, Ruthie was never sick, she was only twenty-two—and my God, when I got to the hospital they said she was dead. Only twenty-two. I didn't believe it. I couldn't believe it."

"What did they tell you was the cause?"

The Byrds looked at each other again. "If there was anything—wrong about it," said Myra, "I suppose we'd better tell them."

"It just didn't make sense," said Byrd wretchedly. "The doctor I saw said, acute alcohol poisoning. Look, it was crazy. Ruthie was pretty straitlaced—we were raised kind of strict. She'd take a glass of wine, like we had for my birthday, but she wasn't—it didn't make sense. I just couldn't believe it. She was just the same as usual, last time we saw her—but—well, we didn't see her all that often, and—" He massaged his jaw again, miserable and undecided as he'd probably been at the time. "You can see. She might have got in with some crowd—not like Ruth, but—"

"Do you know who her friends were? She have many? Going with any men?"

"Dotty Clavering, Marcia Wills, they were about her closest friends," said Myra. "We didn't know them. Didn't they both work at The Broadway, Don? I kind of remember that. She hadn't been going with any boyfriend since she broke up with Jim Noble. Ruth was sort of quiet, not one for going around much."

"Jim Noble. They had a fight?"

"Not really. She liked him all right, they'd been dating about a year, but he got serious and she didn't like him all that much. I don't think there was any fight, she just turned him down. Oh, I don't remember where he worked."

"Some construction company," said Byrd. "He was a nice guy, I liked him. I'd kind of hoped Ruthie would marry him."

"Well," said Mendoza. "Was there an inquest?"

"What? Why, no. The doctor gave me a death certificate—"

"What doctor? If there wasn't an inquest, she must have seen a doctor within ten days of the death."

"Oh. I don't know anything about that. She'd been going to a doctor—his name was Palmquist, up in Hollywood—for her allergies, it was him gave me the certificate. A couple of days later. The hospital asked about a doctor and I told them his name. I tried to pin

55

him down when I saw him—told him I couldn't believe Ruthie'd got to drinking—but he gave me a lot of double-talk. And like I say, right when it happened, we had Cindy in the hospital, we were worried sick—everything coming at once, and the bills piling up—we had to get a loan—Ruthie had some money in the bank, but it took a long while for me to get it, prove I was next of kin. She hadn't made any will, well, why should she?"

Mendoza regarded them meditatively. "Did she ever say anything to you about her job? At the pharmacy?"

"The last time we saw her, she told us she was going to quit it, look for something else. The boss had too many hands, she said. I don't know whether she had. Ah, we should have, you know, been in contact more. But you get busy—"

"You let it go," said Mendoza. "Understandable."

"No, it wasn't," said Don Byrd. "I felt guilty about it later—not knowing what might have happened to her, if she got in with a bad crowd or something. Not like Ruthie to take up with any kind of fast bunch—but that doctor saying—oh, hell. And now police, all this time after—do you think there was something wrong about it? The doctor was wrong? This letter—"

"I couldn't say, Mr. Byrd," said Mendoza, "but you've given us something to think about."

Back in the car, Hackett said, "There seems to be a vague sort of case to look at—as if we needed anything else to work. Though on the face of it, the simplest explanation—Ruthie not used to pouring it down, takes up with a new boyfriend maybe, and when she passes out he doesn't want to get involved."

"*No sé.* I don't know," said Mendoza, "but I think I'd like to talk to this Dr. Palmquist. It's rather a funny little tale, Arturo."

Henry Glasser had come back to work after a day off to find the perennial heists still with them, and a couple of new cases. Phlegmatic plodder that he was, he went out on the legwork philosophically.

56

Now, on the new body last night, the lab had turned up a registration in the car, a John Lockwood, address in Hollywood. Glasser handled that as routine, called and broke the news, and Lockwood showed up at headquarters at ten-thirty. He was a middle-aged man, a very respectable-looking citizen, a CPA, and he was shocked and bewildered. He said since getting up that morning and finding Jim not home, he'd been calling his friends, trying to locate him. Now he identified the body as his son James, twenty-two; he couldn't offer any suggestion as to what might have happened. Jim was a good boy, never in any kind of trouble; he was a senior at U.S.C., a sociology major. His own car was in the garage; he'd borrowed Lockwood's last night. Lockwood wasn't sure where he'd been going—on a date, or to meet a crowd of friends. He gave Glasser some names—Jim's girl was Sue Blaine, his best friend Rex Lejeune. Both were going to U.S.C, too.

Glasser typed out a report. Now somebody would have to find these college kids and talk to them.

He went out to lunch alone—everybody else was out somewhere—and over his sandwich he again studied the postcard he'd had from Wanda Larsen. It had a photograph of some horses in a field, and on the opposite side it said, *Hampton Holt Morgan Stud Farm, Marysville, Calif.* Wanda had appended her neat backhand below that: *"Met some old neighbors unexpectedly. Beautiful place! Am thinking of marrying for money and getting out of the rat race!"*

Oh, really, thought Glasser.

When he got back to the office, nobody was there, but after a while Galeano and Landers came in with a suspect to question. They didn't spend much time talking to him; he turned out to have an alibi of sorts for the job they'd picked him up for. They were all sitting around, disinclined to go out on the legwork in the heat, when about two o'clock a new call went down, and they all cussed.

Landers brought out a quarter and flipped it. "Heads," he said. "Tails," said Galeano. Landers uncovered it; it was tails. "Hell," said Galeano without rancor, and went out, audibly collecting the address

57

from Lake on the way. Apparently it involved two bodies. Well, heat waves—

Five minutes later Mendoza and Hackett came in, and Mendoza said, "Nobody back. I could bear to hear any gossip the boys picked up at Hollenbeck."

"There's a new homicide down," Glasser told him. "Nick went out on it. Something on Geneva Street— two bodies."

"Geneva Street? *Qué es esto?*" said Mendoza, surprised.

4

GALEANO WASN'T FIVE MINUTES AHEAD OF THEM; when Mendoza swung the Ferrari into the narrow street, he was standing on the sidewalk beside his car, the squad car angled in ahead, talking to the patrolman Morales and a tall, black-clad civilian. He looked surprised to see Mendoza and Hackett, but introduced the civilian without comment, a Reverend Mr. Alcott.

"I can't tell you how distressed I am." Alcott was tall and thin with a long pale face and a high voice; he wore a clerical collar. "I was just telling this officer, I knew there must be something wrong when they missed the service. They never missed Sunday service —not in years. Even when Mrs. Burdine was in the hospital with the heart attack Mr. Burdine came faithfully. In bad weather, other parishioners were good about driving them—but of course it's quite close, right up on Third Street, the Central Christian Church. When they weren't at service I knew there was something wrong, and I came around as soon as I could. Terrible—so very sad." He brought out a handkerchief and dabbed his mouth.

"It's pretty clear suicide, Lieutenant," said Morales.

58

"And it is kind of sad at that, all right. They're in the backyard. There's a note in the living room."

Mendoza, Hackett and Galeano went around the little house, through the side yard, led by Morales. There was a patch of brown lawn, untended flower beds; two old aluminum chairs faced an old-fashioned wood glider, a small metal table between. The two old people were side-by-side on the glider. June Burdine had slipped sideways against the cushion at the glider's arm; Guy Burdine was slumped over, head on chest, and a glass tumbler had fallen to the grass beneath one dangling hand. A second tumbler stood on the little table.

"Mil rayos," said Mendoza softly. He bent and sniffed at the upright tumbler, which held a little liquid in the bottom. "I'd say lemonade."

"The back door's unlocked," said Morales. "Kind of pathetic. Seems to've been the other thing, the other old lady getting killed, set it off."

In silence Mendoza led the way inside. The house was very hot and stuffy. On the small coffee table in front of the sagging sofa a typewritten page of cheap stationery was held down by an old-fashioned globe paperweight. They could read it without moving that.

"To the police: What happened to Pearl brought home to us what a terrible world it has come to be. We have worried about one of us going to leave the other alone and helpless. We have had a good life and think this is the most dignified way to go together and make no trouble. God bless all friends, we hope to meet in a better land. Guy and June Burdine." It was all typed, including the signatures.

"You'd better call up the lab," said Mendoza to Hackett. When Hackett came back from using the radio in the squad car, Mendoza was in the bathroom with the medicine chest open. There wasn't much in it, but there was a prescription bottle labeled Nembutal, and it was empty.

"Poor damned old souls," said Hackett. Mendoza said yes abstractedly and wandered down the hall into the bedrooms. The back room held, besides a single bed and dresser, a card table with a typewriter on it, an old Underwood portable.

"Something bothering you about it? It looks pretty clear, Luis. You told me about the Davidson woman—old friends and neighbors so long, it must have set them thinking, worrying—frightened. Poor devils."

"*Así*," said Mendoza. "Two plus two. I've just been reminded of something, Art." He turned and went out the front door, down to the sidewalk.

Ronald Purdy was standing there talking to the minister. He looked very shaken and pale; he said faintly, "I was just coming home—when I saw the police car I thought—another heart attack, a stroke—but this—it's hard to take in. And yet—" he paused, collecting himself—"one can understand how they felt. I—this has been a shock, I had better get on home." He started on slowly, turned up the walk of the house next door, fumbled for keys and went in.

Mendoza went down the block and up the little walk of Pearl Davidson's house. There was a police seal on the door; he slashed it with his knife and went in, back to the kitchen. "Jogging my memory," he said. "Two tumblers on that counter. Both clean. I wonder why." They would have been printed. No other dishes were standing out.

"Oh, don't reach," said Hackett, reading his mind. "An inside job? Somebody she let in? Look at all the other evidence, Luis. The door forced, the place ransacked. Your torturous mind imagining her offering a guest iced tea or something, and the guest yanking out a garrote. It's a lot likelier she'd just washed those glasses and hadn't put them away yet."

"You're probably so right," said Mendoza. "It was just another little thing. *Ridículo*." They came out again and started back up the street. The Hallams and the Millets were out in their front yards, staring at the squad, the lab truck just pulling up; Martha Fogel was on her front porch. There wouldn't be much detective work on this, just the clearing up, collecting the evidence for an inquest. The lab was automatically thorough: that note would be checked against the typewriter, the contents of the glasses analyzed; there

60

would be autopsies. The minister would be asked to make a statement. The inquest scheduled. All the rules and regulations to follow, clearing up after unnatural death.

This was just a rather pathetic instance of how crime, any crime—like other human actions good or bad—created waves: the ripples widening out from the stone tossed in the pond. The poor old people, alone and afraid and worried, taking the dignified way out.

They left the lab to it and drove back to headquarters, and Galeano started to write the report. Reports were beginning to drift in: while they'd been gone, autopsy reports on Coburn and Lambert had come in, and one from the lab. The autopsies read very much alike. All three corpses had been beaten to death. Specific injuries were detailed: what it came to was that their skulls had been smashed in. Traces of wood splinters in some of the wounds: a blunt, fairly heavy weapon. Something like a two-by-four maybe. Both the adults had been legally intoxicated at the time of death, the equivalent of four or five stiff drinks.

Mendoza passed those on to Hackett and glanced over the lab report. Analyzed bloodstains, types O and A, matching the autopsies. No liftable latent prints not belonging to the bodies anywhere in the place. Contents of dirty glasses in the living room, vodka and cranberry juice—*"Por Dios,"* said Mendoza with a shudder.

He picked up the phone and told Lake to get him the coroner's office. For a wonder, he got hold of Dr. Bainbridge himself. "I don't suppose you've had a chance to do the autopsy on Robsen yet, but we asked priority on looking for the slug. Did—"

"Yes," said Bainbridge promptly. "I had a look myself. It was sent over to Ballistics this morning. Looked like a .22 or .25 to me."

"Bueno. Has anybody got to an autopsy on the Davidson woman yet?"

"I think so—business a little slow for once. I don't know if the report's been written up—give us time, Luis."

61

"Well, shoot it over *pronto* when it does get written"

Hackett had wandered out; Mendoza went across the hall to see who was in, just as Higgins, Grace and Palliser came back. Two scruffy-looking young men and an equally unkempt young woman were talking earnestly to Glasser and Conway. Everybody else came crowding into Mendoza's office, hauling in extra chairs.

"We turned up a little something," said Higgins. "It may not be worth a damn. Robsen had been working a forgery case, paper work on a couple of suicides, couple of burglaries, just lately. But he'd made a narco arrest on Friday, a juvenile—it was Hoffman's day off so he hadn't heard about it—and the father made quite a fuss, threatened to get him for picking on the kid. The father's a Manfred Johnson, no record, but—"

"A very little something," said Mendoza dryly.

"Otherwise, just what we heard from Hoffman. Robsen has a very clean record, well liked, easygoing, never any trouble with anybody. In other words, no leads," said Palliser.

Jason Grace sighed. "Rules to follow. We'll have to find Johnson and lean on him, but I don't see it. That would have been the moment's impulse. And who knew Robsen was home alone?"

They looked at him. "Your well-known simple mind," said Palliser, feeling his admirably straight nose. "That aspect of it hadn't occurred to me."

"All cops' home addresses are dead secret," said Grace to his cigarette. "Sure, not to say Johnson or somebody couldn't have followed him home. But in that case, he'd know about the family. If it was anything like that—which it looks like—it wasn't on impulse. Somebody lay in wait a little, to see the wife and kids leave."

That reasoning just took it farther into left field than it had been.

Glasser and Conway came in. "More progress," said Conway. "That pretty trio of riffraff were pals of the Coburn girl and Lambert. All upset to hear about the murders, came in to tell us they couldn't imagine who'd do a thing like that. They saw them on Wednesday night. The only thing they do give us is that Lambert hailed from Clinton, Iowa. I've just been talking to a sergeant there, they'll try to hunt up some relatives to pay for a funeral. Lambert and this Bob Blanchard had hitched out here together last year. They don't know where Blanchard is, he'd been sharing a pad with those two fellows but got fed up and walked away sometime last week."

"Yes," said Mendoza inattentively. He looked at his watch and got up, yanking down his cuffs. "Well, you may not see much of me tomorrow—I'll be out and about, and bringing Alison home from the hospital. You don't need me to tell you what to do." He picked up his hat.

Palliser's car didn't have air conditioning, and he was sticky with sweat by the time he turned into the drive of the house on Hillcrest Road in Hollywood. Opening the back gate, he got a single joyous welcoming yip, but these days Trina, the big black German shepherd, was a changed dog, and greeted him sedately on all four feet. Roberta really had been working with her, by the obedience-training book, and she was getting quite good at Sit and Stay and Down. "Good girl," said Palliser, and she actually let him precede her into the kitchen.

He kissed Roberta soundly. "I want a shower before dinner."

"And a drink. It has been a day. I only had to go out to market, but that was enough. Thank God for air conditioning." Her dark eyes were grave on him. "Have you found out any more about that sergeant?"

"Hardly anything we didn't know, damn it." He went down the hall to look in on the baby, David Andrew, who was single-mindedly attempting to break out of his playpen, and began to shed his clothes before he reached the bathroom. Fifteen minutes later, feeling better and wrapped in a dressing gown, he joined her for a drink. "Here's to crime, Robin." As Mendoza was always saying, tomorrow was also a day.

Higgins got home to a house quiet for once. Mercifully, their musical genius Laura had just graduated to studying written harmony, and these days was oftener poring over music-lined paper than pounding the piano. She was on her stomach on the living-room floor, and just looked up to say hello. Mary came out of the kitchen with the little black Scottie Brucie at her heels, and Higgins kissed her. "Everything O.K.?"

"Except that Steve's not home yet. He knows the schedule, after all." Mary's fine, gray eyes were a little worried.

"He'll be along." Higgins went down to the bedroom to get rid of jacket and tie, and found his darling Margaret Emily crawling around the bedroom floor with a stuffed bear as big as she was. He swung her up in his arms and she giggled at him. She had her mother's eyes.

By the time he got back to the living room Steve had just ridden up on his bike. "Sorry I'm late, Mom—I got yakking with some kids. Hi, George."

"You hurry up and wash—dinner in five minutes." Steve and Laura vanished down the hall.

"I swear he's grown another inch the last month." Higgins didn't add that Steve was looking more like Bert every day.

Mary laughed. "And you may have noticed that he hasn't been spending so much time in that darkroom. I think he's beginning to notice there's an opposite sex. He mentioned quite casually yesterday that he'd have to go to the senior class dance next semester and he'd need a new suit."

"My God," said Higgins, "he's only fifteen. Did you look at houses today?"

"A couple. There's one in Eagle Rock I'd like you to see on your day off."

"Well, all right.'

Matt Piggott and Bob Schenke came on night watch expecting a quiet night; Sunday usually was, after the hell-raising on Saturday night. Schenke had seen their old colleague Shogart in the hospital today and said he was doing fine: going home tomorrow after a final bout of surgery. Neither of them missed Shogart much; he hadn't been much loved in the office, but he had been a good cop and they were glad he was O.K., taking early retirement after getting shot up a few months before.

They hadn't got a replacement for him yet, and very likely wouldn't now, the whole force being shorthanded.

They got a call early, just after nine o'clock; they both went out on it. It was a little market on Fourth Street, and the owner was a Mr. Baumgartner. He was more annoyed than excited.

"The *Schweinhund*," he said. "Five minutes and I am with the doors closed. And the English I do not so good talk, I know, but I *talk*. This guy in he comes and not a word to speak—just like I am *Dummkopf* not good enough his mouth to open at! A letter he gives— a letter yet! Say to give money. Yes, a gun he has—a big black gun so long." He gestured.

As usual, the heister had taken the note away with him. "Can you describe him?" asked Piggott.

"Ach, describe? He is tall, thin, dark clothes, his hair light—I would know if I see him again—" And a couple of other victims had said so, too, but so far nobody had picked a mug shot out of Records; the conclusion was that he wasn't there.

He had got about forty dollars.

They asked Baumgartner to come in and make a statement for the day watch, and went back to the office to write a report.

Half an hour later, when Schenke was down the hall at the coffee machine, a call got relayed up from the downstairs desk. "Robbery-Homicide, Detective Piggott."

"If you want to know who killed that cop on the TV news tonight, I can tell you." The voice was rough, male. "You listen good, I'll say it once. You want Glen Brock. He lives in the Carpenter Arms on Cahuenga." The phone thudded down at the other end.

"Well, well," said Piggott, and wrote down the names. Sometimes useful information came in from such anonymous sources: somebody knowing something and not wanting to get officially involved. More of their useful informants were halfway pros, expecting to get paid for tips. But any tip was automatically followed up; you never knew where you'd hit pay dirt. He told Schenke about it; they hoped it would give the boys somewhere to go on that.

The night wore on and no more calls came in: a quiet night. At the end of shift Piggott drove home to the apartment in Hollywood through the empty streets, traffic signals just flashing amber. He let himself in quietly. As usual, Prudence had left a night-light on in the living room; it illuminated the tropical fish tank, and he stood for a minute watching the pretty colored creatures swimming endlessly, soundlessly around while bubbles rose. Then he slipped into the bedroom and started to undress. Prudence was asleep; she stirred and said, "Matt, you're home," as he got into bed, but she wasn't really awake.

Piggott yawned into the darkness and wished it would cool off, but there was a lot of summer to go yet.

On Monday morning, with Palliser off, there wasn't much to do on Robsen but try for a few bricks without straw, until the lab report came in. The anonymous tip might be their best bet; Hackett and Higgins went out on that, and to look for Manfred Johnson.

There was a lab report and an autopsy report on Pearl Davidson; Grace and Galeano kicked that around, not that there was much in either one. The autopsy put the time of death between nine P.M. and midnight Thursday night. She'd been a healthy old lady, sound heart, except for the deafness and rapidly worsening rheumatoid arthritis. She'd died of mechanical strangulation, the hyoid bone fractured; she had died practically instantaneously, and there were no other injuries.

The lab report amounted to nothing. They had sent some unknown prints to the FBI, hadn't had a kickback yet.

"Well, the routine pays off or we wouldn't do so

much of it," said Grace, brushing his moustache. "One thing occurs to me, Nick. Nobody heard a car along Geneva Street that night. Only about half of the people there own cars, I suppose all the old people are past driving. But everybody we talked to said no car at all drove down there that night. Short quiet street, we can take it they're right."

"So he was on foot," said Galeano. "Yes, I see, Jase. There might be something in it." They went down to R. and I. Phil Landers came up to them; she was a cute one with her flaxen curls and freckled nose, and they smiled at her, but without envying Landers. They told her what they were after and she went off to consult the computer.

Ten minutes later she handed them three names, men out of Records whose last known addresses had been within a mile's radius of Geneva Street. Darrel Foster, a record of armed robbery, had lived on Virgil Avenue a year ago; Carlos Lopez, robbery with violence, had lived on Berendo Street eight months ago; Bruno Franks, B. and E., had lived on Hoover Boulevard two years ago.

It was a very rough first cast, and they might draw a complete blank, but the routine did pay off. They took Grace's little blue Elva and started for Virgil Avenue.

The new corpse, college student Jim Lockwood, had fallen by default to Landers and Conway. They had already left for some unspecified destination.

It was Palliser's day off, but he had to go back to the courthouse this morning, that damned trial. Just in case the lawyers decided to drag it out some more and recall witnesses. He was surprised they had subpoenaed Tom Landers too.

Court didn't convene until ten, and after the lawyers had held a whispered conference with the bench it appeared they were going straight on to closing statements. But the courtroom was nice and cool and Palliser hadn't anything particular to do at home; he sat on of inertia. There wasn't a soul in the courtroom but the bailiffs, the jury, the lawyers and judge and court reporter, and the defendant, who was sitting head down, looking bored.

Palliser wondered just how much all this had cost the unwitting taxpayers. The expense of two trials, all the time put in by the detectives before that, and the time of the attorneys and the judge, the courthouse staff. The prosecuting attorney was going for life; it was a Murder One charge. That would probably depend on the judge's last instructions to the jury. But even if they handed Steve Smith life, it was an empty sentence: he could ask parole in seven years. He had abducted a pair of fifteen-year-old runaways, and raped and strangled one of them. There wasn't any guarantee he wouldn't do that again, or another kind of homicide; and he was only thirty-three now.

The two attorneys were surprisingly short-winded; maybe they were feeling bored with it too. The judge took about five minutes to explain their duties to the jury, and turned the case over to them and adjourned court at twelve-fifteen.

Palliser went out the parking lot and started home. If he wanted to know the verdict, he'd have to call the D.A.'s office; it wasn't important enough a case to rate a line in a newspaper.

Mendoza got up late for once, and after a leisurely breakfast left the twins swinging madly on their double swing in the backyard, the cats spotted about strategically under bushes, and Cedric barking at the mockingbirds again, while Máiri bustled about fussing over the new crib in her room.

Just as well Alison wasn't nursing this one, at that, he reflected. He'd had enough of the two A.M. wakings and howlings from the twins five years ago. Máiri was apparently looking forward to it.

He hadn't been up to inspect the new *estancia* for about a month. It was in the hills above Burbank, an old winery and a hundred-year-old Spanish ranch house on four and a half acres. When he got there, past the place down the hill where the new wrought-iron gates would join the chain link fence, where eventually a blacktop road would replace the dirt climbing the hill, he was surprised at progress.

The new red tile roof was all on. There were three trucks parked alongside the building opposite the house that would be a three-car garage, and a dozen men wandering around purposefully, carrying lumber and hammering. The handsome, old, double front doors had been refinished to a rich teakwood color. There were new iron grilles on the front windows and the balcony upstairs on the long side wing, and new panes of glass sparkled in the sun.

"Here, you—what're you doing here? This is private property, mister." A beefy big man marched at him indignantly. "You can't bring a car up here—"

"This is my house," said Mendoza, annoyed. "Would you be Mr. Hardpenny?"

"Oh, is that so?" He peered at Mendoza carefully. "Now, come to think, you was with the little lady once last month—day I was here late getting them doors fitted. Well, excuse me, but how'd I know?" He looked suddenly anxious. "How is the little lady? You here instead—would she have *had* it, now?"

"Thursday night. Yes, she's fine, thanks. It's a girl."

"Well, that's the hell of a load off my mind," said Hardpenny, and blew out his breath in a sigh. "Her skipping around up here and those stairs not real steady till we got them all fixed last week, and her about ready to have it any minute, I was getting damned nervous, I tell you."

"Oh, so was I," said Mendoza. "We can both relax. I'm supposed to tell you where to put an outlet."

"Oh, yeah, the master suite." They went in past the double doors. The vast expanse of double parlors stretched before them like a desert. The new tile floor was getting laid. The spiral staircase had been beautifully refinished.

"Pleasure to work on a place like this," said Hardpenny. "They sure knew how to build them. Acourse materials was so cheap, they could use the best. Just a question of tightening her all up sound, and putting in all the modern stuff." In the master suite, over the enormous rooms below, Mendoza looked at real mar-

69

ble floors and counters in the sizable bathroom, holes where medicine chests would go, a new east window to match the other, and at random marked that wall for the outlet.

"We've made a start on the other job," said Hardpenny. "The apartment in the other building. You might want to take a look."

Being there, Mendoza went over the hilltop to where the long, low adobe building that had been the winery was.

They had started to remodel it, tearing out partitions, remodeling it into a generous modern cottage for the Kearneys. He seemed to recall that there was now talk of a new stable for the ponies nearby. There had also been mention of a corral on the other side, and a riding ring. The things that girl got him into—

But it was eleven o'clock; he drove slowly down the dirt track, mindful of the Ferrari's springs, and made for the hospital. Alison was all dressed and waiting for him, kissed him enthusiastically and said, "I've been counting the minutes—how I hate hospitals, orange juice at unlikely times and no ashtrays, and lights out at nine o'clock. Let's go home, for heaven's sake."

"They won't let you out until I pay the bill." A nurse brought the baby in, and Mendoza took Alison's bag. Downstairs the desk was obligingly quick with an itemized bill; he wrote a check and said, "I'm parked right outside."

"Oh, I'm fine. Lord, it feels wonderful to look like something again—you don't know how tired I was of being an elephant." For the first time since Mendoza had laid eyes on Luisa Mary, she was peacefully quiet, bundled up in a blanket. He opened the door of the car and Alison handed him the baby while she got in.

He looked down at her. It was too early to tell what color her eyes would be, and she hadn't a hair on her head. Suddenly she gave him a wide, toothless grin and made a little cooing noise. Her face wasn't quite so red.

"Well, *Señorita* Live Wire, you may develop into something worth the trouble, after all," he told her.

"What on earth do you mean by that?" demanded

Alison. "Of course she's worth all the trouble—"
When he slid under the wheel, keys in hand, she was
nuzzling the baby. "She's *Mamacíta's preciosa, ¿cómo
no? Mamacíta's enamorada—querida—*" The baby let
out something like a chuckle. *"¡Tiene mucha sal esta
niña!"*

Mendoza put the key in the ignition without switching on. "Now you listen to me," he said sternly.
"¡Entendámonos! I want it clearly understood that
we're not going that route again, so by the time she's
talking she doesn't know one language from the other.
I'm aware that it's an advantage to know a second
language, but there are limits to all things. After the
time we had with Johnny and Terry—"

Alison sat back and laughed. "Oh, didn't we? But
we needn't have worried at all, Luis—it all came right
as soon as they got into nursery school with all the
other children speaking English. Don't fuss, *amado*—it
doesn't matter."

"¡Anda!" said Mendoza. "On your head be it." He
took her home. In the driveway Máiri was waiting
eagerly to take the baby, and the twins rushed up
excitedly yelling at the tops of their voices. Nobody
paid any attention to Mendoza; they hardly realized he
was there, and probably wouldn't for some time. He
grinned at their backs and got into the car again.

Nobody was in the office when he got there after
lunch at Federico's on North Broadway. He read the
reports that had come in and stared into space for a
while. He was still sitting there when Carey came in
and sat down in the chair opposite the desk.

"You know," said Mendoza lazily, "for all the deal-
ings we've had with each other and all the funny little
problems you've handed me, somehow I've never
heard your first name."

Carey blinked, looking surprised. "Well, I don't en-
courage people to use it, it's a sort of sissy one.
Douglas."

"I suppose you're here to tell me, no ransom demand."

"That's just what. I know we said all along it wasn't

71

a snatch. But damn it, Mendoza, it's five days—and if it was the other thing, you know how that goes. Dead or whatever, the kid should have shown up by now."

Mendoza blew smoke at the ceiling. "Probabilities," he said. "Sure. The pervert. Just happening to be around, spotting the bunch of kids getting out of the station wagon, going into the museum. Wandering after them and somemow managing to isolate Joyce long enough to—mmh—immobilize her. I can see that, just. Art said he could have got her out to a car easily enough. And then what? We know how that goes ninety-nine percent of the time. He rapes her and lets her go—or he rapes her and kills her. That kind don't go in for hiding bodies."

"Not often, anyway. They don't think that far ahead," agreed Carey. "We know what should have happened. We should have found her—somebody should have found her—within a day, two days. And now we both know she's dead. If he'd just raped her and let her go, she'd have found help, identified herself." He brought out a glossy print from his breast pocket, laid it on the desk.

Joyce McCauley had been a pretty child: a kitten's triangular face, large eyes, shoulder-length fair hair. But there was the indefinable mark of illness in her face too: a child who had known pain and misery even in her short life. Carey looked at it in silence.

"People stick to their own little areas of town," said Mendoza. "We're both thinking, if that's his general area, he wouldn't have dumped her body even five miles away. Along an alley that night—in a parking lot the next night. But he might have been a transient, just passing through, you know. He might have taken her along and dumped her a hundred miles up the coast highway."

"We have to go by probabilities, damn it. It had to be a spur-of-the-moment deal. He happened to be there, saw them, got a yen for a kid, followed them and got hold of Joyce. Maybe he's got a room, an apartment, somewhere around there—he wouldn't keep her there. He could have attacked her in a car.

72

Right there in the parking lot. He'd want to get shut of the body."

"There are two answers," said Mendoza. "One, he deliberately hid the body somewhere out of town, in the wilds. Or two, he put it somewhere, not meaning to hide it, where it just hasn't been spotted. Even in the middle of a city, there are places like that."

"As we both know. But in this weather— Damn it," said Carey, "it reminds me of that Mason thing. I never roped you in on that because we started out thinking it was a runaway, and she was fourteen. But—"

"How's McCauley?"

"In the hospital," said Carey. "He collapsed on us this morning—just couldn't take any more strain. He's a very good man, he's been patient and cooperative and listened to the damn Feds, but it's just been too long with nothing turning up. He's not exactly a young man—mid-forties—and the kid's all he's got. The one ewe lamb."

"What are the Feds saying?"

"Oh, they think she's dead, too, and the snatchers got cold feet. Maybe amateurs."

"Nobody plotted a snatch from the middle of fourteen people in a public building."

"Tell the Feds. It's all they think of where a kid's concerned. Alice Mason," said Carey. "It looked like a runaway. Fourteen, and not a very good student at school. Only child—parents both work. Single house up on Ashmore the other side of Elysian Park. Because she was seen coming home that day, from school. Girl friend saw her go into the house—she had a key. When the parents came home from work she wasn't there. They called around some, couldn't find her, called us. And we went looking and asking. I didn't, tell the truth, put much pressure on, because I figured she'd walked out of her own accord. But everybody said no. And all we did turn on it— Magic trick," said Carey.

"*¿Por qué?*"

"Well, nobody on the block saw her after she went

73

into her own house. Doesn't say she didn't come out and just wasn't noticed, but— She wasn't boy crazy, young for her age that way. Not a very pretty girl— little too fat, pug nose and mousy hair. Shy. What she was good at, and liked to do, was housework. Her mother said she was a big help, loved to cook and was pretty good at it. And none of her clothes were missing —just what she had on that day. Brown skirt, white blouse, brown sweater and loafers. Did I say it was about six months ago? She didn't even take her purse —it was lying on her bed, with six and a half dollars in it. The parents are nice people, pretty religious."

"*Extranjero*. She never turned up?"

"We never found out anything. I wonder if we'll ever find out about Joyce."

"I suppose you gave a passing thought to the flesh peddlers up in Sin City," said Mendoza idly.

Carey gave a short laugh. Los Angeles, and the Hollywood area in particular, was coming to be one of the national centers for the juvenile sex-slave rings. The pimps and their adult whores waiting at the bus stations, along the lighted boulevards, to spot the scared runaways running out of money: offering help. Corraling the kids and introducing them to play for pay. It was all pay for the pimps, who found the johns and kept the kids locked up. It was a vicious game, practically impossible to control, nobody willing to testify against them in the rare instances where there was cause for arrest. And some of them dealt in kids as young as Joyce. But—

Carey summed it up. "They don't have to go out of the way picking them up like that. To get noticed." He put Joyce's picture away. "Well, I suppose you've got work of your own to do," and he got up and went out.

He passed Hackett and Higgins coming in. "Accomplish anything?" asked Mendoza, eyeing them. They looked tired and sweaty, his two senior sergeants, dwarfing his office with their twin bulks.

"Nothing," said Higgins. "But we've got a funny story to tell you."

"The damnest story," said Hackett, "I ever heard since I've been at this job."

They had, naturally, started out on that anonymous tip. Glen Brock. At the apartment on Cahuenga, a uniformed nurse looked sourly amused at them and told them that Miss Brock couldn't be disturbed, and they'd find Mr. Brock at an address on Sixth Street downtown.

It was a big, shabby old building; the office they wanted was 611 upstairs. The door was labeled *S. Greenbaum, Candy Jobbing*. Behind it in a narrow cubicle was a middle-aged woman with a long nose who looked at the badges without comment. She got up, opened a door at the back of the cubicle and said, "Police, Mr. Greenbaum."

"So send them in," said a genial voice, and Hackett and Higgins walked into a much larger office, which held two untidy-looking desks piled with papers, and two men. Behind the left-hand desk sat a stout short man, Semitic and bald and friendly-looking. Behind the other desk sat a tall, rangy young fellow with curly black hair and a rugged jaw. Both wore casual sports clothes. They looked at the badges.

"We're looking for Glen Brock," said Hackett.

"Be my guest. I am he," said the young fellow. "I haven't met you before. Who are you?"

"Robbery-Homicide."

Brock looked at Greenbaum. "We hadn't got that high before. Seriouser and seriouser. When am I supposed to have done what?"

"Why should you think—" began Hackett, and Brock cut him off in a tired voice.

"Don't waste time. You got a tip that I'm the boy you want for something. Murder this time? It's been going on for four years. It is one big Goddamned nuisance, and a couple of years ago I spent a young fortune on a private dick, try to find out who the hell's doing it, but he came up blank. Look, we've got a lot of orders to get out today and I don't feel like going down to headquarters to answer questions. I don't suppose you've got time to waste either. When do you want an alibi for?"

They stared at him. "Call it eleven to two-thirty Saturday afternoon," said Higgins.

"Good. This is the hell of a way to live. I was at home up till noon, I suppose you know the address. My aunt and her nurse can swear to that. From noon to twenty past I was driving to the head office of Spinellis' Market on Vermont, and I couldn't have got there in less time—you can pace it. From then till two-fifteen I was discussing an order and writing it up, with Mr. Joe Jenkins in their purchasing department. Then I went home again."

"You've got that pat," said Higgins. "Do you mean to say—four *years?*"

"Oh, it is just a dandy way to live," said Brock bitterly. "You try it sometime. It sounds like such a little thing at first. I have met cops from every force in L.A. County—name it, I've met them. I've been turned in on heist jobs, burglary, auto theft, grand larceny, arson, planting bombs, breaking and entering, anything you can think of. I've seen the inside of most police stations everywhere in the county. I had one hell of a time that first year or so, because I couldn't always show I was somewhere else and didn't know one thing about it."

"I will be damned," said Hackett. "That's a funny one."

"I can think of at least a dozen more appropriate adjectives," said Brock.

"Somebody with a grudge on you—but you've got no idea who?"

"Obviously not, or I'd have taken steps." Brock's expression held hints of what steps.

"Says somewhere in the Talmud," observed Greenbaum, " 'Praise the Lord for the evil as for the good.' "

"Oh, there is that," said Brock. "Generally speaking, I've found all of you to be quite nice fellows. On the whole. There are a few tough customers on the Pasadena force who give me a rough time now and then, and the Santa Monica cops are a little obtuse, while the sheriff's boys tend to use bluster. The Glendale police are fairly gentlemanly, and I must say you've all been quite fair. I've never had a hand laid on me, all of you so nervous about civil rights, but—"

"This is level?" said Higgins. "That's the damnedest tale I ever heard. Of all the queer things—"

"Oh, you are so mild about choosing words," said Brock. "I gave up counting after the first two years, but it's been an average of once every couple of weeks. Police coming, hauling me in to question. Of course in a smaller place, say with only two or three police departments around, they'd soon have caught on to the game, but here—" He raised his shoulders expressively. "Police coming out of the walls. And you and the sheriff's boys the two big ones, all sorts of different bureaus. I haven't met one of you twice, so I was a new face to all of them every time. Of course they never could prove anything, because I'm really quite a straight-living square, but it certainly gave the neighbors something to talk about. Six months ago my wife left me, said she couldn't stand it anymore—she knew I hadn't done anything, but none of the neighbors were speaking to her, the few friends we had had sheered off—being quite as respectable as I used to be. I suppose you know that phrase, no smoke without fire. Me always being hauled in by the police, there must be something behind it."

"Now, boy," said Greenbaum. "Joanie'll come to her senses, it just made her nervous. But you know she had another reason, Joanie's got her head screwed on straight. I've been talking to her like a Dutch uncle —"

"And that, of course, is another thing," said Brock. "If this kosher Dutch uncle here didn't happen to be a sentimental old bastard, I suppose I'd have lost my job a long time ago. Any other employer—police after me all the time—no smoke without fire."

"Now look, gentlemen," said Greenbaum. He spread his hands. "This boy's father was my best friend. I knew Glen since he was in diapers. Do I let him down because some nut with a funny sense of humor is persecuting him? Besides, he brings in orders." He chuckled. "That's a joke—anybody could get orders now. Wait for the crash when it all goes bang."

"You don't have any idea who's behind it?" asked Hackett. "Somebody with a grudge—maybe something to do with your wife, an old boyfriend—"

"No, and no," said Brock. "It started before we were married. I am a fairly easygoing fellow, I never had a fight of any kind with anybody—enough for this. That private eye came up with nothing. But I have got very damned conscious about alibis. The last few years I've become a professional collector of alibis. I've always been something of a loner, but I've had to learn different. Keep a diary of where I was when, with who. Chapter and verse."

Greenbaum put his head to one side. "That was really why Joanie kicked him out," he told them. "She said a wife's word's not so convincing. We've both been after him to go to the police, get them to find out—it'd be what, invasion of privacy, harassment, whatever. She's still a good wife to you, boy."

"Police!" said Brock. "Don't say police to me, Sam! What the hell, they do their job, but this isn't anything they can waste time on, not even a misdemeanor, damn it. Yes," he added to Hackett and Higgins, "and can you imagine what a bind I'd be in, alone in an apartment? I moved in with my Aunt Isabel. She's partly paralyzed, but she's a game old girl, and that dragon of a nurse knows all about it too. I don't get out much anywhere, except to the office here with Sam, business calls with people all around, the apartment. Keeping a notebook up to date, where I was when. One hell of a way to live," said Brock.

"¡*Vaya historia!*" said Mendoza. Galeano and Grace had come in to listen to that too. "But that is a very funny one. A grudge—jealousy—and of course the man's right, none of our business."

"Naturally the tips get followed up, but my God, you can see how it's disrupted the poor devil's life," said Higgins. "Matt'll be interested—he took the call."

"Yes," said Mendoza. "What have you got, Jase?"

"Nothing much," said Grace. "We turned three just possibles on Davidson. One's disappeared from the area, off P.A. now. The other two, one we haven't found and the other's got an alibi."

Mendoza stabbed out his cigarette and said suddenly, "¡Condenación¡ I meant to hunt up that doctor today."

5

ON TUESDAY MORNING BEFORE THE DAY SHIFT STARTED, a call went down: a new body. Hackett and Higgins had gone out on it before Mendoza came in. It was Grace's day off. Galeano had brought Palliser up-to-date on the Davidson thing, and said to Mendoza, "You know there's no handle on it, it'll go in Pending. I had just one little idea that might take us somewhere. No car down that street, Thursday night. Him on foot, Jase thought. It could've been any punk who lives in the general area or once did. And by all the earmarks of the thing, the simple violence, it could also have been a juvenile graduating to the big time."

"Oh, yes," said Mendoza. "Always possible."

"I thought it wouldn't do any harm," said Galeano, fingering his solid jaw that even at this hour looked unshaven, "to talk with Morales, the other men on that beat, ask about any local J.D.'s who come to mind."

"No harm at all," said Mendoza. Conway and Landers came into the office as the other two went out, sat down and lit cigarettes.

"This Jim Lockwood," said Conway. "Bring you up-to-date as far as we've got."

"Anything interesting?"

"Maybe a little generation gap," said Landers. "Lockwood senior told us what he knew, which wasn't much. To start with, the witnesses are N.G.—a couple of people who heard the shot saw a man running away from the car. No description. Not worth getting statements, hardly. This Rex Lejune, supposed to be a pal of Jim's—more likely the only one the father ever met. He admitted he hadn't met Sue Blaine, said to be Jim's latest girl friend. They're really just names to Papa Lockwood, Jim had his own car and ran around as he pleased. Well, he was twenty-two. Mother dead, he and Papa live alone in an apartment on Edgemont."

"We can't get at U.S.C.'s records, the office is closed for the summer," said Conway, "but we got the contents of his pockets from the lab, and about the only thing useful was a notebook." He tossed it onto the desk and Mendoza leafed through it. On the first page were three addresses: *Sue,* a line through an address on Hobart; *Rex,* and a line through an address on Fountain; an undesignated address way out on La Brea. A lot of empty pages, and then at the back a page and a half of phone numbers, just initials identifying them. "The Blaine girl doesn't live there anymore. She had a part-time job at a dress shop, but she quit that last month. However, another clerk there is supposed to be a pal of hers—she was off yesterday, we'll catch her today. Lejune has also moved out of the apartment on Fountain, but we haven't talked to everybody there, somebody may know where he's gone."

"People do move around," said Mendoza, and Duke came in with a manila envelope.

"I thought I'd deliver this personally with an apology. We can't offer you any leads on Robsen at all. Not even any odds and ends. That place was clean, and about all the facts we can give you is the gun. It was a Harrington and Richardson .22, probably one of their target models and for a choice, that little Sidekick. An old gun, but it hadn't seen much action. Find it for us and we'll match it to the slug out of him. We took Mrs. Robsen's prints, and the kids', for comparison, and there weren't any other liftable ones in the place. And that's about it. What it comes to is, somebody just walked in and shot him."

"Well, you can't give us what isn't there."

"What about the other slug?" asked Conway. "Lockwood, the body Saturday night."

"Oh, that one. We're still going over the car," said Duke. "Yeah, the coroner's office sent it over. That's an old Ivers and Johnson .25 automatic. The casing was in the front seat. I'm sorry, Mendoza. Just nothing there." He laid the report on Mendoza's desk.

"Bricks without straw," murmured Mendoza. Conway and Landers went out on their continued hunt, and Mendoza got out the Hollywood phone book. They were busy, but likely not as busy as they would be once the heat wave had been running another month, and he was the lieutenant and could afford to waste some time on a wild goose. The average cases passing through their hands, evidence of the rank stupidity and aimless violence of human nature, bored him; the very occasional offbeat one was a refreshing change.

He had just closed the book and gone out to the corridor when Hackett and Higgins came in. "Well, something simple? You haven't wasted much time on it."

"Oh, another one to work, but it doesn't look very complicated," said Hackett. "A Vincent Pace called in, found his eldest daughter dead when he came home. He's a night security guard at a downtown department store, left about ten last night and she was all right then. Two younger kids, but they were asleep and didn't hear anything. Rae-Jean Pace—she was twenty-two—going to beauty school. Looks as if she was strangled on the living-room sofa. The father says she was going around with a young fellow he didn't approve of, he'd warned the girl about him. Brian Gall. Father doesn't know where he lives but he works swing at Lockheed."

"Open and shut probably," said Higgins through a yawn. "Just the damn paper work."

"We've got the lab report on Robsen—damn all except for the gun." Mendoza handed it over. They both swore.

"Where the hell to go on that—I'd hate like hell to shove that in Pending," said Hackett savagely. "But

81

unless Manfred Johnson did it, which I very much doubt, I just don't see where to go on it."

"Did you ever find Johnson?"

"No, he didn't show up at his job—he works at Goodyear in Compton. We'll find him."

Higgins had started the new report. Mendoza left Hackett fishing for change for the coffee machine and went out to a temperature of ninety-eight at nine-thirty.

There were five Dr. Palmquists throughout the county, but Dr. Arnold Palmquist had an office on Third Street between Vermont and Western, which would have been readily accessible to anyone living in the Winterhaven Apartments who didn't have a car.

Dr. Palmquist regarded a lieutenant of detectives as an unmitigated nuisance on a morning when he had a full roster of patients. He told Mendoza that he had a large practice, he couldn't be expected to remember casual patients that far back when they were no longer his patients, and with all the damned red tape for health insurance and Medicare, he had to pay three girls just for that and they couldn't spare time to look through all the back records.

"Ruth Byrd," said Mendoza patiently. "She had allergies. And she landed in Emergency as a D.O.A. and you got called out to certify the death because she'd been seeing you. Does that ring any bells?"

"Oh," said Palmquist. "Oh, yes. I do remember that. What's the police interest? It's a good while back." He was a middle-aged man with pale blond hair and pale gray eyes in a sharp-featured face.

"I'm not quite sure what kind of case it is," said Mendoza. "I'd just like a few answers. Do you remember enough to give me some?"

"Possibly."

"You told her brother it was acute alcohol poisoning."

"That's right." He shrugged. "I didn't know the girl well, had seen her only a few times, and she'd assured me she didn't drink, but patients aren't always truthful.

She must have ingested something equal to about a fifth of alcohol, and over a short period."

"Excuse me, you're quite sure of that?"

"Certainly. There was an analysis of stomach contents as I recall."

"But not an autopsy?"

"I didn't see any reason to perform one. It was a straightforward case." He looked down his nose, darkly disapproving. "We see too damned much of that kind of thing among young people these days. The unhealthy craving for stimulants of any kind—and complete irresponsibility in using them. I just remember the bare facts of the case, if you want details I'd have to look up records—" He sounded impatient, and looked at his watch.

"I'll let you know," said Mendoza, and stood up. Palmquist looked pleased, stood up promptly himself and then hesitated.

"One other thing I just remembered. A little curious, in a way. The doctor who saw her first at Emergency mentioned it to me—I didn't see her until she'd been, er, cleaned up. Shortly before she died she had engaged in sexual intercourse. For the first time."

"Oh, now, really," said Mendoza. "Thank you so much."

Don Byrd's wife had said Dotty Clavering, Marcia Wills, were friends of Ruth's. He found a public phone booth and again looked at the Hollywood book. Not a usual name; there was a D. Clavering on Ardmore. He tried there; it was an apartment house, and the woman in the apartment next to that marked Clavering told him that Dotty worked at Columbia Records. He drove back to Hollywood Boulevard and that big round landmark of a building, went in and asked. Miss Clavering was in the mail order department. It was a tiny office high up in the building.

"About Ruth?" she said. "You're police? What on earth?" She was a tall rather gawky girl, not pretty or plain; she looked like a sensible girl, and he told her about the anonymous letter. "Well, that's certainly funny, but I don't see how there could be anything in it. Murder? I never hear of a Bill Loring. Ruth died of a ruptured appendix, I know that." The story Don Byrd had given out.

She had a coffee break due, and willingly answered questions. She and Ruth had gone to the First Congregational Church, it was where they had met each other. Ruth was a serious girl; she'd dropped out of high school because she was anxious to start earning, but she'd been sorry, only getting the dead-end jobs, and she'd been thinking about going to night school, getting her diploma, taking shorthand and typing. Yes, she'd have liked to get married, but she always said she'd have to be sure it would be for keeps: she didn't approve of cheap sex or divorce. That was why she broke up with Jim Noble, he was mad to marry her and she wasn't that crazy about him.

"There'd been some talk about her quitting the job at the drugstore?"

She nodded. "She was, as soon as she lined up another. Maybe she already had, I don't know. The boss there had given her a rough time, making passes, you know. She said he didn't really mean anything, just one of those middle-aged men pretending to be fatherly—you know, but she didn't like it, it embarrassed her. There was a girl she met somewhere around there—I think she worked at the place Ruth usually had lunch—told her she used to work at the drugstore and the boss nearly raped her or something. Which I don't suppose was true or he'd have been arrested. But it wasn't long after that Ruth died." She was silent, and added, "It's brought it all back. It was awfully sad, her dying so young. I liked Ruth, she was a nice girl."

"What the hell gave you the idea Sue goes to college?" asked Dolores Higman, amused. "That's a hot one. Sue's got better things to do with her time than read books, for gosh sakes." She batted false eyelashes at Landers and Conway. She was a plump girl about twenty, with a dirty neck and legs with no ankles; she was wearing tight white shorts and a T-shirt bearing the legend, *Try me You'll like me*.

Yesterday they had tried the address for Sue Blaine

in Lockwood's notebook, and they were back here again: the dress shop where she had worked wouldn't open until one o'clock. They had talked to Natalie Dunning, who had been Sue's roommate and hadn't much time for cops. This was a cheap old apartment on Hobart Avenue, and either Natalie wasn't home or wasn't answering her door; Dolores in the apartment across the hall was proving slightly more helpful.

"You know her pretty well?" asked Landers.

"Oh, sure, the way you do, you know."

"Know her boyfriend, Jim Lockwood?"

"Oh, she had a lot of boyfriends. I don't remember the name just offhand. Why? You bill collectors or something?" Evidently Natalie hadn't mentioned cops asking about Sue.

"Or something," said Conway. "Her roommate says she's moved. You have any idea where?"

"Nope. Only she must've taken up with a new man, somebody had money, or she got left a legacy or something, you know? Last time I saw her, it was about a month back, she had on this gorgeous slinky outfit, must've cost a fortune, and a diamond ring— you could tell it was real—and when I walked in—I'd just gone over to borrow some aspirin—her and Natalie were having an argument over how much rent she owed. See, she was moving out then, and she opened her purse to pay Natalie and there was a wad of cash in it. I don't think Natalie noticed, but I sure did."

"That's interesting," said Conway. "She didn't give any hint about this man, where she was moving?"

"Nope. Gee, it's hot. I'll bet she's sitting in some air-conditioned place right now, with her new boy-friend. You fellows like to come in? I got an hour before I got to go to work."

"No, thanks," said Landers. "We've got work to do too."

They were driving Landers' Sportabout; without discussing destinations, Landers drove to the nearest air-conditioned coffee shop and they knocked off for lunch. By the time they'd finished sandwiches and coffee it was after one, and they went back to the dress shop, which was a hole-in-the-corner place called Ann's Fashions on Santa Monica Boulevard. It was open. Natalie had grudgingly mentioned the name of the girl here, Jean Taylor.

If there was an Ann, she wasn't in evidence. And Jean Taylor wasn't exactly a girl; at least she looked as if she'd lived a full life, if she deserved the title. She was thin to emaciation, with greasy dark hair and sallow skin, and she looked at them suspiciously.

"So what do you want with Sue? I don't know where she is and I wouldn't tell you if I did. All I know is, she had some luck come her way and could quit this lousy job, which she did last month. And if you think I can't smell fuzz when it's under my nose you're dumber than most cops. Sue's had enough trouble with the fuzz—" She stopped abruptly and shrugged. "Look, I got customers coming in—I can't talk anymore."

"Females, they will open their mouths," said Landers in the car. "Where do you want to go next?"

"To see your wife," said Conway deadpan. "She is an adorable girl, I could fall in love with her."

Landers laughed and headed the Sportabout downtown. In the R. and I. office business appeared to be brisk: a couple of detectives from Vice were in a huddle with a brunette policewoman at one end of the counter, three witnesses were bent over books of mug shots, and Phil was talking with Captain Patrick Callaghan of Narcotics, huge and fierily red-haired. She went away and came back with a Xerox copy of something for him, and he started out, spotting the men from Robbery-Homicide.

"And how's our Luis these days?"

"Same as usual," said Landers. "He's just become a father again."

"He would take up with an Irish girl," said Callaghan, amused, and got into the elevator.

"And what can we do for you?" asked Phil.

Conway leered at her. "I've been leading your husband into low company, Phillippa Rosemary. Not that we've caught up to the girl yet. Her name's Sue Blaine, and we'd like to hear if she's on the books."

"Can but look," said Phil. "You still playing the field, Rich? You ought to find a nice girl and settle down."

"Give me time." They waited, and five minutes later she came back with a Xeroxed sheet. "Well, there we are," said Conway. "Just following our noses."

Sue Blaine was in Records as a J.D. first, soliciting and one narco count; as an adult, since two years ago she'd been picked up on charges of prostitution, shoplifting and petty theft. She'd served little stretches in the county jail, the last time eight months back.

"Dear me," said Conway, "where do you suppose a clean-cut college student met up with this one?"

Hackett and Higgins landed at Lockheed at three o'clock. It was a good fifteen degrees hotter in the San Fernando Valley. They hadn't talked much on the way, in the new Monte Carlo; they knew each other so well they didn't need words to communicate feelings, and right now they were both feeling disgruntled and unhappy about Sergeant Walt Robsen. It didn't look as if there was anywhere to go on that, no leads at all. There was, of course, one set of neighbors they hadn't talked to; they hadn't found them home yet, and probably they hadn't been home at the time of the murder and didn't know anything. To be thorough, the detectives would see them. But they could foresee this shapeless thing ending up in Pending, and that was never a thing they enjoyed seeing; when it involved the senseless murder of a good cop, they'd enjoy it even less.

The badges got them into Personnel, and they asked for Brian Gall. They were shepherded into a large, bare employees' lounge and waited ten minutes before he came. He was a large, blond, gangly young man with steady blue eyes that held bewilderment at the badges.

"Police? What do you want with me?"

"When did you see Rae-Jean Pace last?" asked Hackett.

"Rae? What's the matter with Rae?—what's happened?" he asked sharply. "We're engaged—we—I

87

saw her last Saturday night, we went to a movie—"

"What about last night?"

He shook his head. "I'm on here till twelve— I went straight home. What's—"

"Where's home?"

"What is this, anyway? Arden Avenue in Glendale."

"Anybody there to say what time you came in?"

"Yes—my mother was up, my young brother'd been sick, and he could say too—it was about twelve-thirty. What's wrong with Rae, for God's sake?"

They told him, and he said, "Oh, my God. Oh, my God." He turned away, shoulders shaking, and after a long minute he added dully, "I suppose her father gave you the idea I—he never liked me, but he wouldn't like anybody Rae might have married. Her mother's dead, you know, and she takes care of the house and the younger kids. He never let her have any boyfriends when she was in school—but—but—" He blew his nose; his hands were shaking. "She was right in her own house, you said? After he went to work? But she wouldn't open the door to a stranger at that time of night—she had some sense—and nobody she knew would have done that—oh, my God, I can't take it in."

Hackett and Higgins exchanged a look. Possibly this wasn't so cut and dried after all.

Matt Piggott had been profoundly shocked by the note Hackett had scrawled to him yesterday. He'd been a cop a long time, and all cops get cynical very quickly on the job. But Piggott was also an earnest fundamentalist Christian, and as far as his thought processes went, the victimization of Glen Brock came under the heading of bearing false witness.

He told Prudence about it next morning, when he was up. And of course she felt the same way. "And I can see it's hardly police business to investigate, but there must be some way to find out who's behind it and why."

"You'd think the man would know who might have that much of a grudge on him," agreed Prudence.

That afternoon Piggott went down to Greenbaum's office and talked to Brock. He asked the obvious questions, and Brock, friendly enough, turned impatient.

"You don't suppose I haven't thought of all these points for myself? Anybody I ever had a serious disagreement with—any girls before I was married—there weren't any serious affairs, damn it. I've never had that big a fight with anybody, to warrant a thing like this—this campaign against me. I appreciate your interest, but—"

"Don't discourage him," said Greenbaum. "Somebody official taking an interest."

Piggott sat silent, thinking. Naturally he thought like a detective. And if there was one thing any detective of experience knew, it was that the motive for any action depended on who had it. Some very small and slight motive might trigger A into action, which would never move B.

He said, "Do you mind if I talk to your wife, Mr. Brock?"

"Not at all, not that she could tell you anything." He gave Piggott her address.

It was a slightly crazy way to victimize a man, Piggott thought; so it was probably somebody slightly crazy who was doing it. And somebody like that wouldn't really need much of a motive at all; it needn't be a motive that a sane man like Brock would even recognize as a motive.

Mendoza landed back at the delicatessen at five o'clock. The two women looked at him sourly and he regretted his random excuse of the other day; but of course they were leery of him too, and answered questions reluctantly. The older, fatter woman was the owner of the place.

She'd hired a good many girls, she said. They were mostly flighty; they didn't stay long. One who used to work at the drugstore? Oh, her. That one had been the flightiest of all. Couldn't depend on her to pick up a dish without dropping it, and an awful liar too. She'd said terrible things about Mr. Snyder in the drugstore, and he was a perfectly respectable man, owned that store for years.

"What was her name?" asked Mendoza. "Do you know where she lived?"

"You're after *her* now? Well, let me think." She didn't, long. "Charlene Williams. I happen to know where she lived then because she said at first she'd liked the drugstore job, she could walk to work from right over on New Hampshire. But she was no good to me, forgetting orders and breaking things, I fired her."

Mendoza reflected that his wild goose was leading him quite a chase. Again he found a public booth and looked at the Hollywood book. There was a Robert Williams at an address on New Hampshire a few blocks away, and he drove over there, rang the bell of a modest frame house. Nobody was home.

Tomorrow was also a day. He went home.

It would be some time before Johnny and Terry grew blasé about the baby; they were continually being shooed away from the crib in Máiri's room with admonitions to let the wee lamb sleep in peace. Mendoza had vaguely, through the mists of sleep, heard one howl in the middle of the night, quickly stilled; maybe this one was going to be easier than the twins, at that.

At the moment he surveyed his household, as he came in the back door, with mixed gratification. The twins swarmed over him, were persuaded back to coloring books in Johnny's room. They had already been fed. The baby, less red-faced than ever, was sound asleep. Alison, wearing the new housecoat, was stretched out on the sectional, and cats surrounded her, purring contentment that one of the principal laps was back home. She didn't stir as he bent to kiss her.

"Heavenly to have a lap again," she said dreamily. Cedric came in panting and flung himself down beside them. "Let's have a nice leisurely drink before dinner, *amado*."

"Margaritas?"

"Mmh. Lovely."

"I'll join you for once." He went out to the kitchen and got in Máiri's way, getting out ingredients. Inevitably he was pursued by their alcoholic cat El Señor, who got on the counter, his Siamese-in-reverse mask creased to a scowl, and flicked his tail dangerously near the coffee maker until Mendoza poured him half an ounce of rye in a saucer. Máiri snorted at him.

They sipped their drinks. The cats purred, Cedric panted. The children were all peacefully quiet. It wouldn't last; it wasn't exactly the natural state of his household, but for the moment Mendoza relaxed and enjoyed it.

On Wednesday morning a messenger came in just after the men began to drift into the office and left autopsy reports on Mendoza's desk. The Burdines and Lockwood.

"Well, there you are," said Hackett, as Mendoza passed the first two over. "The Burdines all kosher. Just as we thought, the overdose of Nembutal. Neither of them was in very good shape, I see—enlarged heart, developing tumor, kidney stones."

"The lab report came in last night. The suicide note matches up with the typewriter all right. The Nembutal had been dissolved in lemonade mix, they even tell us the brand."

"So that's that. Luis, where do we go on Robsen?"

"Round and round," said Mendoza. "You deride my torturous mind, but on a thing like that—" he sat back and blew twin jets of smoke. "How does it strike you, and I know it'd be damned offbeat, somebody he'd put away a while back, holding a grudge and just getting out?"

"And stalking him. Now that is a thought. Pretty damned unlikely, but it could happen, and it'd give us somewhere to look, sure. I suppose it's *possible*."

"I think I like it," said Palliser, coming in behind Conway and Landers.

"So what did you and Nick accomplish yesterday?"

"Not much. We got a few names from the patrolmen on the beat, young punks who've been in trouble— petty theft, gang rumbles. Where's any evidence? We talked to a few of them. But when nobody can say what might be missing from the Davidson house, unless one of them should come apart and confess— There just isn't enough to go on."

"*Conforme*. You can all go and share the work, digging up Robsen's past arrests. It might take a while."

"You missed a lab report," said Landers. He lounged against the desk, looking a little pleased. "Came in just before end of shift. The report on Lockwood's car. They found some specks of angel dust in the front seat."

"Now that is a step forward," said Mendoza. The angel dust—technically, the PCP, Phencyclidine—was the latest street craze in drugs, and about the most dangerous one the dopies had gone for yet. It was cheap, it produced a fast high, and it could be made by anybody who had a few bucks for the ingredients. It was also, as some of the experimenters had sadly discovered, highly explosive in the process of manufacture, owing to the fact that one of the ingredients was ether.

"We've got a line on Lejune," said Conway. "He'd moved out of that apartment on Fountain, but we went back last night to catch tenants at home, and one of them had helped him move—Lejune's stereo was too big for his sports job, and this fellow has a wagon. Lejune's living in a very classy new pad out on the Strip. About five hundred per."

"Mmh, yes, so you'll go and ask him where it's coming from," said Mendoza. "If they're dealing in the angel dust, they'll be dealing in the more profitable stuff too. They way it shapes up, they've just got into the business. I wonder if Narcotics has anything on them."

"It's the homicide we're working," said Conway. "Keep your fingers crossed. We can always rope Narco in when we've collected more evidence." He went out with Landers.

They all dispersed, Galeano coming in late with Glasser, on the various jobs. Mendoza sat on awhile, thinking about Joyce McCauley. It was the seventh day since she had vanished. It was almost a foregone conclusion that she was dead; but where was her body?

And was there anything to his wild goose at all? Enough to venture out into the heat wave? He decided reluctantly that there might be.

"Say, this is just the hell of a thing about Jim," said Rex Lejune boyishly. "I'm sorry as hell to hear about it, but like I say I don't know a thing about it. I hadn't seen him for a couple of weeks." He glanced at the gold watch on his wrist.

"Have a fight with him? We understood you were best pals," said Conway.

"Oh, sure, no, nothing like that. I guess he was just busy, chasing around, you know, and so was I. I talked to him on the phone a couple of times. My God, I can't believe it, old Jim shot—who'd do a thing like that?"

Lejune was trying to sound convincing, but he was jittery. He was a fresh-faced young fellow in expensive sports clothes, a little too handsome, a good deal too winning of manner. This ultramodern apartment high up in a new building on the Sunset Strip was a good setting for him: he was as phony as the plastic-topped bar simulating marble, the plastic furniture imitating wood. They doubted very much that he was a student at U.S.C.; his wariness was straight out of street experience.

"It's the hell of a thing," he said, "but I'm afraid I couldn't tell you anything about it. I mean, he knew a lot of people beside me. And I'm sorry, but I've got an appointment. That's O.K., isn't it? You really want to talk to me about it some more, kick it around, you could come back later. I'll be back about three, but right now I've got a date. Is that O.K.?"

"Sure," said Conway heartily. "That's fine. You can maybe tell us about other fellows he knew, about his girl friends and so on. It looked like a personal motive."

"Well, I'd sure like to help you, I'll try. Thanks, fellas." He shut the door behind them gently. They rode down in the elevator. They had routinely spotted

Lejune's car in the apartment parking lot at the side before going upstairs. He was driving a little bright-red Datsun. They got into the Sportabout and Landers drove around the block to double-park illegally at the back entrance to the lot, where they had a view of the front entrance.

"Pair of fools we'll look if he doesn't show," said Conway.

"Oh, he was really anxious. He's a damn bad actor. Could be he's got a buyer set up," said Landers. "He's hardly big time. Did you see the autopsy on Lockwood?"

"And neither was he. Oh, yes, absolutely clean—no sign of drug use at all. It adds up, Tom."

"Here he is."

Lejune got into the Datsun and backed it up, headed for the front entrance with his left-turn signal on. Landers turned into the lot and let him make his turn onto Sunset before following. It was the hell of a place to turn left into traffic, the narrow bottleneck of the Strip, but Landers ruthlessly cut across an oncoming Mercedes, causing indignant braking. The Datsun was three blocks up.

Landers stayed well behind all the way up to Western, where the Datsun made a right. It was tricky trying to time the lights, keep the Datsun in sight but not on his tail; but they stayed with him down past Olympic to Pico, where he made a left. A few blocks on he turned left into a narrow side street; Landers hung back and slowed past the corner. "Where is he?"

"O.K., he's pulling in. House about the middle of the block, this side."

Landers made a U-turn at the next corner, swung back, turned up the side street and immediately parked. It was a street of shabby old houses, a couple of apartments at the other end of the block.

"Blaine, I wonder?" said Landers. "If so, she's not throwing money away on a pad."

"Business office maybe," said Conway tersely. "You want to walk in and surprise them? Maybe witness a buy."

"Damn it, why not?" said Landers. "He's nervous. He might come apart right away."

They started up the block rather fast. The heat was appalling; it beat at them from the broken concrete of the sidewalk, the blacktop street. They passed the house two down from the house Lejune had presumably entered: plenty of parking spaces, and the Datsun was right in front there.

Landers never knew what made him stop right there, unless it was his guardian angel. Whatever it was, it was as if he ran into an invisible fence, and he stopped dead and grabbed Conway's arm.

"What's the—"

There was a sudden shocking WHOOMPH, and the house came apart. It split open, sending bits and pieces of roof and walls skyward. Landers dived face down behind a hedge alongside the sidewalk and Conway dievd past him; they lay prone on dusty brown grass. Things stopped falling, and a loud crackling began instead.

The house was on fire.

"The gas," panted Landers, and they got up and ran, cowering from the heat. They had reached the corner when the gas line went up, a duller WHUMPF. There was a large piece of roof lying on the Sportabout's hood. Landers pulled it off, they climbed in and he backed out fast. There was a fire box at the next corner.

"They were making the stuff," he said unnecessarily when he'd called in. "The Goddamn fools, playing around with that—"

It was Higgins' day off, and he went with Mary to see the house in Eagle Rock. It was an older frame house, the rooms a good size, four bedrooms, on a quiet dead-end street. They were asking eighty-five thousand for it. If Mary liked it, it was all right with Higgins.

"The realtor said we ought to get a good price for our place, maybe more than that," she said. "Just for the land. All of those apartments going up in the next block—" She was silent, and he knew she was thinking of the house being torn down to make way for a concrete block. That she was thinking of old days in the house, when Bert Dwyer was alive, and Steve and Laura were babies. There wasn't anything he could say to her, but he put his arm around her so she knew he knew.

"Things change," she said. "You can't go back. It's a nice house, George. We can paint, and fix up the yard."

At two o'clock on Wednesday afternoon Mendoza finally caught up with Charlene Williams. He had started out at the house on New Hampshire, where a vague-eyed woman said she was Charlene's mother, and Charlene was working at a gift shop up on Wilshire but she wouldn't be there till noon, she was probably at her girl friend Wilma's right now, the house across the street. There, an incurious Wilma said Charlene had gone uptown shopping a while ago. He gave it up, went back to headquarters and spent a vain hour in Carey's office. Nothing at all had turned up on Joyce. McCauley was still in the hospital.

He missed hearing about the explosion; he went on to the gift shop on Wilshire and asked for Charlene. An exasperated proprietor said she wasn't there. Yet. "I expect she will be. Just forgot she was supposed to be here at noon instead of two o'clock—that's on Fridays when we're open later, but time means nothing to Charlene. She means well, and heaven knows she's obliging and honest, but not the biggest brain in the world."

Annoyed, Mendoza took himself out to lunch and dawdled over coffee. When he got back there, the nearest parking space was two blocks away, and the temperature had gone up to a hundred and two.

She was there, explaining breathlessly, "I'm so sorry, Mrs. Pollock, I forgot it isn't Friday, I guess. It sounds silly but one day's kind of like another, and I was looking at dresses at Magnin's, only I think these blouson things are hideous and I—"

"All right, all right," said the proprietor. "This gentleman wants to see you for some reason."

Charlene looked at Mendoza with large, inquiring eyes. She was very pretty in a soft, babyish way, like a plump kitten: big brown eyes and a wave of reddish-brown hair, very white skin and a soft, little red mouth. "Oh, what about?" she asked.

He judged that any circuitous approach would only confuse her. He said persuasively, "It's rather confidential. Is there somewhere we could talk privately?"

Mrs. Pollock looked him up and down. "Well, you look the part a bit too much actually to be a con man. You can use my office if you like." It was a tiny, square cubicle at the back of the shop, with a small desk, an armless chair. He sat her down in the chair, leaned against the desk.

"What do you *want?*" she asked. "I ought to be working."

"Well, I'm a police officer," and he showed her the badge.

She was entranced: a nice honest girl. "But what's it about?"

"It's about Mr. Snyder," said Mendoza.

"Oh, my goodness!" said Charlene. "Has he done it to some other girl? That terrible old man!"

"It's possible," said Mendoza cautiously. "We'd like to know something about your experience with him, Miss Williams. It seems you'd told a couple of other girls something about it—" he paused encouragingly.

"Oh, I did," she said earnestly. "I tried to *warn* them. Oh, dear, it's awfully embarrassing, but a policeman isn't like an ordinary *man,* are you, sort of like a doctor really, I suppose—"

"Exactly like a doctor," said Mendoza firmly. "You used to work at Mr. Snyder's pharmacy. And—?"

"I just thought it was fair to warn them," she said. "That girl named Ruth. She worked there after I quit. I got the job in the deli then, and she used to come in for lunch, and after I knew she worked in the drugstore, I told her. Only I don't think she believed me. I don't know why. Then she quit working there and another girl came, and I told her. I mean, I didn't really know them, but girls have to stick together, don't you?"

"Yes, of course," said Mendoza. "What—"

"I mean, it wasn't right. I know some girls don't think a thing about it, I mean if they like the boy, even, but I wasn't brought up like that and I don't care, I don't think most girls are like that. Oh, dear," and a great crimson blush enveloped her face. "It's awful to have to tell you. But it wasn't my fault, of course."

"Of course not," agreed Mendoza. "Mr. Snyder—?"

"Oh, I suppose I've got to." She fixed her eyes on her clasped hands and proceeded to do so while the blush grew and deepened. "He seemed nice and kind at first, he called me dear and it wasn't a hard job except for the cash register—I never could get used to its snapping at me—and of course it was nice not having to take the bus. And there wasn't anything wrong at all, I liked it fine—it was my first job, you know, I'd just got out of high school—until Mr. Snyder's birthday. It was sometime in December. We always closed at six, and that day he said it was his birthday and he wanted me to share a little toast with him, and we went in the back office and he gave me some brandy—he said it was brandy, I'd never tasted any before. And— oh, dear—I don't remember one thing after that till I sort of came to, and I was on the floor there and my watch said it was nearly midnight! I felt just terrible, so sick, and I don't know how I got home, I really don't. There wasn't anybody around, I must have been staggering all over—I just remember *crawling* up the front steps, and—and—oh, dear—my panties were gone, and—well, you know what I mean—"

"Yes, yes," said Mendoza soothingly.

"And Mother was in such a state, no wonder, thinking I'd been run over—oh, it was so lucky Daddy was working nights, he'd have had a fit. Just a fit. Of course we never told him. The way Mother said, it wasn't my fault, and Daddy'd have killed him or something and got in trouble."

"Didn't you think," asked Mendoza, "of reporting it to the police?"

"And have everybody *know?* It wasn't *my* fault.

That terrible old man—I never went back there, and I just thought, later on, I ought to tell those other girls. That worked there. In case he—you know."

"Yes. You told Ruth Byrd about it. And another girl?" He remembered suddenly that that blonde in the pharmacy had said she was new at the job. "I don't suppose you knew her name?" A forlorn hope.

"It was Barbara Fogarty," said Charlene. "We got talking in the deli when she was late once, and I found out she lived a block away from us." She sniffed into a Kleenex. "She said she liked the job because she could walk to work—just like me—" she raised solemn eyes to him—"but believe me, there are other things a girl's got to think about too."

6

"MY GOD, YOU NEVER SAW SUCH A MESS!" SAID LANders. "There wasn't anything left bigger than a matchbox. It was just damn lucky we got the alarm in so soon, that whole block could have gone up."

Mendoza had come back to his office to find Pat Callaghan and Saul Goldberg there with Conway and Landers, telling Glasser and Lake about the narrow escape. "Anybody who was in there went up with the house. The bomb squad's out on it now, but it's still hot, it'll probably be tomorrow before they can get into it. And we know what it's bound to have been."

"And I needn't ask," said Mendoza, "what you two are doing in on it. Get out of my chair, Saul."

"Narco business in a way," said Callaghan. "Your two boys have applied for a search warrant, and we'd like to have a look at what may be there—this classy pad on the Strip."

"I swear to God it must have been my guardian

angel," said Landers again. "I just stopped, for no reason, and the next second it went up. Even twenty feet farther—"

"So, praise heaven for small miracles. We couldn't afford to lose both of you at once, we're always short-handed."

By the time the search warrant came through and they took off with it, nobody else was in; they left Mendoza staring out his window smoking.

The ultramodern apartment on the Strip yielded this and that. They found a modest cache of cocaine, morphine, various barbiturates and Methedrine. Buried under a pile of shirts in a dresser drawer, they came across an old Ivers and Johnson .25 automatic, and Landers said tenderly, "Come to Papa, baby. Oh, isn't that nice. Want to bet, Rich?"

"No bets," said Conway. "It's got to be the gun that took off Lockwood."

"How do you read it?" asked Callaghan. "They were in the business together, had a fight over the take?"

"You could build a lot from a little." Landers considered. "I didn't get the impression that Lockwood senior is loaded. It's likely enough that Jim Lockwood met Lejune through the girl, and that she and Lejune were dealing in a small way, and Lockwood the smart college boy had the notion to parlay it into the big time. It's just funny how Papa shunted us at those two. As I said, Jim evidently didn't bring friends home, and my guess'd be that they just happened to be there one day when Papa walked in unexpectedly, and they got passed off as pals from college. Probably the only pals Papa had ever met. Way I say, generation gap. And it seems likely that after they got the business on the upswing—rented that house down there as a business office, place to manufacture the angel dust, Lockwood got to thinking he was worth a bigger cut because he was masterminding it."

Callaghan regarded a row of natty sports jackets in the wardrobe thoughtfully. "They will do it. What'd you say this Lejune looked like? . . . Um. Boyish and winsome—yeah—nice wave in his blond hair—slight

100

cast in the left eye, maybe, and one eyebrow higher than the other? Um. I just wonder, Saul, if he wasn't that Jack Moritz we grilled in the Sanderson case about six months ago. Sounds like him."

"Could have been," said Goldberg.

"Well, we'll never know now," said Callaghan cheerfully. "Whoever went up with that house, he's got no fingerprints left. I suppose we turn the lab loose here, for all we know there was a bigger ring involved. It may be the end of a job for you, Landers, but maybe the beginning of one for us."

The gun was all that concerned Landers and Conway. Landers took it back to headquarters and dropped it off at the lab. It was a quarter to six. He went down to R. and I. and told Phil he'd take her out to dinner, to celebrate.

"Celebrate what?" she asked suspiciously. "We can't afford it."

"Celebrate me being still alive," said Landers. "You nearly got to be a lovely young widow today."

Hackett didn't really think much of Luis' idea on Robsen, but it was worth a cast maybe. He went over to Hollenbeck with Palliser and Grace and put it to some of the men who'd worked with Robsen. "Your lieutenant's got the hell of an imagination," said one of them.

"I know, I know, but it's just possible." They talked around it, and the other detectives recalled a few cases out of the past. It wasn't a very likely idea because on any case it wasn't going to be just one detective responsible for an arrest and charge, for a grudge-holding criminal to blame. "Luis goes far out sometimes, but sometimes he's right too," said Hackett. "We can look."

The only way to look, of course, was to hunt up some records. The business of any LAPD precinct tended to be pretty hectic, and none of the detectives' memories could be trusted for what cases Robsen might have been partly working last year, five, six years ago. They'd have to go down to Welfare and Rehabilitation where all the relevant papers would be filed away: charge, arresting officer, trial personnel, sentences, date of parole and so forth. It would be a hell of a job, just pawing for records of arrested men who'd passed through Hollenbeck station's hands, come in contact with Walt Robsen. Men in for this or that sentence on Robsen's testimony or detective work.

Hackett talked with Hoffman a few minutes, at Hoffman's desk in the communal office. "You don't think much of the idea. There's no place much to look. The lab didn't give us a damn thing."

"I was afraid they might not. Nothing disturbed there, just—" Hoffman lit a cigarette and looked at the half-finished report in his typewriter. He looked older and tired today, eyes a little bloodshot. "Oh, hell and damnation. We've been helping Cathy—all the arrangements— The funeral's tomorrow. She'll have to decide whether to sell the house—she probably can't afford the payments. She'll have to get a job—when he wasn't on active duty there won't be a pension. Insurance, but how far that'll go— Hell."

"At least she's lucky to have you and your wife to help," said Hackett conventionally.

"Well, we'd all been good friends awhile. Give and take," said Hoffman. He pressed one temple with the heel of his hand. "Walt wasn't as good with his hands as I am—I helped him put in those louver windows. He was good at figures—always did my tax returns." He laughed without humor. "Saved me from making an expensive mistake just a couple of weeks ago. I'd been thinking of putting in a pool. Larry—our oldest boy—he's on the champion swimming team at school, has big ideas of getting into the Olympics someday. Walt showed me what a fool idea it'd be—the neighborhood running down, we won't be there forever, and it'd up the taxes. Damn it, I'll miss him—and he'll be missed here. And what Cathy's going to do— Well—"

"You never know," said Hackett meaninglessly. "Something may break."

"Yeah," said Hoffman.

The Robbery-Homicide men spent most of the day at Welfare and Rehab, turning up old records and hunting for Robsen's name. The computer wasn't any help on that. In the end, they came up with a handful of names, none of the owners sounding very likely; but of course they wouldn't know until they found them and looked at them.

Hackett got back to his own office to hear about the explosion; everybody was gone then except Mendoza, who hailed him into his office to hear about the wild goose.

"Oh, for God's sake," said Hackett. "Of all the— yes, I see. If the same thing happened to Ruth, only a little more serious—it could even add up to Murder One. It'll have to be followed up. And damn it, nobody's got back to those neighbors of the Robsens', and there's the Pace thing too—I wish to God things would come one at a time." He'd been reading the lab report on the Pace house, and now took off his glasses and folded them away. "We'll waste a lot of time looking up these old cases of Robsen's, and it'll fizzle into nothing, only two of them have any history of violence at all. But you had to have the idea."

He felt a little better, driving home in the smooth-running Monte Carlo. He'd noticed he got the stares, stopped at traffic lights: the paint job. He didn't mind. Tomorrow was his day off. He wondered if Angel had found any more houses. She was looking down toward the beach now—a good many areas down there weren't much better. Well, wait and see.

On Thursday morning, as Mendoza laid a hand on the garage door to open it, most of Los Angeles was slightly shaken by a little earthquake. It wasn't enough to do any damage; it rattled windows, toppled an ornament here and there. There wasn't any follow-up, and ten minutes later most residents had forgotten about it—the kind of thing that happened fifty times a year.

At the office, Lake said Higgins and Palliser had already gone out. Conway was up in Callaghan's office. The inquest on Pearl Davidson was scheduled for ten o'clock that morning, and Grace would cover that. Arthur Banks was to be arraigned in another court at the same time, and Landers would cover that. Mendoza took Glasser and Grace into his office and told them about the wild goose. They were amused and incredulous.

"Kind of like a Victorian melodrama," commented Galeano. "But I see it, we'd better locate this Fogarty girl and hear what she's got to say. I suppose it amounts to bodily harm, some degree of assault. And with the Byrd girl dead—though it'd probably be impossible to prove anything on that— Well, we'll have a look around."

As they went out, Mendoza was taking the pack of cards from the top drawer and beginning to shuffle them. Glasser said, "You know, Nick, I can't make this out about Wanda."

"What about her?" asked Galeano.

"Well, she said she was going to Carlsbad on her vacation, and here she turns up way up in Marysville." He pulled out the postcard and showed it.

"Oh," said Galeano. "Well, I wouldn't worry, Henry. She's due back on Monday, we'll probably hear all about it then." There had, of course, been a little speculation on the office grapevine about Wanda and Glasser.

At ten-thirty that morning Gil Lane was sitting as usual at his table behind the long counter past the double doors of the Museum of Natural (North American) History, working the crossword puzzle in the *Times*. As usual, it was very quiet; there'd been only one party in since he opened up. If this had been a private business, he'd often thought, it would be losing money hand over fist; there hadn't been twenty people in all week. Well, it was an easy job in a way.

The party that had come in consisted of two women, a man and a couple of kids. They hadn't been there very long, and he was faintly surprised to see them coming out again. They all went out except for one woman, who came up to the counter. He got up.

"I'd just like to say I'm surprised, and I don't like it," she said. She was an angular, thin woman in a red pantsuit. "I think it's very poor taste. I've always enjoyed the exhibits here, and my husband's sister and her family are visiting from Illinois, I wanted them to see the museum. Well! I don't know what your designers or whatever they're called are thinking of, but I call it very poor taste. Gruesome—the children were quite upset, I suppose they'll have nighmares about it." She turned to march out and then fired a parting shot. "Besides, it's unscientific—eagles don't carry people off, they're not strong enough!"

"Ma'am?" said Lane; but she was gone. He stared after her. Eagles? he thought. There was an exhibit of eagles, a new one, but he didn't remember anything gruesome about it.

After a minute—there wasn't another soul in the public rooms—he got up and came out from behind the counter, and went down to the hall of North American wildlife. The eagle display was the first on the left as you went in. He looked at it. And then he said, "Oh, Jesus! Oh, Lord God!" That kid there'd been a fuss about last week—

He ran for the telephone.

Mendoza was practicing the crooked deals when Lake came down the hall and said, "The kid at the County Museum, Lieutenant—they've just found her, right there. The beat man said—" He looked sick.

"*¡Vaya!*" said Mendoza, and got up in a hurry. "Right there? *¿Qué es esto?* All right, call Carey—I'm on my way!"

He used the siren all the way down Figueroa to Exposition Park. As he swung the Ferrari into the big public parking lot, very briefly there slid across his mind a small memory of some nonsensical case that had started here—Alison's car being stolen out of this lot, and that was before they were married— There were only a few cars here now. There was a squad car with doors open up at the front of the lot.

He knew this city like the palm of his hand, but he couldn't remember ever going into the County Museum. It was a complex of grounds and buildings on at least twenty acres in the middle of town: there was the state Armory, the famous rose gardens with every known variety, the Coliseum, a big sports arena, and besides the County Museum, the Museum of Science and Industry. A uniformed patrolman was standing at the top of a flight of broad steps in front of the first big building beyond the parking lot; that would be the Museum of Natural History. Mendoza ran up the steps. It was very hot again today, but the sweat on the patrolman's forehead was not from the heat.

"My God, Lieutenant," he said. "My God, I never saw anything like this—" He swallowed, turned and led the way.

It was a huge building with high ceilings—"like a church in the middle of the week," he remembered Carey saying. There was a wide corridor leading off in two directions. The patrolman led him straight down past a counter beyond the entrance, down a corridor where glass cases lined the walls. A hundred feet up they passed a stout man in blue uniform leaning on the wall. He looked frightened. There was a wide doorless entrance to the right of this corridor, and suddenly Mendoza found himself in a long, high, wide hall in very subdued light, like a theater before the curtain goes up. On either side of the hall and at the far end was a series of huge displays of mounted creatures behind glass. Each display must be twenty feet high, twelve or fifteen wide, and the only light was inside and above the exhibits. They were a series of brilliant, realistic, three-dimensional still lifes. Appropriate scenic backdrops behind, actual simulated rocks, trees, forest or desert growth in the foreground, surrounded the mounted animals. A snarling mountain lion lay along a tree branch, a grizzly bear stood upright on a hillside, a family of deer paused in a forest glen, chipmunks chattered silently in trees above.

To the left of that entrance, the first display on the wall, a bevy of birds was artistically arranged. The scene was a mountaintop with rolling slopes in the distance, a forest marching down a mountainside far below, in the foreground a conical rocky crag, rocks and rough earth around it: an eagle's nest at the top, one great bald eagle poised with wings spread in the air, the female resting on the side of the crag. At the other side, three or four different birds on the ground.

The slender little body was lying, head down, just to the side of the steep crag. *"¡Jesús y María!"* said Mendoza softly. "She was behind that all the time, and that quake—" He swung to the patrolman. "Get on to my office. Tell Sergeant Lake to shoot everybody out here as they show up!"

It was a while before they could even get at the body. The head curator was on the premises, a Mr. Aubrey Keogh, and shaken and astonished as he was, he managed to answer questions as they were fired at him. He was tall and elderly, quiet-voiced, authoritative. The exhibit—"It was finished just last week, the glass should have been reinstalled on Wednesday but it was still open Thursday morning, I think it was put in that day. Mr. Van Tine will know—the men who worked on it." The exhibits were not changed often, perhaps twice a year. They were arranged by the assistant curators, wildlife experts; the old display would be dismantled, the case opened from both front and back, and when the new exhibit was finished the glass reinstalled. There was access to the back of the cases from a narrow corridor behind. That would be the only way to get into a case without removing the glass.

"But the glass was still out of this one last Thursday morning?"

"Yes," said Keogh; until a new exhibit was finished and ready, the front opening of the case would be covered with a heavy canvas drop. The work would be done at night when the museum was closed to the public; normally it might take a couple of days to mount a new exhibit. As far as he recalled, this one had been finished on Wednesday, the glass reinstalled and the canvas removed on Thursday.

By then Carey was there, a lab team was called up, and Conway had come out. Keogh produced keys and led them through a small door off the main hall to a long, narrow corridor lit with naked bulbs at the back of that wall of display cases. The back of each case was a wide door folding flat against the wall; as this one swung open, it showed on its inner side the painted

107

mountain vistas and forested slopes that formed a background for the eagles.

"Christ," said Scarne. He climbed gingerly up to the three-foot-high platform, Horder after him. They approached the body carefully; after a few minutes Scarne backed out. "There's hardly any decomposition," he said. "All but sealed in here—cyanosis—but it looks to me as if she'd been strangled. The doctors'll say. I don't know if any of that stuff in there would take prints."

"Have a try at it anyway."

"So now we know," said Carey. "And what a damn fool thing—but we said that kind never thinks ahead."

They left the lab team to the routine, and started gathering information from Keogh. He had already called the assistant curator responsible for the display.

There was, he explained, a regular staff of general workmen. A good deal of rough work to be done, the regular maintenance, jobs like these exhibits; and maintenance of the basement rooms, where exhibits not on display were stored. Sometimes, as on a job like the mounted animal exhibits, they worked under the direction of one of the curators. There was a regular schedule for the cleaning work, the floors, cases, windows. Of course the men were screened before being employed, they couldn't have any irresponsible person even occasionally handling valuable objects. He didn't recall that they'd added a new employee to the staff in several years. But there were records on all the men: previous employment and so on.

There was a separate staff of gardeners for the rose gardens; the Armory, the Museum of Science and Industry had their own staffs of maintenance men. Keogh could see where they were heading, and he was upset, but he went on answering questions. There were twenty men on the staff here, and two all-night security guards. The guards had keys for all the locks in the building except those of the glass display cases. The maintenance staff held only certain keys: those to the rest rooms, basement doors, supply closets.

And by then Martin Van Tine, the assistant curator, had got there, shocked and shaken. He was younger than Keogh by thirty years, and if anything his mind moved faster. "I see how you're thinking on it—there was only that one period—but my God—"

"Exactly, Mr. Van Tine," said Mendoza. They were all in Keogh's private office at the front of the building, waiting for reinforcements from headquarters, waiting for a preliminary report from the lab men. Mendoza had called the coroner's office and routed out Bainbridge. "According to the information you've given us, if I understand it, that display case was open for only that Thursday morning, a week ago today."

"It had been open a couple of days, while we were working on the display. I started work on it Tuesday night. It was finished by Wednesday night, and the men could have put the glass back then but there really wasn't any hurry about it. I told them next day would do. We wouldn't be getting many visitors until the weekend."

"How do you arrange the night work—some of the men regularly on nights?"

"Yes, the regular clean-up crews, all that has to be done at night. It would have been a couple of the day staff put the glass back—it's a job for at least two men."

"You're thinking one of our staff is responsible for this terrible thing," said Keogh.

"It's really the obvious answer, you can see," said Mendoza. "All the easier for him to get hold of the child—in uniform, looking like authority to her. And later on, when he wanted to get rid of the body, a staff employee would have been most likely to think of that open display case. In fact, with the canvas over it, only an employee could have known that the case was open."

"It was a damn fool thing to do because it points straight at one of the employees here," said Carey.

"I can hardly believe—they've all been with us a long time, all quite reliable—I follow the reasoning," said Keogh, "but it seems incredible."

"Do the maintenance men have keys to that back corridor?"

"No," said Van Tine. "Only the museum staff."

Mendoza shrugged. "The front was open. He had only to wait until there was nobody around, get under the canvas drop and stash her away, out of sight from the front. How long might it have been before you opened the back of that case again?"

"It might have been months," muttered Van Tine miserably.

Keogh had been on the phone at intervals, and said now, "Those two men are here—Adams and Pickering. They're the ones who put the glass back."

They looked like ordinary honest men: both in their forties, Adams balding and stout, Pickering taller and thin. They had heard about the body; Keogh had closed the museum to the public without being asked. They were looking shocked and curious. "When did that glass get reinstalled?" Van Tine asked.

"We've been trying to pin it down," said Pickering, blinking. "My God, if we'd had any idea—there didn't seem to be any hurry, we don't get a crowd except at weekends. You'd left orders to put it back, but we didn't get to it till just before lunch."

"That's right," confirmed Adams. "It was on to noon, we'd been in the basement moving some stuff around like Mr. Gibson told us day before. We were going to knock off for lunch and I said to you, 'Let's get that glass in, it's a bastard to fit back and we won't have to think of it after lunch.' So we did it, and then knocked off."

"How long had you been together in the basement?" asked Mendoza.

They consulted each other. "Since nine-thirty anyway."

"Well," said Mendoza as they went out, "that's two eliminated anyway." Nobody else had shown up from headquarters, and he was debating calling Hackett in. Every single one of the staff here was going to be questioned thoroughly.

The door opened without ceremony and Dr. Bainbridge came in. "I'll tell you more when I've had a better look. But she was strangled all right, Luis."

"And raped? Molested?"

110

"I couldn't say right now. It looks like that kind of case, doesn't it? I'll get to her right away."

"Oh, my God," said Van Tine.

Keogh answered the phone again. "Some more of your men have arrived, Lieutenant."

"You understand that we'll want to look at your records on all these men, and I'm afraid we'll be interrupting your routine here while we question them."

"Certainly, Lieutenant," said Keogh quietly. "The only consideration must be to find out who committed this crime, though I can't believe it was one of our men. But of course we'll give you every cooperation."

Mendoza drove out to Brentwood Estates in the late afternoon. He hadn't felt inclined to break the news in person and waste time watching even the disciplined emotions of the sisters at St. Odile's; he had phoned the Mother Superior an hour before.

It was an old and beautiful little estate behind its wall, old trees in manicured grounds, several large Spanish stucco buildings with red tile roofs. The iron gates were locked, but there was a bell; he was expected, and a silent novitiate came to let him in, led him past a separate chapel into the first building. It would be, he recognized, the sisters' dormitory. Undoubtedly some of them quartered in the girls' dormitory; where would the classrooms be? Ground floor perhaps, bedrooms above on two top floors. He was tired, his mind reaching for trifles. They climbed bare, polished stairs.

The novitiate knocked at a door, was bidden to enter, stood back to let him in. And this would be the Mother Superior's office. It was a pleasant room, rather bare without being ascetic, with a view over treetops. She was a little woman with black eyes in a very white face, and she smiled at him serenely. Sister Mary Katharine and Sister Mary Constance sat side-by-side under the window. They had both been crying.

"You gave us very sad news, Lieutenant. But we must abide by God's will, and I believe we had all

111

known—guessed—when so much time had passed. I must ask you—" she compressed her lips—"was she raped?"

"We don't know that yet."

"Ah, I see. If there is any way we can help you— Please sit down."

"I don't know whether you can or not. Do you remember—" he looked at the two sisters—"seeing that canvas drop over one of the display cases that morning?"

"Oh, yes," said Sister Mary Katharine. "I'd been there before when an exhibit was being changed. I remember noticing it that day. Just casually."

"I don't suppose you can give me any idea at all of which girl was where at any given time while you were in that particular room?"

They looked at each other. Sister Mary Constance looked pale enough to faint. "Mother of God," she said, "haven't we been asking ourselves—if we were to blame—not watching carefully enough? But who could suspect, in a public place and no one else there—no, I can't remember. I know Paula went in ahead of me, and I'm almost sure Joyce and Peggy were with her. Magda was walking with me. I remember seeing Peggy a little later, with Ann Garner, looking at the elk— Joyce wasn't with them then. And then Elsa asked me something about the mountain lion and I went over there with her—"

"Would this Paula remember anything?"

A little pause. The Mother Superior said, "You had better see her if you like." At her glance Sister Mary Katharine went out quietly. "I had better explain to you that Paula is my great-niece. She is retarded mentally, but a very docile, gentle child and as she is an orphan it seems to me that this is a better place for her than an institution. She is very good and kind with the young children. She is fifteen."

"I see." Nothing to be had from her, then. Nothing definite to be had from any of them, and now, thinking about that place, he could admit that it was only natural. The great darkened echoing hall, the light

112

from the tall cases illuminating only its own vicinity. The children wandering back and forth, distracting the sisters' attention with questions. And so far as anyone knew, a very safe place: a very innocent place.

"Do you remember seeing any of the uniformed attendants?" he asked Sister Mary Constance.

"No, except for the man by the entrance. Oh, when we were in the weaving and pottery room one of them passed the door." She was fingering her rosary. It came to him irrelevantly that they must have the baby baptized. If he had time, he would call Father Donovan tomorrow.

"Here's Paula," said Sister Mary Katharine.

She wasn't a bad-looking girl, large for her age, smooth pale skin, smooth brown hair neatly combed. But her round face was curiously blank and innocent. "Perhaps I'd better—" said the Mother Superior. "It's about Joyce, Paula. Do you remember being at the museum with Joyce and the others last week?"

"Oh, yes, Mother." She had a clear thin voice; and suddenly her expression lit up, and she smiled. "To the animals. We always like to see the animals."

"When you went to see them, you went into that room first, with Peggy and Joyce—Sister Mary Constance was behind you?"

"To the deers," she said happily. "Yes. The deers with the horns. But poor Joyce, she was scared. She told me she was so scared—because the doctor was going to stick needles in her again, and it hurt. Poor Joyce." The doctor's appointment that afternoon, remembered Mendoza. "She wished she didn't have to go."

"Did she stay with you, after she said that, dear?"

"Oh, no," said Paula definitely. "She went away— because she wanted to. And I went to look at the lion with Peggy and Ann."

"Where did Joyce go, do you know?" Paula looked uncertain and then shook her head. The Mother Superior looked at Mendoza; he shrugged and got up. He had had some idea of talking to the rest of the children, pinning down memories; but it would be an exercise in futility. The Mother Superior nodded at Sister Mary Katharine, who took Paula's arm and led her out.

"Another thing," said Mendoza. "When you said the children were told to keep together, did you mean they were together in each room at all times?"

"Well, the little ones," said Sister Mary Katharine. "They all knew they weren't to leave the building. But some of the older ones were a little bored with the animals and went back, I believe, to the pottery room. I know Magda was there when I was—collecting them all to leave."

All he could do was thank them. They hadn't anything useful to tell him. Poor women, he supposed they'd go on blaming themselves for it; but they couldn't have known that evil was anywhere in those quiet halls. Danger, in a friendly blue uniform. Because that had to be the answer.

He had left Hackett, Higgins and Galeano down there, Grace coming in an hour or so ago, to ask questions, try to pin down times and facts. There'd be more to do on it tomorrow. The novitiate let him out through the gate silently. He got into the car and started home.

Before all that broke, Nick Galeano had taken over Mendoza's wild goose. He had gone looking alone, because a new call went down just as he and Glasser were leaving, and Glasser went out on that. Galeano rather liked Mendoza's wild goose; it was something different. He found a Dennis Fogarty in the phone book, at an address on Ninth, which was close enough to that pharmacy, and tried there first. A pleasant-looking gray-haired woman admitted that she was Mrs. Fogarty and had a daughter named Barbara. "But she doesn't live here now, she has her own apartment with another girl. Why do you want to know?" Galeano showed her the badge and first she looked a trifle less alarmed and then a trifle more. "Police?"

"It's just a little matter of something she witnessed," said Galeano easily. "Nothing important."

"Oh, well," she said. "Well, it's on Ardmore. But as

a matter of fact I don't know whether she's there. She's taking a vacation and she said something about going somewhere for a few days. But Rona could tell you—the girl she lives with, she works nights at the phone company so she'll be home."

She was, and annoyed with Galeano for ringing the doorbell. "I'm sorry," he apologized, "but I won't take five minutes. I'm looking for Miss Fogarty."

"Well, you can't see her till next Sunday," said Rona. "She's on vacation. She went off with Bill to Catalina."

"Bill," said Galeano with interest.

"Yes, Bill Loring, she's engaged to him. Oh, there's nothing wrong about it," said Rona hastily. "They're with his parents. The Lorings have a summer cottage over there, and a boat. At first Bill thought he couldn't get away, but he did, so they went. But Barbara has to be at work on Monday so she'll probably be back Sunday. Now you've got me wide awake, what's it all about?"

"Just a few questions for her," said Galeano, and turned away from her curious eyes.

He'd just got back to tell Mendoza about that when the McCauley thing broke, and he spent the rest of the day at the museum with Hackett and Higgins, and later on Grace. The boss went off about four o'clock to see those sisters at the convent.

By then they'd got the thing sorted out and had a better idea what to ask.

"Damn it, it's the only possible answer," Higgins was saying now. "Ten men on the regular day staff, and we haven't checked thoroughly but their records look clean on the surface. Which says nothing. They were wandering all over this place, except for those two in the basement, claim to have been cleaning rest rooms and checking supplies, God knows what—why the hell do they need ten men in this morgue? Any of them could have been anywhere anytime. But—"

"Morgue is about right," said Hackett. The curators had gone away and they were using Keogh's office; they'd done a first round of questioning those men without getting anything suggestive. "I'll say something

115

else. This place must be full of nooks and crannies where he could have taken her. They've all got keys to the inside doors, most of 'em anyway. As far as we've sorted it out, there were only three of the museum staff here that day—Keogh and Van Tine and this Gibson fellow—and they were all down in the basement—"

"And not," said Galeano, "together."

"God, yes, I suppose we keep that in mind too. But all those men will know this place like their own homes. Lane tells us as far as he remembers there weren't any more outside visitors until after two o'clock."

"It had to be before twelve, if Adams and Pickering are right," said Galeano, and discovered he was out of cigarettes.

"All right—all right. That still goes. The nuns and the kids were here for an hour and a half. He still had time. He took her off to a back supply closet or somewhere, and then he came back and saw the nuns and kids were gone and stashed the body in the display case."

"He had luck," said Galeano thoughtfully. "Bum a cigarette from you, Jase? He probably didn't know when Adams and Pickering were going to replace that glass—they didn't themselves. There wasn't any hurry about it. But it must have been a near thing they didn't spot him. He couldn't very well have stashed her there much before a quarter of twelve."

Grace had been sitting listening, smoking quietly. "You still aren't thinking simple enough," he said now gently. "We're told the maintenance staff doesn't have keys to open that back corridor behind the cases. Not necessary because it's used so seldom. Well, I'll remind you first that obviously they've got keys to the front doors, to get in—they're the first ones in every day. Me, I don't know how a child rapist might feel, but I kind of think I'd feel mighty damn nervous carting that body around here right at noontime. He'd have no guarantee one of his fellow employees, or a visitor, or Keogh himself wouldn't turn up round any corridor. There seem to be about twenty different curators, assistants, here—attached to the place, biologists, geologists, naturalists, God knows what—and you're not going to tell me it'd be so damn difficult to get hold of a key to that back corridor, all the staff have 'em. I don't know whether you noticed, but when Keogh left awhile back—" Grace reached out lazily—"he left a whole ring of keys hanging from the drawer of his desk." He dangled them in the air.

"By God!" said Hackett and Higgins together.

"Now if it were me, stuck with that body," said Grace, "I'd have stashed it under some cartons of toilet paper or something, locked in a supply closet, and hid it away in that case after everybody else had left. The night crew doesn't come on till ten. And by then, of course, the glass was back—but that wouldn't matter. It wasn't really such a damn fool hiding place—she might not have been found for months, and no way to pin things down by then. I'd have gone looking to see if Keogh had left his keys—ten to one it's a habit of his—and after the place was closed and everybody gone, I'd have come back and gone in. Between the museum closing at five and the night crew coming on."

"By God," said Hackett thoughtfully. "I'm inclined to think you've got something, Jase." He looked at his watch. "Lean on all of them again tomorrow. We might get an autopsy report—Bainbridge was getting right on it."

Galeano went home to his bachelor apartment, showered, shaved again and got dressed, and went to pick up Marta Fleming. There was only one place to go on a summer night, the Castaway up in the hills above Burbank, where you had a view over Hollywood and L.A., over the hills beyond right down to the beach: a million lights; and up here you couldn't read the silly things the lights said, it was just a million jewels against the dark sky.

"You were late because some important new case came down?" asked Marta. She looked very delectable in a pale-green sleeveless sheath, pearl earrings, her tawny-blonde hair loose-waving about her face. Her dark eyes were serious on him as she sipped her cocktail.

"Went down," corrected Galeano, smiling. Suddenly he remembered that Tom Landers and his Phillippa Rosemary had got engaged right here one night. He didn't want to tell her about Joyce McCauley; it would cast a pall over the evening, she'd be harking back to that unhappy marriage and the baby she'd lost. "It was kind of funny," he said, and told her about the anonymous letter and Mendoza's wild goose.

Marta was amused. *Es ist drollig.* Oh, it is not so funny for those girls—I should not laugh. But so naïve—the toast for the birthday!"

Glasser, good harness cop that he was, plodded out on the new call routinely. It didn't look like the making of much work, a clear-cut suicide. There was a note left. An old lady, she'd been, and by the looks of the place living pretty close to the bone. Maybe you could understand it.

"She just didn't have anything to live for," said the woman who had found her, a neighbor, another old lady. "Poor old soul—not but what it's a shock, just seems like we're going off one after another. I hadn't seen her out in a few days, just came over to ask how she was keeping, and when I didn't get any answer— I knew she was home, she never went out. My husband said we'd better call you, she had a bad heart—"

"Yes, ma'am," said Glasser. Going by the routine, he called the lab out, and went back to the office to write the report.

It just added a little to the small worry in his mind. He and Wanda had dated, and he'd settled on her as his girl and thought she'd sort of settled on him, though nothing had actually been said. The only relative he had in the world was a cousin riding a squad car in Hollywood. That poor old woman—*"nobody to miss me,"* she'd written in the note— Well, if you were married you had somebody at least. And that postcard—

On Friday morning Mendoza came in energetically and listened to what they told him about that museum crew, and Jase's little idea. *"Muy posible,"* said Men-

118

doza. "All I know is, we're going to haul in those men and go at them hot and heavy. Look back to see if any of them's ever been in this kind of trouble before. Because one of them is the answer—whether your fiddling about with keys is valid or not, Jase, but I think you could be right."

"Robsen," said Hackett. "If we're going to follow up—"

"Por Dios," said Mendoza, "everything to work at once—I know, Art. But let's get on this. Eight men to look at all told—"

"Oh, yes?" said Hackett. "We can't rule out the curators because they've got university degrees. And all the staff have got keys. If one of them was there for some reason that morning—"

"Probabilities, *por favor.*" Mendoza glanced over the night-watch report. Another heist; as expected. There was an autopsy report in. Rae-Jean Pace. He looked it over rapidly, handed it to Hackett. "You went out on this."

"Hell," said Hackett, reading the name, "and we never followed up on that either—I will be damned!"

"Why?" asked Higgins.

"Estimated time of death," said Hackett, "between seven and ten P.M. Monday night."

"Oh, isn't that interesting," said Higgins.

Mendoza cocked his head at them. "Say something?"

"Something loud and clear," said Hackett.

7

THEY HAD TALKED TO THIS MAN BEFORE, IN THE SAME shabby living room, with the quiet body of the girl sprawled across the couch under the window. His name was Vincent Pace, and he was a heavy-shouldered dark man with a bad-tempered mouth. He scowled at Hackett and Higgins.

"I just got home, I got to get my sleep. What the hell do you want?"

"Some straight answers," said Hackett. "You told us you left for work about ten last Monday night, and Rae-Jean was all right then." The other two girls appeared in the kitchen door; they were about fourteen and sixteen; he didn't remember their names. Both were in too-short shorts and T-shirts.

"That's right."

"Was it Brian killed her?" asked the older girl casually. "Pa was always arguing at her not to marry him."

"I was glad she was getting married," said the other one. "Always bossing us around. Just because she was the oldest."

Pace swung on them. "You two get in the kitchen and do up them dishes!"

"Just a minute," said Hackett. "You two were out that evening? What time did you get home?"

The older one shrugged. "Big deal. To a movie. About eleven-thirty, and for once Rae hadn't waited up to see we was in, we thought. Next morning Pa found her."

"You go do them dishes."

"O.K., O.K." They went out.

"I told you all I know about it," said Pace.

"I don't think so," said Hackett. "She was dead before ten o'clock. You knew that. Before you left."

"That's a—how did you know that?"

"The doctors can tell, Pace. They told us. You were arguing with her, weren't you? Then what happened?"

Pace's face suffused with a rush of dark blood. "She hadn't no call!" he said chokingly. "She hadn't no call, walk out on me—she had a duty to me! Who's gonna keep the house and fix meals and all? Those two lazy sluts, catch them! She wouldn't listen—she wouldn't— I just took hold of her to shake some sense into her—oh, my God—I never meant her no real harm—" Suddenly he collapsed onto the couch and just sat there, head hanging.

Hackett and Higgins got rather tired of human nature sometimes. They gave him his rights, with the girls looking on in silence; they couldn't tell how the girls were feeling. They took him down to the Alameda jail and booked him in, went back to the office and applied for the warrant. Higgins began to write the final report and Hackett talked with Juvenile division about the girls. It didn't occupy much of the morning to disrupt and change all those lives, but of course Vincent Pace had done the original disrupting.

It was just after ten-thirty when they joined the rest of the men on the McCauley case.

It was Glasser's day off, and a new call had gone down at eight-thirty so Conway and Landers had gone out on that, but everybody else was out on Joyce, one way or another. They had commandeered the museum's records on all its employees, and Palliser, Galeano and Grace were out checking those, looking back on those men as it was possible, talking to former employers. None of them, of course, had any police record. On the face of it, they all looked equally unlikely. One of them had been working there for nineteen years, one for five; the rest for various periods in between.

They were brought in to question in batches, and they were cooperative. But as one of them, Joe Sullivan, said to Mendoza, "I know how you're thinking, and by God I'd be thinking the same way, sir. I'd have said I know all these men inside out, working with 'em for years. But men can go off the rails like. But the trouble is, you can ask where I was and I can tell you, damn it, what good is it? I was down in the basement unpacking all those damn crates Mr. Gibson sent back from that dig in Arizona, just like he asked me to. It was really a two-man job, but I tell you no lie, some of them goof off on slow days. I was there to about eleven-fifteen, and I went to the rest room down there and ran into Holderby, and he said he'd been there an hour cleaning the place, the night crew was getting sloppy and it'd been a mess. But I don't *know* he'd been there—he just said so—and you don't *know* I'd been where I say. Nothing to prove it." He was a big bulky man, and he looked angry and apprehensive. "My good God, Lieutenant, I'd cut off my right hand before I hurt a kid, I got grandchildren of my own—and I'd take an oath, before this, any man on the crew felt the same way. But it's easy to talk."

As the morning wore on and their list of timetables grew more complicated, the picture came clearer. Mendoza was annoyed. He disliked untidiness in general; perhaps one reason Luis Rodolfo Vicente Mendoza had stayed at the thankless job was his hatred of loose ends and vaguenesses; a detective was committed to precise answers. With the discovery of the body, the one pointer was fixed squarely toward the staff in the museum, and it was turning out to be impossible to show any definite evidence. Only Adams and Pickering alibied each other; the other eight men had been alone at various places in the building. They said. Keogh had been in his office. Van Tine had been in his office in the basement, doing some writing. They said.

This was the second time they'd talked to all these men. At one o'clock they went up to Federico's for lunch—Mendoza, Hackett and Higgins. They ran into Conway and Landers just entering.

"What was the new one?" asked Mendoza, uninterested.

Conway said laconically, "A hooker. Name of Jeanette Remling. About thirty, not a bad looker. She was in business for herself, so the girl friend indignantly informed us when we asked about a boyfriend, read that pimp. Neither of them let any man run them, and it was a free country. They had apartments across the hall from each other at a place on Commonwealth."

"What'd it look like?" asked Higgins.

"Somebody roughed her up and probably strangled her. Hazard of the job," said Conway. "I just put the lab on it." They sat down at a big table in the back.

Hackett got out his glasses to study the menu. He was used to them now, and the others used to the vaguely scholarly appearance they gave him. The waiter came up with coffee. They ordered more or less at

122

random, and Mendoza sat back and lit a cigarette. He said abruptly, "So all right, who don't we all like?"

"Whom," said Higgins. "Clyde Moore."

"*Exactamente.*"

"Time, opportunity and proximity," said Hackett.

"And how do we prove it?" asked Higgins.

Clyde Moore was the one who had been on that crew for five years. He was a man about forty, and he was one of two unmarried men in the bunch; the other one, Grimalski, was a widower. Moore said he had been busy that morning washing the glass cases lining the halls; he had worked his way up from the side wing of the museum to the main corridor, and he admitted that he had noticed the party of nuns and kids in the wildlife hall as he passed up that corridor. He would be the attendant Sister Mary Katharine had seen. He had been busy over the cases until he knocked off for lunch, he said.

"*¡Diez millón demonios!*" said Mendoza. "There's just no solid evidence. Unless the lab gives us something to put him on the scene—but I like him, I like him." Not that you could pick killers on looks. Moore was a dark, taciturn fellow with deep lines of bitterness carved in his face and dark, sunken eyes. "Has anybody checked back on his employment record yet?— no, we're doing it alphabetically and the boys won't have got to him yet. I could bear to know more about Moore's past."

"He admits he was on the spot," said Hackett, "but he couldn't very well claim he wasn't, because he went straight past Gil Lane out there in the lobby and Lane spoke to him. Asked him something about the crossword he was working. And that was about an hour, or less, after the nuns and kids had come in. Say ten to eleven."

"But," said Higgins, "Moore had been—or so he says—working in that corridor down from the lobby, so he'd have seen them come in at ten o'clock. If he had a sudden yen for a little girl, he knew they were wandering around in there."

"Oh, I like him," said Mendoza. "We'll take a long,

hard look at him, boys. If we can dig out anything suggestive on him at all, and lean on him hard enough, we might get him to come apart. Of all those men he's the likeliest, by the little we've turned up." But they were still talking to them, getting estimates of where each man was when, what other men they'd seen when; Higgins had started to draw up a timetable that looked like something out of an old-fashioned detective novel.

After lunch Conway and Landers went to see the immediate reference Moore had given when he applied for the museum job five years ago. It was an office-cleaning service operating out of a cubicle on the top floor of an old building on Western; the boss and also owner was a Peter Salvatore, a shrewd-eyed, swarthy man who listened to their questions in silence and grunted. They didn't tell him anything about the case.

"Moore," he said. "He in some trouble? Forget I asked. I don't want to commit slander, but I'll tell you so much. I never had any fault to find with his work, but I got the idea he was the one responsible for some petty theft we kept having. Nothing much—few cleaning supplies, little cash out of the office box, a flashlight—like that. I don't know it was him so I couldn't accuse him. I told him business was slowing up and let him go. But naturally I couldn't put that in the reference I gave him, he'd have sued me."

"Do tell," said Landers. Of course it didn't say anything about Joyce. They went back to pass that on to Mendoza, and help out on the questioning.

By late afternoon Higgins was muttering and tearing his hair over the timetable; the other men were back with everything they'd gathered on the men's backgrounds, and Hackett was drawing up a list of names with all the information they had appended to each.

"Moore sticks out like a sore thumb," he said, sitting back after adding the latest news. "By his own admission he was fifty feet away from the door to the wildlife hall between about ten-fifty and eleven-thirty. And the nuns tell you, Luis, that all the kids might not have stayed in there. Most of them. But say Joyce

didn't. She started back to one of the other rooms—
and he'd see her come out. She'd be right there under
his hand, for long enough."

"You don't need to convince me," said Mendoza.
"It adds up like two plus two. But as to evidence—"

As if on cue, Scarne and Horder walked in.
"Thought you'd want to know," said Scarne, "that we
picked up some dandy latents in that display case.
Mostly from that back panel, both sides, some on the
inside of the glass. The rough plastic stuff used for the
rocks and so on, none of that would take any. We
collected everybody's to compare—all the men, Van
Tine's, Keogh's. Haven't got to that yet."

"Anybody offer any objection?"

"No," said Scarne, "all nice and cooperative. Bowed
to the inevitable. By the way—" he took something out
of his pocket and dropped it on the desk in front of
Mendoza. "It was lying right beside her, I guess—that
is, where she'd been, back of that artificial mountaintop." It was a rosary made of plain, carved wooden
beads. "No prints on it, they're too small to show
anything."

Mendoza picked it up absently and fingered it.
Joyce's rosary, maybe fallen out of a pocket as she was
lifted in there. At night? he wondered suddenly, thinking of Grace's deductions. He dropped it in the top
drawer; he must remember to give it to the sisters, or
Carey; doubtless McCauley would like to have it.
"Well, that's something," he said. "If you can show
Moore was anywhere near that exhibit—he shouldn't
have been. He didn't do any work on it at all."

"You've spotted him as X?" asked Horder.

"Damn it, he's obvious," said Mendoza, and Bainbridge came in.

"Conference?" He looked around at the little crowd;
they were bunched together in Mendoza's office, chairs
at odd angles. Galeano offered the doctor his, and
Bainbridge sat down, stuck out his short fat legs and
got out a cigar. "Well, she wasn't raped," he said.
"Little surprise, hah? She wasn't molested in any way.
Just strangled."

"*¡Parece mentira!*" said Mendoza. "You don't say."

"That puts a little different face on it," said Hackett, taking off his glasses.

"Oh, I don't think so," said Bainbridge comfortably. "It didn't take much to kill her. She was a chronic asthmatic, and if she'd been my patient I'd have diagnosed incipient T.B., couple of other possibilities. She wasn't, as they say, a good life. And small and thin even for her age. What could have happened, and what I think did happen, was that she died the minute after he took hold of her. A man with any strength—he grabbed her, squeezed her throat a little to keep her quiet, probably meaning to pick her up and take her somewhere private for the attack—and all of a sudden found he had a body on his hands. It would happen just like that," said Bainbridge, and snapped his fingers.

"I'll be damned," said Hackett. "So he was stuck with the body—all for nothing."

"My guess is, that's the size of it," said Bainbridge.

Piggott went to see Joan Brock that afternoon. She was living in a small apartment on Mountain Avenue. She was a pretty, fair girl with large hazel eyes, and she was surprised to see him.

"Don't tell me somebody's taking some official action on it? That's a switch." Piggott didn't waste time enlightening her. "Oh, I'm going back to Glen," she said wearily. "I don't like living this way. It was a gesture, really. Sam said it might stir him up to do something. But after that private detective couldn't find out anything— Do you have any conception of what it's been like? I even had a fight with Mother—she always liked Glen, but after a while she started saying it, no smoke without fire. And we sold the house—the neighbors— And Jay and Betty Reed, Betty and I were at school together, but they started turning down invitations and—"

"Yes," said Piggott. "Mrs. Brock—I'm going to be seeing your husband and I'll ask him this too—can you think of any little, unimportant difference your husband ever had with anybody?"

She stared at him, at his earnest, undistinguished face with the rather snub nose and serious blue eyes. "But that's what we've been saying all along! There's never been any important trouble with anybody, enough for anybody to be doing this—"

"I said little," said Piggott. "Something maybe he didn't think twice about. You see, Mrs. Brock, whoever's been doing this—it's a slightly crazy thing to do, so he may be too. So, when there's nothing else, the reason may be a little crazy in itself. It could be something that happened, something really petty, that Brock scarcely gave a thought to at the time. A—" he cast around in his mind—"a political argument, or a little minor traffic collision—almost anything. Sometimes, you know, people build things up in their minds that haven't any basis in fact."

She looked at him curiously, seriously. "I never thought about it that way," she said slowly. "I don't think Glen ever did. I—now that you put it that way—I can see there might be something in that."

"Listen, I'm telling you all I know, honest," said Nita Stone. "Jeanette was a good friend of mine and I'd sure like to see you get the guy who did it. I been honest with you, didn't try to cover up. She was on her own, like me, and believe me it's no easy life. She never had much."

It was Saturday morning, and Landers' day off; Nita had come in to make a statement about finding Jeanette Remling's body, and Conway was listening to her. "Well, I'm not going to arrest you on a soliciting charge right now," he said.

"I should hope not. Girl's own business. Different when it comes to a pimp beating you up, or those poor little kids you hear about." She was little and dark, with nervous eyes.

"All right," said Conway. "I just want a statement about your finding the body."

"Well, like I told you, I went across to borrow some instant coffee, I was out. And the door was unlocked, which was funny, so I went right in. And there she was

127

on the floor, and I knew right off she was dead. So I called the cops. That's it."

"Not quite," said Conway. "When did you see her last?"

"That noon. About. We had a cup of coffee together. She had her regular coming in the afternoon, and when I went out about six I tapped on her door, we'd said maybe we'd meet in Tobin's bar, middle of the evening, for a drink. But I guess she'd left already, she didn't sing out."

"Was her door locked then?"

"I don't know, I didn't try it. I'd sure think so. She was careful—you got to be."

Conway didn't laugh. "Who's her regular?"

"Oh, a guy named Roger Marsh. Every Thursday afternoon. Usually between, oh, two and three."

"Do you know what time she came home that night? Hear her come in?"

She shook her head. Conway sighed. He had an address book from Jeanette Remling's apartment, and unless they got lucky there was going to be a lot of legwork on this, looking at everybody in it, finding out where they were first: a lot of names had only phone numbers attached. All for a cheap whore. And the likelihood was, of course, that it had been some john she'd picked up that evening; she might not have known his name. But of course you couldn't have people running around killing people; that was one reason there were policemen. He supposed Matt Piggott would say, equal in the eyes of the Lord. He typed up the statement, and she signed it and left in a hurry. And the sooner some work was done on it the sooner they might wrap it up.

The R.M. in the address book was probably Roger Marsh, then. There were fourteen numbers with only initials attached; he got the appropriate phone company office and read them off. Eventually they'd get full names and addresses.

He looked up the address and went off to see if Tobin's bar was open. It wouldn't be until one o'clock. Conway took himself out to lunch wondering what was going on about Joyce. And they had dropped

Robsen; there was a lot more work to do on that; but of course a thing like Joyce rather took precedence. He expected Lieutenant Carey had had to break the news to McCauley, and didn't envy him the job.

At one-fifteen he was talking to the bartender in Tobin's, which was a small neighborhood place.

"Yeah, I know Jeanette," said the bartender, instantly recognizing Conway for what he was and taking him in stride. "And you don't have to get any funny ideas. She never picked up any johns in here, the boss, wouldn't like it. She used to come in about the middle of the evening, have a quiet drink or two, rest her feet."

"Was she in on Thursday night?"

"No, she wasn't. I remember, sure. It was a slow night, Thursday usually is."

Conway came out of the place, and passing a phone booth told himself he was losing his grip: age coming on probably. He looked, and a Roger Marsh was listed at an address on Clinton Stret down near Echo Park.

He drove up there; it was a little house at the rear of a larger house. Nobody was home at either place. He decided to leave it lay; maybe the lab would tell them something. The other boys could probably use some help.

Reluctantly, because they'd have liked to nail Moore for Joyce right away, Palliser, Grace and Galeano had gone back to the Robsen case and started following up all those old cases of his. It was heartbreaking legwork in the heat; they hadn't current addresses for half of them, and it came to looking up known relatives, old associates, old neighbors. About the middle of the afternoon Palliser suddenly remembered those next-door neighbors of the Robsens, who hadn't been talked to yet, and drove up there; but nobody was home. He wondered who they were and if they were ever home.

Out of curiosity, he tried the house next door. "Oh, them," said the woman who answered the bell. "They're all Vietnamese—refugees, you know. Hardly talk a word of English. But they're usually home on

Saturdays, I don't know where they'd be. They all work in a market someplace, for another Vietnamese."

Probably a waste of time to talk to them, thought Palliser.

Mendoza, Hackett and Higgins had been busy. They got a search warrant for Clyde Moore's apartment; it was a cheap one—if any apartments were cheap these days—on Citrus Avenue up in Hollywood. They went through it with precision and the tenacity of pack rats, not that they had to dig deep. Moore, living alone, wasn't covering up after himself.

"My God, isn't it always the earmark!" said Hackett. "I've never come across a sex nut yet who didn't have a closet full of the porn." There was quite a lot of it, the cheap stuff, crude and unimaginative, lying openly around the place. Moore, however assiduous he might be at his cleaning job at the County Museum, wasn't a very neat housekeeper for himself. The place was dusty and untidy, dirty dishes in the kitchen, dirty clothes in a laundry bag on the closet floor, a pair of dirty pajamas thrown across an unmade bed.

There wasn't a scrap of correspondence, or any books, not even an address book. They hadn't, of course, expected to turn up any evidence on Joyce here; what they had hoped to find was some clear-cut evidence of his perversion. The ones interested in sex with children sometimes spent years fantasizing it before carrying it out; the fact that he hadn't any record of that was meaningless. None of the pornography here stressed that.

But they went and got him again, brought him down to headquarters and took him into an interrogation room.

"We can guess the hell of a lot about it, Clyde," said Higgins. Everybody knew all about civil rights these days, but a lot of people on the wrong side of the law would still be leery of a cop like Higgins, who had a blunt, rugged, tough face, wide shoulders and a convincing sneer in his voice. "She came out of the animal hall and you spotted her, didn't you? You had a yen, and you took the chance and grabbed her right then."

"What the hell?" said Moore. The two deep lines in his saturnine face tightened as he looked at them in turn: the twin looming bulks of Hackett and Higgins, the slender, dapper figure of Mendoza standing apart. "The kid? What do you think I am—a nut? You're crazy."

"There's a lot of hard-core porn up there in your pad, Clyde," said Hackett in a hard voice. "It's about all you read, isn't it? Brood over it a lot, don't you? Nothing else to do off the job?"

"You grabbed her right there," said Higgins, "and you had someplace in mind to take her—where was it?" Since yesterday there had been lab men swarming over the museum, looking for any scraps of evidence that that little body had been hidden away somewhere—a supply closet, that narrow corridor, anywhere out of sight. Grace's little idea was probably right; he'd have done the final hiding when the place was empty. "Only right away you found she was dead on you—you don't know your own strength."

"What the hell are you talking about?" asked Moore. "I'd get the hots to do it with a kid? A little kid like that? That's weird. I know you're lookin' for one like that on that kid—but my God, nobody at the museum—why you landing on me, for God's sake?"

"Only somebody at the museum could have put her where she was, you stupid bastard," said Mendoza softly. "And you were right there, weren't you? Right up the corridor when she came out. There wasn't much time for her to vanish—it had to be there and then. And you were the only one there. That's how we landed on you, Clyde. And we're going to keep after you until you tell us all about it, so the sooner you decide to open up, the happier these two big tough cops will be, Clyde. You don't suppose the doctors don't cooperate with the law? You'd be surprised how many people fall downstairs here and break legs and arms." Very carefully he lit a new cigarette and held the lighter to squint at the flame. "Or get burned by defective lighters."

Moore went slightly gray. "But no kid ever came out of there!" he said loudly. "She never—no kid. Sure I was there, I was up from that door washing the cases— I—my hands were all wet, I had the bucket and rags there on a dolly—I wouldn't have, in the middle of that— I was facing that door and *no kid ever came out!* They were chasing all over in there, I heard 'em—a racket— Listen. Listen." He breathed hard, regaining some control. "A man'd have to be crazy, want to do a thing like that. Listen, I've got a couple of girl friends, I can get it anytime I want for free. You go and ask them, I'll tell you their names, they'll tell you—ask if I've got any kinky ideas! Listen, you can ask me till doomsday and you don't hear any different. No kid ever came out of that hall when I was there, and if one had come out I wouldn't've touched her."

They kept prodding at him most of the afternoon, and he kept saying the same things. He wasn't the biggest intellect in the world, but when they let him have cigarettes, and water, and use the rest room, it came to him that they weren't about to lay a hand on him, because if he should give them a confession, a defense attorney would be on that like lightning. He sat there gray and tired and scowling, and went on saying it all over again, he wasn't that kind of nut and he didn't know anything about the kid.

They let him go at the end of shift, and Mendoza went home in a disgruntled mood. He snapped at the twins for yelling, and snapped at Alison's innocent hope that he'd had a profitable day. It didn't improve his temper that the baby was howling at the top of her voice.

Alison exchanged a look with Máiri, who went hastily in to the baby, and brought Mendoza a double jigger of rye. "We had a shrimp salad and a casserole, but I can do you a nice steak. With asparagus and Hollandaise sauce?"

Mendoza swallowed rye and after a moment laughed. *"Lo siento tanto, mi corazón*—I'm an old grouch, and didn't I warn you at the start about taking on a middle-aged husband? It's a hell of a day, that's all. And that is the bastard who accounted for Joyce, but I swear to God there'll never be enough evidence to nail him."

She said lightly, "Leave the office downtown, *amado*. These things come along. Do you want the steak?"

"No, no—whatever you've got." He finished the drink, and went to make peace with the twins. The baby stopped howling, and they sat down to dinner in peace, except for cats prowling underfoot and Cedric begging for handouts.

After dinner Máiri brought Luisa Mary in, sleepily cooing and friendly, and regarding Mendoza severely said, "We'll need to see about getting her baptized."

"I suppose so. As her mother's a heathen you'd better see to it," said Mendoza amiably.

Later on, Alison came into Máiri's room with the baby's bottle, and sat in the rocker holding her. Máiri watched her for a moment and said cautiously, "I wonder now, *achara,* if you've been noticing a little something—right at the back it's starting in, and—"

Alison gave a little chortle. "Oh, indeed I have. Indeed. And I do wonder what he's going to say about that?"

On Sunday morning, as usual, Mendoza was late in. Everybody else had gone out on current business by the time Conway had told Landers about Jeanette, and they had decided they'd better do a little legwork on that, when a report came in from the lab. Conway looked at it and said, "Well, finally. As if we didn't know, that gun in Lejune's pad was the one that took off Lockwood."

"So that's one off the books anyway. I wonder if the bomb squad shoveled out enough of those bodies to bury. I suppose we ought to see Lockwood senior and tell him about it."

"He'll never believe us, you know. Jim the clean-cut college boy."

"I suppose not."

The phone company had come through with some addresses, but Conway wanted to look up Roger

Marsh first, to find out what time he'd left the girl on Thursday. They went up to Clinton Street, to the little rear house, hoping there wasn't a wife and family to evade.

There wasn't. Marsh answered the door, which was open beyond a screen, and admitted his name. They produced the badges and he said, "How can I help you?" He was a man about forty, short and weedy, with myopic eyes behind thick lenses; he held a book in one hand.

"I think you called on Miss Jeanette Remling on Thursday afternoon," said Conway. "I'm sorry to tell you that she's dead, and we'd like to ask you some questions."

"Oh," said Marsh, and after a moment, "You'd better come in." It was a tiny living room, sparsely furnished and very hot, with a small fan aimed at the one comfortable chair. He sat down there rather suddenly and looked from Conway to Landers. "D-dead?" he said.

"I'm afraid so, sir. It looks as if someone she brought home with her strangled her. We'd just like to know what time it was when you left her on Thursday afternoon."

"Oh," said Marsh. He took a long breath and held it. "I am so very sorry," he said quietly. "So very sorry." He hesitated and then went on painfully, "I should explain to you, my wife is confined in a mental hospital. She's a manic depressive—occasionally they let her out for a little while but it never seems to work. Fortunately we have no children. She knows me, and I try to save to bring her little presents—that pleases her. I—"

"You don't have to explain, sir."

"I have a job in men's suiting at Bullocks'. But the price of everything—Mrs. Bollings told me just the other day they'll have to raise the rent again—" he looked around vaguely—"I would just take a room, but I must have someplace for Bernice, when— Well, that was it, you see."

"What, sir?" Conway at at sea.

"Why, the reason," said Marsh. "Maybe you won't

134

believe it, but I have a very quick temper. I went to see Jeanette—as usual on Thursday—and after we, er, that is as I was preparing to leave, she told me, well, that she was raising her price. Because of costs going up—inflation. And I couldn't have afforded—and really when I've sacrificed so much—it was just the last straw and I'm afraid I, well, lost my temper and went for her. It was about four o'clock Thursday afternoon," he added helpfully, "and I most certainly did not intend to kill her. But I suppose I must have, losing my temper like that. I am so very sorry— I—I liked Jeanette, she'd been very kind to me."

Conway and Landers looked at each other.

"I suppose you want me to come with you. And what Bernice will do—the hospital—this will be quite an upset for everyone," said Marsh mournfully.

Mendoza marched into the office at three o'clock with Hackett and Higgins at his heels and proceeded to pace. He listened to the pathetic tale of Roger Marsh without a smile, and trailed smoke behind him like an angry dragon as he paced. Hackett and Higgins sat and watched him, looking gloomy.

"And so now we know he's got away with it!" said Mendoza. "Now we know there isn't a piece of any of his prints anywhere in that case. Sure, sure, by then he'd had time to think about it, so he was careful. That Goddamned bastard is the only answer on Joyce, and there is just no damned evidence at all. I don't need to call the D.A.'s office. They'd laugh in my face. The lab hasn't turned a damned thing to say she was ever anywhere in that mausoleum except that damned display case. Moore was on the spot, he was the only man on the spot, he has got to be the answer, and we'll never be able to charge him."

"It's happened before," said Hackett. "How many times are we morally certain and can't bring any charge?"

"I know, I know! But in a case like this—that kind, once he's tasted blood he isn't going to stop. *Pues sí,* he probably never meant to kill her, but—"

"Calm down, Luis," said Higgins, sounding tired.

"There isn't one damned thing we can do about it. Nobody likes it, but there it is."

"Continue to haul him in and put the pressure on?" said Hackett. "We've had several rounds of that and I don't think he's going to break, Luis. He knows he's got a clear record and we've got nothing to hold him on."

"He's not going to break," said Mendoza. "Oh, no. *¡Diez millón demonios desde infierno!* So we have to forget it, mark the case closed, and go on to the next job *¡Por el armor de Dios!*"

"Look, we all feel the same way," said Higgins. "Personally—" he got up—"I am going to knock off early and go home." Hackett got up too.

Mendoza stopped in his tracks. "Don't tell me not to get emotionally involved, *amigos*. As I won't tell you. Like the people who don't want to get involved in anything controversial—calling for cops, politics, religion, whatever—They're involved. So long as we're all breathing, we're involved." He stabbed out his cigarette in the ashtray on Palliser's desk and picked up his hat. "Let's go home, boys. *Mañana es otro día*—tomorrow also a day."

Galeano had been pounding pavements down on Second Street in the merciless heat, hunting for a man named Paul Shelbarger, who had once been arrested and testified against by Walt Robsen in a case of armed robbery. Shelbarger was now off P.A. and nobody knew where he was living, so Galeano was looking around the neighborhood where he used to live, trying to get a line on him. He wasn't having very much luck, and he didn't really think that Shelbarger was the X who had stalked and shot Robsen, but this was the job he'd been given to do.

He gave up on it at five o'clock and started back to base; and suddenly, as he drove through the hot, dirty, downtown streets, he remembered Barbara Fogarty and Mendoza's wild goose. They'd all been so busy over Joyce the last few days, that had passed right out of his mind.

"Be damned," he said to himself. He'd been interested in that too. Go and see if she is home, anyway.

He drove up to the apartment on Ardmore. The girl who answered the door wasn't Rona, and he assumed it was Barbara: a very pretty girl, little and brunette with green eyes framed in long lashes. She was wearing blue shorts and a Hawaiian shirt and thong sandals, and she had very nice legs—but no nicer than Marta's.

The minute she saw the badge she seized his arm and pulled him into the living room. "I've been simply dying of curiosity ever since Mother and Rona told me—you're the same one, by what they said— *Police! Is* it about—I couldn't believe it was because Bill wasn't going to do anything, he just laughed—and if it is about that, he'll be here any minute because we're going out, he'll just have to wait while I get decently dressed— But what *is* it about? And what's your name?"

Galeano told her, feeling slightly breathless. "It's about," he said cautiously, "a place you used to work. The Wilmont Pharmacy."

"I knew it—I knew it!" There was a brief touch on the doorbell, announcement of arrival; she'd left the door open, and swung to it dramatically. "So there, Bill! *So there!* I was imagining things, was I? Building a fancy story? Well, Randy believed me and now you'll have to too! And I hope you saved those vitamins. This is Sergeant Galeano of the police, and he's—"

"Detective," said Galeano.

"Investigating it. Mr. Snyder, and that drugstore. So you see!"

"What? Well, I'll be damned." The young fellow who walked in was about twenty-five, tall and well built, with short brown hair and tortoiseshell-rimmed glasses. "Now calm down and tell it like it is, Barb. Are you really—" he looked at Galeano.

"We've been looking into certain occurrences at that drugstore," said Galeano. "We'd very much like to hear what Miss Fogarty has to say about the time she worked there."

"And what a time!" she said.

"You'd be Mr. Loring?"

"That's right. How did—"

"Never mind for the moment. If you'd like to tell me your story, Miss Fogarty—" There was, apparently, a story.

"I certainly will." At Loring's urging she sat down on the couch, and calmed down a little. "I was still living at home, and taking shorthand and typing at night—I've just got a better job now on account of that. Well, the job at the pharmacy was close, and I thought it was going to be fine. He—Mr. Snyder— seemed nice and kind, sort of fatherly, you know. And then one day when I was in the deli having lunch that girl came up and talked to me. I don't know what her name was, but she rambled on telling me a confused sort of story about working at the pharmacy and saying she wanted to warn me—she said Mr. Snyder had raped her, honestly—asked her to drink a toast to his birthday and got her drunk—and she said another girl named Ruth who used to work there had quit all of a sudden and never came back, and she thought probably the same thing had happened to her—"

"Female rigmarole," said Loring indulgently.

"Well, now we know it wasn't," said Barbara. "I didn't pay much attention to her then. I just thought she was a little weird, it went out of my mind. But when Mr. Snyder started to try to put me off Bill I got annoyed. You see, Bill's taken a year off from teaching to get his master's degree, he's at Western University right near there, and a few times he picked me up after work. And Mr. Snyder started to talk about these perennial students, he'd expect me to support him, I was foolish to take any interest in him— I got mad. But I'd better tell you about the vitamins—"

"That's ridiculous," said Loring. "I went to that picnic the day before, and you know Millie, she'd probably used last year's eggs in the potato salad or—"

"It isn't either. Bill's a nut on vitamins," said Barbara, "and Mr. Snyder gave me a discount, so I used it to get them for him there. And one day Mr. Snyder gave me a little bottle and said it was a sample of a new brand of vitamins and he thought Bill might like to try them. I didn't think much about it, *then*. I

138

gave them to him—and you know very well, Bill, it was the very day you started to take them you got deadly sick and had to go to the hospital— It was nearly a month ago," she added to Galeano. "But it was before that I quit that job. I've just got a new one, you see—typing and receptionist at a stockbrokers' place, I start tomorrow. But—this was just after Bill was in the hospital—a Friday night—just as we were closing up, Mr. Snyder said to me it was his birthday and he'd like me to drink a little toast with him. It didn't ring a bell then, but about three minutes later when we were in the back office, all of a sudden I remembered that girl and what she said. He gave me a glass and said it was brandy—but it didn't taste like brandy, it was terribly strong—and honestly, it was just like one of those times you feel you're living something over again—what the girl had said, you know. The birthday and the brandy. And I was scared to death. So I put the glass down and just said I was sorry, I wasn't feeling well and I had to get home, and I *went*. I was a little unsteady on my feet, but I got home all right. I'd just moved in with Rona then."

"Imagination," said Loring.

"Oh, and I suppose your coming down with gastroenteritis was imagination?" she said fiercely. "That old man's crazy, to my mind, and I wish I knew that girl's name so I could thank her. What do you think of all that?" she asked Galeano.

"Miss Fogarty," said Galeano, "I can only say it's a very interesting story, and we'll be taking a look at Mr. Snyder."

8

SUNDAY NIGHT STARTED OUT QUIET AS USUAL. PIGGOTT told Schenke about his reasoning on the Brock thing, and Schenke said he might have something there. "It's a queer one all right," said Piggott, "and you've just got to figure that queer people do queer things."

"That is for sure," said Schenke. "You never know what the hell people are going to get up to, Matt."

About ten o'clock a squad called in to say that some mayhem had gone on at a disco out on Third, and they went to look at it. There was one corpse, female, with her skull smashed in, and a couple of young men ready for an ambulance. The uniformed men had had some trouble subduing a big, blond young fellow obviously high on something; they'd had quite a battle with him and had to take him down, and he was unconscious, in cuffs, awaiting transportation. Various patrons of the disco stood around watching in silence; but it wasn't silent, for the hard rock sound blared out of the open door of the place, and the men had to shout at each other.

"He seems to've gone berserk," said Patrolman Zimmerman, sucking grazed knuckles. "Just started swinging that thing around without any warning—" A rough length of two-by-four wrested from him had blood and hair on it. The corpse was one Maureen Daly.

"Who is he?" asked Schenke. "He'd better go to the guarded wing at the General."

"The only I.D. on him is an Iowa driver's license out of date. Robert Blanchard."

"I'll be damned," said Schenke. "That's the one on that Coburn thing they never turned up."

Nothing else called them out up to the end of shift. Of course on Saturday night there had been four heists and a knifing in a bar.

On Monday morning Wanda Larsen came in early, bright-eyed and her usual neat, blonde self in her navy uniform. Glasser, coming in a minute later with Landers and Grace, tried to scowl at her. "Well, so you came back after all. What you wrote on that postcard, I was thinking we'd seen the last of you."

"Don't be silly, Henry," said Wanda.

"Have a good vacation?" asked Grace.

"Oh, marvelous. Just as I was going to leave for Carlsbad, Mother called and she and Dad had an invitation from some people we used to know in Marysville, the Brinleys, and they asked me too. It's a gorgeous big ranch—Morgan horses—of course they've got scads of money. We rode and went on picnics and saw a local horse show, and the scenery's beautiful, and I'd just decided it would really be worth marrying their son for the money—if I could stand him that long, he's pretty yokelish—only I found out he was already engaged. What," asked Wanda, "has been going on? Have I missed anything interesting?"

When Galeano came in he found Hackett in Mendoza's office futilely discussing Clyde Moore, and diverted them with Barbara Fogarty's tale.

"For God's sake," said Hackett, amused, "did you say something awhile ago about Victorian melodrama? But a rape charge'd never stick now, when that Williams girl didn't yell rape at the time."

Mendoza was looking cynically pleased. "Yes," he said, "but there is also Mr. Loring—and Ruth Byrd. That is a very funny little story, Nick, and I think we'd better do something about it. Where do we find Loring?"

"I thought you'd want to talk to him," said Galeano. "He's working at home today—apartment on Oakwood in Hollywood."

Bill Loring looked at Mendoza's gray Italian silk and Sulka tie with respect, and said, "I can't take this in. You think it's for real? Barb's got an imagination." He had, however, kept the bottle of vitamin capsules, though he admitted he hadn't taken any more; he handed it over willingly. "If there is anything in it—of course Randy was all for calling the cops right then, as soon as he heard Barb's wild tale, but he's as bad as Barb." Randy, it appeared, was one Randy Fischer, who lived in the next apartment. "He's the one called the ambulance for me. I thought it was summer flu or something, thought I could make it home, but I passed out in the lobby and Randy found me. Nice fellow, if a little excitable—he works in an occult bookshop on the boulevard, which may account for it. I don't get this," said Loring. "How could anybody be so stupid as to—"

But he hadn't their experience of the stupidity of human nature. "Which bookstore, Mr. Loring?" asked Mendoza.

It was, in fact, a rather sedate bookstore that specialized in classic parapsychology, but dealt in other reference works too; and Randy Fischer all but jumped out from behind the counter in excitement when he looked at the badges. He was built long and thin like a crane, with a shock of wild black hair.

"I told Loring there was something funny about it, but he's got no imagination. As soon as I heard the story that girl of his told, I said there was something fishy and they ought to tell the law. But Loring kept talking about food poisoning at some picnic, and these damn fool doctors never look beyond their noses, of course. I told Loring—"

Mendoza regarded him interestedly. "So, if I'm deducing with my usual brilliance, you decided to take matters into your own hands and tell the police yourself. That anonymous letter—all your own idea?"

"Well, I've got some imagination," retorted Fischer. "What the hell good would it have done for me to come to you and pass on that story? It was all third-hand—hearsay! And with Loring dead set against talking to you, and I suppose having some influence on the girl, I didn't know but what they'd back down and refuse to tell you anything at all."

"I see that," said Mendoza, "but what about Ruth, Mr. Fischer? Why did you mention Ruth? And murder being done?"

"Oh, well," said Fischer. "I thought if I put it that way you'd be more apt to look into it—after all, if I was right, murder'd been attempted. The Fogarty girl mentioned this Ruth, that tale the other girl told her, and I just put that in—I mean you could find that a girl named Ruth had worked there once—I put it in for verisimilitude." He brought that out with dignity.

"*Maravilloso,*" murmured Mendoza. "It's possible, of course—" he looked around the ranks of books on parapsychology—"that your daily surroundings have encouraged your natural ESP. We don't approve of anonymous letters, Mr. Fischer."

"Well, I don't suppose you approve of murder either," Fischer shot back neatly.

They dropped the bottle of vitamins off at the lab to be analyzed.

They were now about at the tail end of that handful of far-out suspects on Robsen, and of course nothing had come of it. There was the new routine to be done on the new heists. Mendoza had handed back the County Museum's records without comment; today it would open its doors as usual for the handful of visitors on a weekday.

There was an inquest scheduled on Guy and June Burdine today; Hackett would cover that. It was Palliser's day off.

Mendoza went through an empty office, Sergeant Lake hunched over a paperback about some new faddy diet—like Hackett he was usually dieting—and sat at his desk staring out over the hills, today shimmering in heat haze. After a while he swung around, opened the top drawer and brought out the cards to practice crooked deals; domesticity had ruined his poker, but he still thought better with the cards in his hands. But what his hand met first was Joyce McCauley's rosary.

He had thought, see McCauley got it back. Keepsake? But now, he dropped it back in the drawer. Officially, the case wasn't closed; unofficially, there was nowhere else to go on it. But superstitiously, he felt if he handed over the little memento, the thing would be ended right there. Something could still turn up— He laughed a little savagely at himself and began to shuffle the cards.

The hospital sent over word that afternoon that Blanchard was conscious and coherent, and Hackett and Grace went to see him. He lay flat in the hospital bed, the curtains pulled around, and looked at them

143

incuriously. He was supposed to be twenty-two, but he looked twenty years older, gray-skinned, sunken-eyed, with a fuzz of blond beard hardly staining his jaw. He said, "You're cops."

"That's right."

"It's funny," said Blanchard before they could start to ask questions. "I been thinking, I guess that doctor was right. I thought he was talking a lot of bull. I guess not."

"About what?" asked Grace.

"Oh, the stuff. Sayin' how dangerous it is. Well, I'd been using since I was fifteen—a lot of stuff, the grass, barbs, speed, whatever came along. No sweat. I had a few bad trips like anybody, but mostly it was O.K. But I been thinkin'—maybe it all sort of builds up, like, inside you. Because there wasn't no reason for me to do like that, before the cops come down— I guess it was last night, was it? I got a kind of picture of myself—that piece o' post I picked up somewhere— and that was crazy. I didn't know any o' those people there. Just all of a sudden I felt like my head was gonna explode, and next thing I had that post and—"

"None of it's much good for your brain," said Grace. "You had to find out the hard way, Bob. We've been looking for you, you know."

"I been—around," he said. "Around. I been tryin' to think about it. If I could do without the stuff. They say it's like goin' to hell, you been using. But it shook me right up. That first time it happened."

"When was that, Bob?" asked Hackett. "You beat up somebody else?"

"I don't know why," he said. "There wasn't any reason. It didn't seem like me doin' it—like I was standin' outside just seein' it. I and Jerry were good pals—I like Jerry. And his new girl, she was an O.K. girl. And the little kid. I don't mind kids. I hadn't any reason to do that, I just don't know why I did." His eyes shut, and after a minute, incongruously, tears began to slide down his cheeks.

"Well," said Hackett in the hall outside, "another one off our hands, Jase. He'll get called incompetent, and put away in Atascadero. And they used to be

144

pretty tough about letting them out of there, but these days— Do you want to bet he'll kick the habit?"

"Few do," said Grace. "Few do."

Aside from that it was another unprofitable day, and when Hackett and Higgins, Landers and Conway landed back at the office at five o'clock, they looked wilted and discouraged. "I'll tell you, Luis," said Higgins, "we're wasting time. This isn't the place to look on Robsen—there isn't any place to look. There's no handle at all."

"John was mentioning those next-door neighbors we never talked to," said Hackett, "but I don't suppose— The people on the other side didn't see anything."

"There's nothing to go on," agreed Landers. "Nothing to get your teeth into."

Mendoza looked at the poker hand dealt on the blotter. "Another one to shove into Pending and forget about—*¿cómo no?*" He was still seething quietly over Joyce and Moore.

"Sometimes there just isn't anything to get hold of," said Hackett heavily. "I hate like hell to think we'll never get anybody for Robsen, but if you ask me, Luis, I think it's the hell of a lot worse to be morally certain on one like Moore and have to leave him walking around loose."

"*¡Está claro!*" said Mendoza viciously.

"We'll go on working it as we can—something could still break," said Higgins, "but right now—"

Mendoza folded the cards back into the deck and slapped them together. "The weather's got us all down, *compadres*. Hold the good thoughts and the guardian angels will reward us."

Duke wandered in and put down a little bottle on the desk. "That was a simple little job. Have you run across another mass murderer?"

"What was it?" asked Mendoza and Galeano simultaneously.

"Pure white arsenic. A lethal dose to about three capsules. There were some prints on the bottle, not known, nothing but smudges on the capsules."

"And isn't that pretty," said Mendoza. "Attempted

homicide, and the evidence nice and straightforward. We'll talk to Mr. Snyder before we ask the D.A. what he thinks about Ruth. Fischer and his unconscious ESP—now that's a strange one if you like." He laughed.

"This is one for the books," said Galeano incredulously.

On Tuesday morning, in Galeano's old Dodge, they parked in front of the pharmacy at nine A.M. and walked in. There weren't any customers in the place. The vapid-faced blonde started toward them, but they made for Snyder behind the prescription counter. There was a framed license, the glass dirty, hanging on the wall behind him: *Southern California School of Pharmacy, Gustave L. Snyder.* He looked up with an automatic, meaningless smile. "Yes, gentlemen?"

Mendoza showed him the badge. "You can tell your clerk to go home, Mr. Snyder, and lock the door. You're coming downtown to answer some questions. Attempted homicide, Mr. Snyder."

Snyder's face went pastier, but his expression didn't change. "I don't know what you mean, gentlemen." But he had recognized Mendoza now.

"Oh, let's not waste time," said Mendoza cheerfully. "There's Charlene Williams too. And Ruth. Come on, we're going to have a long talk."

His eyes shifted on both names, but he never said a word. Moving like an automaton, he told the girl to go; she protested, asked questions, but he just shook his head. He locked the front door of the store with a hand that shook, and rode downtown in the back seat of the Dodge in silence.

He didn't say anything when they sat him down in one of the little interrogation rooms; he listened while they started to tell him what they knew. At last, with an effort, he dredged up one thought. "You can't accuse me now—when Charlene didn't complain then. I never—I never meant any harm. I just wanted—I was lonely. She didn't complain."

"But there was Barbara Fogarty," said Galeano, "later." And they were wondering, of course, how many more. Whatever kind they were, a majority of rapes never got reported.

"I never did anything to her," said Snyder.

"But you took a dislike to her boyfriend, didn't you?"

"I—I didn't like to see a nice girl throw herself away on a worthless—"

"Oh, come now," said Mendoza, "that's a rather feeble reason for trying to feed him pure arsenic, Mr. Snyder." He brought out the little bottle and put it on the table.

Snyder slumped over the table, deflated as he realized how much they did know. "That we'll have tied up nice and tight," said Mendoza, "with the kind of evidence even the stupidest judge can comprehend. But just for the record, we'd also like to talk about Ruth Byrd."

Snyder shook his head numbly. "You don't understand. I never married—never had anybody. I was lonely. I—just—wanted—a little affection. And no woman would look at me—like me." He regarded his paunch, his large, freckled hands. "I never meant any harm."

"Ruth. I can make a pretty good guess at it, you know," said Mendoza with his one-sided smile. "It's very possible she was the first one—because you misjudged the dose, didn't you? What did you give her—pure ethyl alcohol? And overdosed her badly. You were frightened when you found she wasn't breathing, weren't you? You'd have her address, of course. You took her there in your car, used her key to get in, and found her brother's phone number in her address book. Easy way out—then."

"I—never—meant—any—harm. I'm sorry. I'm sorry."

Mendoza looked at Galeano and shrugged. You could interpret that as a tacit confession. He didn't think the D.A. would.

"But Mr. Loring, now. Just what was in your mind there? You were jealous of him?" That seemed an impossibility—but of course he hadn't been thinking rationally.

"She's—a very pretty girl," said Snyder dully. "If he hadn't been there—" He licked his lips.

"You thought if he wasn't there, Barbara Fogarty would—" They were incredulous.

"I don't know," he said. "But she—went away. I couldn't—" There was a long silence. Mendoza lit a new cigarette.

But Galeano had to know. "For God's sake, Snyder," he said, "why all this rigmarole when you can buy female company on any street corner? Why—"

Snyder sat up a little and grasped for vanished dignity. He fixed Galeano with a cold stare. "I'm not interested in associating with any dirty whores! I like good, pretty, respectable girls, don't you understand that? I've always been a respectable man."

Mendoza didn't laugh until they were in the outer office. "*Dios,* the characters we do run across, Nick. It'll get booked as attempted homicide, and I don't dare guess what he'll get. I doubt very much that the D.A.'ll try to do anything about Ruth. After all this time, an exhumation might not prove anything."

Galeano agreed thoughtfully. "That," he said, "was about the damnedest wild goose we ever went chasing."

Mendoza started to laugh again.

The day wore on; Snyder was booked into jail. All the men but Hackett and Palliser had given up on the far-out possibles on Robsen, and were back to hunting the possible heisters—there were now four more to hunt, since Saturday night. The warrant came through on Snyder, and Mendoza talked to the D.A. about Ruth. The D.A. decided to let Ruth rest in peace. Then Mendoza went out to lunch with Galeano and Higgins.

Hackett brought in one of the last men from that abortive Robsen list about two-thirty, a professional burglar who was taking a vacation while he was still on parole, and talked to him without much interest. It was immediately obvious that the man didn't even remember the name of the detective who had arrested him, and like most pro crooks he took arrest and the joint as a normal hazard of life. He hadn't harbored any resentment against Walt Robsen.

Hackett told him he could go, and stood in the communal office wondering what to do next. There were heisters to hunt. He could see the handwriting on the wall; the Robsen case was dead. The only one in the office was Glasser, peacefully typing a report. Even Wanda was out somewhere; she was so hot for street experience, she'd probably attached herself to Conway or Landers.

A uniformed messenger came in and handed a manila envelope to Lake, who sauntered down the hall with it to Mendoza's office. Glasser stopped typing, sat back and lit a cigarette.

Two minutes later the silence was shattered by a wounded roar. "¿Qué demonios—? ¿Cuándo ocurrió eso? Por el amor de Dios— Henry!"

Glasser and Hackett both jumped. Mendoza came charging in at a lope, a report in one hand. "When the hell did this happen? And why didn't I know about it?" He shook the report at Glasser.

"What?" Glasser looked. "Oh, that. Why? It didn't look like anything much—pretty plain suicide. An old lady, and there was a note left—"

"Oh, my God," said Mendoza, "you weren't in on the other ones—Davidson and Burdine. It didn't mean one damned thing to you, of course, and all the rest of us were so busy over Joyce and Robsen and I wasn't keeping a check on what was going on. My God—"

"What is it?" asked Hackett.

Mendoza thrust the report at him. "Martha Fogel—an autopsy report, for God's sake! I don't like it—I don't like it one damned bit." He took the report back and looked through it rapidly. "Digitalin poisoning. Oh no. ¡Porvida—qué disparate! Lemonade! Lemonade, I ask you!"

"What the hell's he talking about?" asked Glasser. "Davidson—I heard somebody mention that, it was a break-in—"

"Where's the suicide note?" demanded Mendoza.

"I suppose the lab's still got it. I turned them loose, just being thorough, but there wasn't anything in it.

149

The house was locked, the beat man had to break in. We figured she'd been dead about twenty-four hours."

"And that was Thursday. My God. Come on—I want to have another look around there. What about the note—what did it say?"

They followed him out. "Far as I can remember," said Glasser, "it was just a line. Something like, 'It's too much trouble to go on, nobody to miss me.' It was just kind of scrawled on a single sheet of paper."

"*Por Dios*," said Mendoza. He prodded Glasser into the jump seat of the Ferrari, Hackett into the front, and headed for the little backwater. It wasn't far. The quiet little street with its few houses was still in the afternoon heat, nothing moving along it, not a sign of life at a window.

Mendoza parked in front of Martha Fogel's house. "Who found her? When?"

"A Mrs. Millet. Neighbor across the street. On Thursday morning. Well, it all looked kosher," said Glasser. "How could it not have been? She was locked inside— The report said digitalin poisoning? Well, there was an empty bottle in the medicine chest, digitalis— her prescription. The lab's got that too."

There was a seal on the front door. Mendoza broke it and they went in. But of course there was nothing to see in the house. Old, shabby furniture, a single bed made up in the front bedroom, everything neat if looking old and tired.

"It's queer all right," said Hackett. He had fished out his glasses and was reading the autopsy report. "But what's worrying you about it? It surely is queer— chain reaction—but you remember what we heard from everybody along here. Old friends, old neighbors, knowing each other so long. What the Burdines' suicide note said—it was Pearl Davidson getting murdered like that sent them into shock and depression— losing an old friend like that. I can see this Fogel woman—"

"Damn it," said Mendoza, "it's usually the old people who are tough. The really old ones, so tenacious of life they hang on to the bitter end, come hell

150

or high water. Queer—that you can say again. Art—Lemonade! The digitalis was in lemonade. Just as the Nembutal was in the Burdines' lemonade."

"It's hot weather. Common sort of cold drink."

"Damn it, it's the wrong shape!" said Mendoza. "I want to talk to people around here."

It didn't do him much good. Ronald Purdy wasn't at home; he was probably, said Mrs. Hallam, at the library, where he went a lot to sit and read. Well, of course everyone had been shocked at the third suicide, but not as surprised as if it had been someone else. Martha Fogel had always been one to look on the dark side of things, and it was Mrs. Hallam's opinion that the Burdines had given her the idea. But it had been a little shock, coming so soon. Seemed as if everybody was dying off all at once. Pearl getting killed like that—and of course the Burdines and Martha had been such old friends of hers—

"Yes," said Mendoza. "There was another woman—lived next to Mrs. Davidson—we didn't talk to her, I seem to—"

"Mrs. Babcock," said Mrs. Hallam, nodding. "She went to stay with her daughter that very day Pearl got killed. I don't suppose she'd know anything about it. She'll be home tomorrow, I think, she was only staying till her daughter got back on her feet again."

The Millets said much the same thing. "Though of course it was a shock, her going like that. If she hadn't left the note, I guess we'd have took it for granted it was her heart—it was in bad shape, she always said."

"Women," said Mendoza back at the Ferrari, "always leave suicide notes. It'd have looked even queerer if she hadn't, because of course the autopsy would still have showed up the overdose of digitalis. *Pues sí.*" He marched back into the Fogel house and began hunting for a sample of handwriting, a grocery list, a letter, anything: but the house was bare. "Like this on Thursday?" he asked Glasser.

"Well, of course, damn it. We have to go through the motions. If I'd noticed any letters or anything around, I'd have sent them in with the note for comparison."

"What the hell is in your mind, Luis?" asked Hackett. "A vendetta of some kind against the old people? How wild can you get? It's a bit funny, but the evidence—"

Mendoza didn't answer him. He went back across the street to the Hallams' and asked Mrs. Hallam if by any chance she had any samples of Mrs. Fogel's handwriting.

She looked at him as if he was mad. "Handwriting! You don't write letters to people living across the street—"

"I just wondered—mmh, possibly—if any of you exchanged recipes occasionally."

"Oh." That was clearly a new thought to her. She thought. "I declare," she said after a moment, "now you mention it, I do believe I've got a recipe of Martha's that she wrote out for me a couple of months ago—a two-egg lemon cake, it was." She had quite a hunt for it, but finally came back and gave it to him. "Though what in time you want it for—"

"The evidence," said Mendoza, jerking open the door of the Ferrari, "is the least of it, Arturo. Damn it, it's the wrong shape—whatever's behind it, there's something—" He was silent and added inconsequentially, "That break-in at the Davidson house was a little early in the evening compared to the average— The next-door neighbor, yes. Already conveniently gone? I wonder."

"Oh, boy," said Hackett, "don't reach so far."

"It is," repeated Mendoza, "the wrong shape."

Again Piggott sat in the cluttered office and talked to Glen Brock. Brock had called and asked if he could come in. As he had before, he was looking at Piggott curiously. "You have a funny way of looking at things, Mr. Piggott."

"Just thinking like a cop," said Piggott.

"That it might be something petty behind it. Two-bit. That I hadn't thought twice about. You turn it upside down—but the thing itself's so crazy, could be it makes sense." Greenbaum wasn't in the office today.

152

"Have you thought of anything?" asked Piggott. "Some little thing that happened just a while before it all started?"

"Well—" Brock dug a ball-point pen into his blotter thoughtfully. "I've had my share of little arguments, disagreements, petty troubles. Political arguments and so on. And—if this character did some brooding before he started after me, I couldn't guess how long before that something had triggered it off. But I've been thinking, and I haven't come up with much—say in the three, four months before it started. I don't think any of these is worth a damn, but you can hear about them."

"O.K."

"One, a guy rear-ended me on Sunset. Not much damage done to me, but his radiator stove in. It was his fault, I hadn't stopped on a dime. He was mad—tried to start a fight—it was a new car. I couldn't even tell you his name, I just referred him to the insurance company."

"Possible," said Piggott. "And?"

"The two fellows who lived in the next apartment. I think they were fags." He mentioned the address. "They used to run a stereo on high volume, I was always going over there to complain. They didn't like it. One of them was Archie Collins, I don't know the other. Place was owned by a corporation, no landlord to complain to."

"The queers can be spiteful," said Piggott.

"Yeah. And that girl. Pauline Dunn. I was introduced to her at some party, she was cute and I took her out once. Never again. She was a nonstop talk and neurotic as they come. But evidently—" Brock grinned —"I'd made an impression. She kept calling me, asking me over—she lived with her father in a house in West Hollywood, I gather there was money, she didn't work—she got to be a regular pest, I even stopped being polite to her after a while. Then Joan and I got engaged, and when I told her that I guess it did the trick, she never called again. But just little things like that—I suppose you think you know what you're doing, but I can't believe it."

153

"Almost anything," said Piggott, "is possible with people, Mr. Brock."

It was Grace's day off. He sat in the air conditioning and watched plump, brown Celia Anne playing some game of her own that involved pushing a toy horse about in complicated patterns. Virginia had gone out to market. When she came in, he drifted out to the kitchen and watched her put things away.

"I wonder if it'd be any use to go down and jigger up the adoption service," he said.

"I know—they said they'd call as soon as they found something suitable— Suitable!" said Virginia. She laughed. "Well, they're not as fussy as they used to be, Jase. And it's not as if we're being fussy about age or sex, really. I expect we'll just have to be patient."

Palliser had gone back, with Conway and Landers, to the heist jobs. It was boring, routine work, chasing down the men from Records, bringing them in to question; none of them were great brains. Like the rest of the men he was feeling unhappy about the Robsen case; his mind kept worrying at it, trying to come up with some new angle.

For a wonder he dropped on one of the right answers that afternoon; a punk still on P.A. admitted the job at the dairy store the previous Saturday night, so Palliser booked him and applied for the warrant, which took him to the end of shift. And as he was driving home he thought, damn it, it was just the one thing that hadn't got done, and there was a thousand-to-one chance that there was anything useful to be got but just on that chance—Those next-door neighbors.

"You're a glutton for work," said Roberta when he told her about it over dinner. "It's a pity you don't get paid overtime." But of course she knew why. He left her loading the dishwasher, while David Andrew crawled rapidly around after Trina, grabbing for her tail. It wasn't dark yet at seven-forty-five, but the city lights were starting to come on.

The house next to the Robsens' was a square-old-fashioned frame house. No lights showed in the front.

Among the shrubbery he couldn't tell whether there were lights in the Robsen house, but he supposed Cathy Robsen and her teenagers were home now. Maybe not for much longer; she couldn't afford to keep that house. He pushed the doorbell and the door opened, a light went on in the entry hall. The young man facing him was slim and brown, with bright, intelligent eyes. He wore a white shirt and dark trousers.

Palliser held out the badge. "Police," he said. "I'd like to ask you a few questions."

The young man stepped back at once, a tacit gesture asking him in, and said carefully, "One minnit. Yes? Soth Eir." He repeated that down the hall. Palliser waited apprehensively. The next minute four people came down the hall, chattering in some impossible-sounding language, and revealed themselves as two more young men and two young women, all slim and brown and quite good-looking. They all looked very clean, in American clothes, and they all looked at him with intense interest, and he felt rather helpless. He cleared his throat, resisting the impulse to start shouting.

One of the women said, "I have the English, some. I and—no, Lim Kuon and I—" she gestured at the other young woman—"we had been at university. I am Soth Eir. We are most pleased to meet you." The oldest man, who was perhaps twenty-five, spoke rapidly to her. "You are policeman?" She peered at the badge. "Very good. We expected perhaps—but it is not to put oneself to the—forward." All the men chattered at her insistently. She laughed. "Please, you come in." She ushered him into the living room. It was barely furnished, but adequately: folding chairs, card tables, a studio couch. She made him sit down, and they grouped around him. She pointed to the oldest man. "My brother, Dhat van Thone." The next: "My young brother, Da Nal. My sister Lim Kuon. The husband of my sister Cheny Vibol."

Palliser said uncomfortably, "John Palliser."

"Before you ask the questions, Dhat van Thone says we must thank you. An American. We all thank you.

For the hospitable of your great country. Only so few of us get away. But here we are safe."

"Vietnam," said Palliser, nodding.

They shook their heads vigorously. "What you call—Cambodia. We are not here long time—but my brothers, Cheny Vibol, study now the English. Soon can speak. We have had the great fortune, Vietnamese gentleman here much more time has given work in c—the city." She laughed almost mischievously. "Not easy to my great smart brother Dhat van Thone, who studies to be doctor at home! Me, am sec-re-tary"— she pronounced it carefully—"in city. But here, so good—free—and people kind, to help. We can rent house, begin again. We wish to thank you. You have given us our lifes back."

"Oh—yes," said Palliser. It came to him suddenly, appallingly, that he had come here to ask these people questions about the death of a single man, when they had come through the merciless slaughter of millions. There wasn't anything to say to them that meant anything. He looked at them helplessly, and she said, "But you have come for a reason. We have heard—the gentleman in the house next—he is killed. You are the policeman who looks for him who killed?"

"One of them," said Palliser. Young as they were, they had lived once in a country where killings were punished by law, where the law hunted murderers. He said, "He was killed one week ago Saturday." She nodded quickly. "Were any of you here?"

"Yes. A person was seen to go into that house. Dhat van Thone and Da Nal have seen. We thought a policeman come, and Dhat van Thone has said one will come, we wait."

Palliser felt doubtful excitement. "When was this person seen?"

"I did not see." She asked questions, and the two men answered quickly. "It was a time after one o'clock. Ten minutes after. Dhat van Thone and Da Nal are—were—in the front garden, bring water to flowers. The person was a young man, a boy—they say perhaps age like Da Nal." Nineteen, twenty?

By God, thought Palliser. It would have been about the right time. The autopsy on Robsen had put the death between twelve and two. "Can they—tell what he looked like?"

She questioned them again, got a spate of answers. "He is tall—even for American, a little. I do not know your measurement." She looked at him, talked to the men. "A little less tall than you." Palliser was six one. "He had fair hair, long. You understand, they see only across front garden, it is not important then. He comes on a bicycle, it is painted green. He walked up the stairs to the house and inside the door. He is not in the house long time—ten minutes. He comes out and rides away on bicycle."

By *God,* thought Palliser. And they'd been going in circles on the futile job of looking into Robsen's old cases! "Was he carrying anything?"

She asked, spread her hands. "They do not see. He has white shirt, pants like—" she paused and thought. "Chocolate?"

"Brown."

"Brown. Ah." She studied his expression. "You are happy."

The unexpected word raised an unexpected laugh from him. He seized her hand and shook it warmly. "I am very happy, Soth Eir. Tell them they have helped us very much. What they have told us—I hope it will help to show the truth."

She smiled delightfully at him. "The truth—that is great word." She spoke to the others, who beamed at Palliser, pleased with themselves.

He was pleased with these people. They were delightful people. "There's no way to thank you," he said. "You have helped to further justice."

"Ah!" she said gravely. "That is also a great word. We are happy too."

Somehow reluctant to leave, he said, "I was here last Saturday to talk to you—no one was home." The silent Lim Kuon burst into laughter and relayed that the rest, who laughed gleefully. Soth Eir's beautiful brown eyes brimmed with mirth.

157

"It was a party. It was my betrothal. We are Christians, the priest is there to bless, was good party. I will marry the son of Vietnamese gentleman who own market."

"I hope you'll be very happy," said Palliser.

"Will be happy always—in freedom, in America," said Soth Eir.

"Well, by God," said Hackett, hearing about Palliser's visit on Wednesday morning, "it's a handle, John. Which we didn't have."

"Don't build any dreams on it," said Mendoza sardonically. "Not much of a description."

"Damn it, it's something we didn't have. I'd say, put it to Hoffman first. He lives in the same general neighborhood, he might recognize the description. Some young punk around there—"

"With a conceived reason to walk in and shoot Robsen? Not much time for an argument—ten minutes—"

"Damn it," said Palliser, "the time fits. This has got to be relevant."

"*Así así*," said Mendoza. "It's something."

Palliser called Hollenbeck, but Hoffman was in court downtown, testifying on a murder case. He would be back by four.

Piggott told himself he was seven kinds of fool, going out of his way in weather like this, on something that wasn't any problem of his. But, he thought, isn't it? If you were going to accept any sort of Christian duty, well, there was a good deal said in the Bible about brotherhood.

He got to the apartment where Brock had lived before his marriage about three o'clock. One of the mailboxes still listed an A. Collins. One of the possible fags, still there after a couple of years. He climbed stairs and rang the bell.

The man who answered the door might be, or might not. You couldn't tell by looks. He was medium-sized, thin, blond. "I'm looking for a Mr. Brock," said Piggott. "Do you know if he lives here?"

There was no recognition or interest in the pale blue eyes. "I don't know at all, I'm sorry."

"Oh. Thought he lived here," said Piggott stupidly. "He said it's a nice place except there used to be some neighbors played their stereo too loud, he was always complaining."

"Oh, that must have been some time ago. That was Denis—a friend of mine who used to live here. I don't care for it on loud either. I remember there was someone who complained—I think he moved away some time ago." He wasn't interested.

"Thanks very much," said Piggott.

It was getting hotter and hotter. He decided to go home to Prudence and his tropical fish. He'd just acquired a couple of new Damsel Barbs, and of course it was a lot of work and trouble, but he'd been thinking it would be interesting to try some breeding again.

Palliser finally got Hoffman on the phone at five o'clock. "Goddamn lawyers," said Hoffman. "I was on the stand an hour when they finally got to me. Hell, I know any punk's entitled to legal defense, but when it comes to trying to stack the deck against us—"

"Haven't we all been through it," said Palliser.

"Murder Two," said Hoffman tiredly. "He's got a pedigree from here to there. He just happens to be black. They'll probably give him a five-to-ten and he'll be out in a couple of years. Did you want anything special?" He'd been desultorily kept up on the case, and knew it was dying a natural death.

"Well, we've turned up something," said Palliser. "Something damn unexpected, from Robsen's next-door neighbors." He told Hoffman what it was. "Ring a bell at all?"

"Nary a bell," said Hoffman. "Description like that—not much in it. I never heard whether your lab picked out a gun. Meant to ask."

"It was an H. and R. .22, for a choice that Sidekick target pistol."

"Oh," said Hoffman.

"If you think about it, and come up with any idea on that description—something may come to you."

"Yeah," said Hoffman. "O.K."

"Well, O.K. then," said Palliser. He felt oddly deflated and discouraged.

9

PIGGOTT AND SCHENKE HAD HAD A BUSY NIGHT: A HEIST at an all-night drugstore with the clerk shot dead, a gang rumble down near the Plaza with another D.O.A. They had sealed the drugstore for the lab and that was the first order of business on Thursday morning. It was Hackett's day off; the men drifted in and went out again, on the old heists, the new jobs.

Higgins, coming in late, looked in at Mendoza's office and said, "Well, we clinched the deal on that house—papers all signed. Now I just hope we sell the other one reasonably quick. The whole thing is ridiculous, you know. Bert paid twenty-one thousand for that house seventeen years ago, and the realtor says we should ask eighty-five."

"Inflation," said Mendoza tersely. He was hanging on the phone, and apparently it had just got activated after a wait. He said, "Macinnes? Have you got to that handwriting comparison yet?—Well, why not?—Yes, I'll ask priority, get to it as quick as you can, damn it." He put the phone down. "Do I remember that there were some prints in the Davidson house sent to the Feds? Did we ever get a kickback on it?"

"Helpful," said Mendoza, and his phone rang again. Higgins went out and started down to R. and I. after some names and addresses to look for.

It was an assistant D.A. on the phone, and he wanted to talk about Gustave Snyder. He kept Mendoza listening for half an hour, talking about the crowded conditions of the courts, the advisability of a plea bargain in this case, the man having no previous record. "Look," said Mendoza, "it's up to you. Unfortunately. It's out of our hands, let the lawyers gnaw over the bones."

He was annoyed at the waste of time; the boys could use some help ferreting out all these damned heisters, and he wanted to know what the lab was getting on the drugstore job. But he'd just put down the phone when he got a buzz from Lake at the desk.

"Squad just called in on a new one. Attempted homicide. They're holding him."

"Oh, hell. All right, I'm on it, Jimmy. What's the address?" He reached for a memo pad. Ashmore Avenue.

As he went out, he thought absently, somebody had mentioned Ashmore Avenue to him recently: he couldn't pin it down, who or why.

It was an old street above Elysian Park, a block of modest homes neatly enough kept up. One squad was standing in front of the house on the far corner, another behind it. A few neighbors were out, staring curiously. Patrolman Bill Moss was waiting on the sidewalk beside the second squad, and eyed the big black Ferrari with gloomy admiration as it swept up. "So what have you got?" asked Mendoza.

"A nut, probably. We've got him cuffed, in case. He owns this place—an Alfred Shaw. Lives here alone, works for Parks and Recreation. This is his day off. He got into the hell of an argument with the neighbor on that side over the neighbor's tree dropping leaves into his yard—the neighbor's wife told us all about it—and biffed him with a shovel. It looked to me like it could turn into a homicide. Neighbor is Percy Griscom. The ambulance just took off, wife went with him."

"People, people," said Mendoza. He followed Moss around the side of the house—the front yard was immaculate with mown green lawn, clipped shrubbery—to a neat, rectangular rear yard, and Patrolman Echeverría standing beside a hulking elderly man in neat, tan work clothes. A stout woman and another man stood by talking volubly, and shut up as Mendoza and Moss appeared.

"Mrs. Stote, Mr. Vanderveer," said Echeverría.

"They heard most of it too, from the two yards back up here."

"He oughta be shut up," said the woman agitatedly. "He's always been sort of queer, but he's got worse since his wife died—they never did have anything to do with neighbors—and he's a real nut on everything being neat. Fanatic like they say. Going on at Percy about that tree!"

"I heard all the ruckus, I was mowing the backyard," volunteered Vanderveer, "and I saw him hit Percy with that shovel—"

"You just need me to book him in," Mendoza told Moss. "Read him his rights and fetch him down to the Alameda facility, I'll check with the hospital."

Shaw growled, looking down at the cuffs on his wrists. "You can't arrest me!"

"You'd be surprised what we can do," said Mendoza.

"I'm not goin' anywhere with you," said Shaw.

"I'm afraid you haven't any choice," said Mendoza uninterestedly.

"But I can't leave my house! You can't take me away from my house!"

"He never does go anywhere," said Mrs. Stote. "To work and home. Got about six locks on all the doors, we often wondered if he's got a lot of money hid away."

"Oh?" Mendoza paused in the act of lighting a cigarette. "As long as we're here let's take a look." He started for the back door.

"You can't go in my house!" Shaw let out a roar and made for him like a bull, head down. Mendoza sidestepped him neatly, and Echeverría grabbed hold of him.

"You simmer down! You can wait in the squad— I'll keep an eye on him, Lieutenant."

The screen door on the service porch was unlocked; they went in, and into a large square kitchen immaculately clean and neat. "Funny the things you meet on the job," said Moss, going from there across a hall into a back bedroom. "You suppose he's got a hundred grand sewed into a mattress?"

162

"I should very much doubt it, but you never know." The single bed wasn't made up here, just had a thin bedspread neatly covering the mattress. The front bedroom was occupied, and the few signs of occupancy—brush, comb, dresser tray—were exactly aligned with military precision. There were no books, no newspapers in the house. The living room, shrouded in gloom with thick drapes pulled, was a period piece of antiques with not a speck of dust showing, the old wood polished to a dull gleam.

"What's that?" said Moss.

"What?"

"I thought I heard something." They listened, and somewhere heard a faint, insistent, distant pounding. Tap-thud, it came; tap-thud, and it was somewhere in the house. "What the hell—" said Moss.

They followed it by ear, and it was loudest in the back bedroom. There was a walk-in closet; Moss jerked open the door, and the next tap-thud was right under their feet. He pushed aside a huddle of clothes, and there on the floor of the closet was a trapdoor with a sizable padlock on it.

"Go see if he's got any keys on him," said Mendoza, and Moss went off at a run, came back three minutes later with a ring of keys and knelt there while he tried one and another. Finally, the padlock came apart and he lifted the trap.

From the darkness down there, something said, "Please—please—" Moss reached down both hands, and pulled up onto the closet floor something at once ludicrous and incredible. It was wearing rags that had once been clothes; it was holding a dilapidated loafer in one hand, which had evidently made the pounding. It collapsed on the floor in a little heap and looked at them wildly through tangled brown hair.

"What the *hell?*" said Moss.

"Oh, I heard voices—not *him*—and I thought—*try,*" said a strangled little voice. "Oh, is he gone? Please—*I want my mother!*"

Five minutes later Moss was calling up another ambulance, and Mendoza was on the phone to Carey.

"What do you want? I'm busy as hell—"

"I thought you'd like to know," said Mendoza, "that we've found Alice Mason."

They had a look at the little half basement, or quarter basement, under the house, built in before Shaw's time: snugly lined, plastered walls, no windows, about five feet beneath the house flooring. It was a space about sixteen feet square, originally intended for God knew what: wine cellar, storage. There was a camp cot there now, with blankets, a tin bucket for a commode, a gallon jug half-full of water, and that was all.

"My good God in heaven," said Carey. "Things like this don't happen."

They heard about it a couple of hours later from Alice, as she lay clean and tidy in a hospital bed. Her mother and father, hastily summoned from their jobs, were close beside her, still alternately raging and weeping. She was a plain girl with insignificant small features, brown eyes in sallow skin, but she looked nearly radiant, back in the world again, her hand tightly clasped in her mother's.

"He didn't hurt me at all," she told them earnestly. "He just wanted somebody to do all the housework." She told them how he had come to the back door that day, just after she'd got home from school, and asked if she'd like to do some work for him, he'd pay her. They didn't know him even if he lived almost next door, one house down, and everybody said he was a queer old man. But she'd been more than willing to earn some extra money, and she'd gone with him right then to his house, and he'd told her he wanted that basement room cleaned, got her to go down the little ladder, and then slammed the trapdoor.

"He only let me out at night, when he was there, and he watched me all the time. I had to fix his supper, we ate together, and that was the only time I had anything, at supper. Then I had to clean the house. At first I tried to think of how to get away, but there wasn't any way—he kept all the curtains pulled and everything locked, and he was always right there. As soon as I'd finished, dusting or washing floors or vacuuming, he'd put me back in the basement again."

The father was breathing fire, and mother half weeping over her. "Oh, baby, we prayed so hard for you—knew you'd never leave us the way they thought—"

"Oh, I prayed too," said Alice. "It was sort of the only thing to do. I guess that's how I could stand it. I minded the dark most, I guess, but I kept thinking about the valley of the shadow of death in the Bible, and the Lord was there, it says, so I knew some time I'd get out. He didn't hurt me at all, really—he let me take a bath once a week, and sometimes he'd get things I asked for, but he wouldn't get me any other clothes, and they were sort of falling apart."

"God in heaven," said Carey.

"He was awfully grouchy, everything had to be just so, but he did pay me." Alice actually giggled. "He did. Every Friday night he gave me a dollar. They're all under the mattress on the cot, it was the only place I had to put them."

"Baby, we prayed so hard," choked her mother. "I just knew the Lord would send you back—"

The doctor had been slightly surprised. "Considering what she's been through, she's in quite good condition. A lot of adults would have broken down mentally in that kind of confinement, but she seems quite stable. Got a lot of guts, if you ask me."

They went over to the jail to arrange for Shaw's transfer to the psychiatric ward at U.C.L.A. Medical Center; he certainly didn't belong in jail. He glowered at them almost plaintively. "The house, it just got beyond me since Mary died—like to drove me wild. I hadda have some help. Heard she was a good little worker, and she was. I paid her!" he said. "I paid her!"

He had. Under the thin mattress of the old cot were twenty-seven dollar bills. She'd been in that house for twenty-eight weeks.

Angel had found a house, and had an appointment to let Hackett see it. "Though what the real-estate agent will think when we drive up in this circus wagon

I can't imagine," she said, getting into the front seat of the Monte Carlo.

"I like it," said Hackett firmly.

"And I know it'll be a drive—but it isn't really terribly far from the Pasadena freeway." She'd given up looking in the other directions: undesirable elements creeping in down toward any of the beach towns and environs. The place she'd found was high above Altadena, in fact just short of the boundary of the Angeles Forest, and she recited all the advantages. "It's so high, we'd be out of the smog and the worst of the heat. It's the last street north in Altadena, and it ought to be quiet and utterly safe for the kids. Though as a matter of fact—the lot's seventy by a hundred and ninety—I had thought about a dog."

"The things you get me into," said Hackett. "How do they want?"

"Seventy thousand, but we ought to get more than that for ours. It does need some painting and a little general fixing up," said Angel.

Hackett groaned, switching on the air conditioning.

Piggott drove up to the house in West Hollywood about three o'clock. It wasn't a mansion, but a nice old house. There wasn't a sign of life about it; the garage was closed; but he went up on the porch and rang the bell, and after a moment the door opened.

"Well?" The man who stood there was perhaps thirty-five, a man with heavy-lidded eyes and a down-turned mouth.

"Miss Pauline Dunn here?" asked Piggott. "I'd like to see her."

"Well, you can't see her. She'd dead," said the man. "Who are you? Who told you to ask for Pauline?"

"A friend of hers said if I was ever in California to look her up. I'm sorry to hear she's dead. Er—how did it happen?"

"I didn't know she had any friends," said the man bitterly. "All of them letting her down, never coming near her. I don't know what the hell business it is of yours, but some bastard she was engaged to jilted her and she killed herself."

Piggott looked at him, head on one side. "His name wouldn't be Glen Brock, would it?"

The man jerked back convulsively and said, "Who the hell are you? What business—"

"Police business, in a way," said Piggott. "I think you'd better let me in, Mr.—" He got out the badge.

"Dunn. I'm her brother. What—" Dunn looked at the badge and turned away; Piggott followed him into a dim living room. "I suppose the bastard's found out," he muttered. "I don't know how he could. I had to get back at him some way. Poor Pauline, the way he treated—"

Piggott didn't attempt to enlighten him. Brother and sister a pair when it came to being neurotic, he thought. The girl fantasizing over Brock, who was indeed a good-looking young fellow, telling wild tales. He said, "You'll have to stop it now, Mr. Dunn. Now we know you've been behind all this."

"Come interfering," said Dunn savagely. "Cops, interfering—last ones should come round—" But having started, he went on talking disjointedly. He and Pauline always close—he was living in Pasadena then and never met that bastard—only when Pauline killed herself, she left him a letter all about it. The bastard, making Pauline do that—had to get back at him some way.

"It was a little trouble," said Piggott, "keeping up with him, wasn't it? When he moved, when he got married?"

"What else have I got to do? Dad left plenty of money. It was a *pleasure*," said Dunn. "I liked doing it."

"It was a funny sort of thing to do. What made you think of it?"

Dunn smiled, not a nice smile. "I got picked up by the cops, mistaken identity, once. I didn't like it much. I didn't figure he would. And it wouldn't be just one time—I could make it over and over. I enjoyed it."

"Well, you understand it's got to stop now. Now we know it was you. Don't you think you've done enough to him?"

Dunn considered. "I suppose," he said, "he'd sue me. And the lawyers coming into it." His narrow

167

mouth drew tight. "He isn't going to get any money out of me. You can tell him that."

"I think he'll be just as happy to forget it," said Piggott, "if the whole thing just comes to a stop, Mr. Dunn."

After a moment Dunn gave a grudging nod. And as he got back into his car, Piggott felt at least a small satisfaction with himself. A funny little business it had been. He thought he'd see if Brock was at his office and tell him about it; he'd be interested, and even more interested to know that his strange persecution was ended.

It was hotter than ever; he could hardly touch the steering wheel. Also, he thought, switching on the ignition, leave a note for Hackett. The other boys would be interested too. So much of what they were dealing with, day in, day out, was the crude and sordid humdrum violence; the offbeat things were always interesting. In a way.

At the moment Higgins and Galeano were dealing with a crude and violent new one, as if they needed anything else, with that new homicide on the drugstore heist as well as all the other heisters to hunt, and Robsen still up in the air. The call had gone down just after they got back from lunch, and nobody else was there so they went out on it.

It was a little duplex on Fortieth, just down from Santa Barbara, and the corpse was a fat old black woman with a knife in her back. The knife had slashed and stabbed her a good many times, and the little, hot living room where she lay was bloodstained—walls and carpets. It was a shabby old place, but they could see it had been clean and neat before the violence struck. She was decently dressed in a cotton print dress, low-heeled sandals. She was a Mrs. Rebecca Woods, and it was her daughter who had called in, Mrs. Rachel Holly.

A lab truck had just arrived and they'd taken Rachel Holly out to sit in Higgins' Pontiac while they talked to her.

"It looks as if she let him in, Mrs. Holly. Neither of the doors were forced. Was your mother careful about—"

"Of course she was! You got to be careful these days—never know who's around. And her living alone like she did—I told you she was having trouble with the arthritis, couldn't get around so good—I came by as often as I could, and Mr. Smith was that good to her, but of *course* she was careful about—she wouldn't have let a stranger in, and nobody she knew would have *killed* her! I told you about the Social Security—" She was a plump, pale-brown woman, agitated and half-weeping, her words tumbling over each other. "She hadn't cashed the check yet, maybe it was somebody knew about that, or no, it'd be the other way round, wouldn't it, because they'd be after the cash— I was coming to take her to the bank today, that's why I came by, she expected me— I was late, the kids were fussing so—and I expected she'd be all ready and waiting and then I saw the door was open—"

"Who is Mr. Smith?" asked Galeano.

"Why, her tenant on the other side. She owns the duplex, her and Dad put by everything they could to keep the payments up, and they got it paid off the year before he died. Mr. Smith's been on the other side for a good ten years and he's such a help to her, don't know what she'd do without him— What? Oh, Mr. Clarence Smith—he drives a truck for the L.A. *Times,* good, steady, reliable man, he's a widower, and he mows the lawn and does a lot of yard work and empties her trash for her and all—lucky to have such a good tenant— But who could've done such an awful thing—" She started to cry again. "It's just terrible the things go on, and to think of her—that knife— But she'd never've let anybody like that in— Oh—oh—oh!" she sobbed. "If Mr. Smith had been here it'd never have happened!"

"I thought you said—"

"Because it's his day off, he gets double time to carry all the Sunday papers around on Saturday nights, and he'd have *been* here! People on both sides work, nobody to hear her scream—which she must have—but if he'd been here he'd have come running— Oh—oh—oh!"

"Why, where is he?" asked Higgins.

"He's—oh, oh—off on vacation," sobbed Rachel Holly. "He's gone to see his brother in San Diego—"

They wouldn't get much out of her now; later on they'd ask her to go through the house, spot anything missing. Mrs. Woods's handbag was gone, and as in most of these cases it had probably been some punk after the easy loot. The only thing was, she had apparently opened the door to him; so they'd want to hear about any neighborhood punks, people she might have opened up to unsuspecting.

They asked her to come in to make a statement tomorrow, told her where to come, and she agreed. They left the lab team poking around and went back to base to write the initial report.

Two of the interrogation rooms were in use, so somebody had found somebody to talk to. Galeano started the report and Higgins went into Mendoza's office to tell him about the new one. Palliser was there, hip on one corner of Mendoza's desk, and they were talking about the suicides. Higgins had heard about that from Hackett.

"But what the hell could be behind it, Luis? I mean, there's no reason for anybody—not as if there was any money involved."

"Reasons are good to who has them," said Mendoza ungrammatically. "I don't know, George. There may not be anything behind it—I may be seeing ghosts. I just feel—mmh—that I'd swallow two suicides, but not three."

"That may be queer enough," said Palliser humorously, "but wait until you hear what he stumbled across this morning, George."

"Oh, yes, you haven't heard about that." Mendoza laughed. "Well, nothing very funny to laugh at, at that—that poor girl is damned lucky to have come out of it as intact as she did. The damnedest thing—" He told Higgins about Alice Mason. "She seems to be a

170

nice little girl," he added thoughtfully, "but somehow I wonder if she'll be so interested in housework and cooking from now on. Of course the old fellow's way off the beam, and they'll tuck him away. When you come to think of it, as the doctor said, it's a miracle she's still sane. At least it took a load off Carey's mind. He said he'd been worrying at that case whenever he had a spare minute—now we know how the magic trick was worked." He sat in silence for a minute.

Higgins yawned and said, "We've got a new knifing, by the way. Looked fairly fresh."

"Oh, fine," said Palliser. The phone buzzed on Mendoza's desk and he reached for it.

"Yes, Jimmy?" He listened for a moment and his face hardened to sudden grimness. "They didn't say—I see. I see, O.K., we're on it." He put down the phone and stood up.

"Something?" said Higgins.

"No sè. A beat man just called in—some kind of fracas—two cars sent out. They haven't sorted it out, but they've ended up at the Receiving hospital and Mrs. Hoffman asked them to call us."

"Mrs. *Hoffman?"* said Higgins.

"I think we'd better see what it's all about," said Mendoza.

The old Receiving hospital on Wilcox Street in Hollywood was used to police cases. The white-clad staff coming and going in the lobby wasn't paying any attention to the two uniformed patrolmen there. Mendoza knew both of them, Gonzales and Beecham. They looked past him to Higgins, and Gonzales said, "She asked for you, Sergeant."

"What's all this about?" asked Mendoza sharply.

"I haven't got the slightest idea," said Gonzales. "We got sent to this address out in Silver Lake. There was the hell of a ruction going on—woman screaming, a man yelling—so we went in fast. This guy was knocking a teenager all over the place—looked like the usual family fight. We pulled him off, the kid was a mess, and the woman screaming he was going to kill him. The guy put up one hell of a fight, we had to

171

knock him right out, he's pretty much of a mess too. We called an ambulance and tried to get some sense out of her, but she was too upset. She went in the ambulance, and we came down to talk to her some more—we've got to put in a report. That's when she asked us to call you, and seeing she knew Sergeant Higgins—"

"Did she say why?" They were in the elevator then. Gonzales shook his head.

"I just—" he stopped, and then he said, "Only, if I ever saw a woman looking into hell, it was her."

Up in the Emergency wing, she was sitting all alone in a straight chair against the wall. She was staring right ahead of her, sitting up straight. The only other time Palliser and Higgins had seen her, she had been a smart, good-looking blonde, rallying around Cathy Robsen that day. Now she looked, suddenly, like a death's head. She might have been a dead woman, by her eyes, except that she was breathing. Her hair was tousled; she had on a navy-and-white nylon dress, and the collar was ripped on one side; there was a darkening bruise on one cheek. She held a big, navy bag upright on her lap.

"Mrs. Hoffman?" said Mendoza.

Her eyes focused on him, but he didn't mean anything to her and they moved on to Higgins. Her lips opened stiffly and she licked them. "He—" she said. "He—would have killed him. I didn't know—until I saw—" She stopped as if her mind had gone blank.

"Has a doctor seen her?" asked Mendoza.

"I guess so. She didn't want any kind of treatment. They got busy on the other two."

Higgins bent over her and took her shoulders. "Mrs. Hoffman. You've got something to tell us. Just take it easy now." She was used to cops, to cops' ways. She nodded dumbly.

"Sorry. They gave me something—sedation of some kind, I think. In a minute." She was breathing more quickly now; she kept a death grip on the handbag. After a moment she was shaken by a long, convulsive shudder, and then she fixed her eyes squarely on Higgins' tie clasp and began to speak in little jerky phrases.

"There was—something on his mind. I know him—so well. Something. As if—worried about—I don't know. Last night. But he—went off to work—this morning— same as always. Then he came home—he came home—too early, before—end of shift. Larry —was there, just came home—from the swimming pool. Mike was over at the Crawfords'—oh, God, he'll wonder where I am—and Bill—and Bill— There was something wrong. As if—get up courage to look—at something he was afraid of—I know him. He went straight to the closet and got that out—and then—he just dropped it—and he screamed at Larry—he screamed *Judas Judas Judas* and he started beating him—he'd have killed him, he'd have killed him— I had to call help—tried to pull him off but he didn't know it was me, he—" One hand slid up to the bruise. There was a moment of silence, and then slowly she took her other hand from the bag and opened the flap and reached in and held out something to Higgins. "You'd better have it," she said.

Higgins took it. It was a Harrington and Richardson .22, the little Sidekick target pistol. He swung the cylinder out, and there was one slug missing.

"Oh, Christ," said Palliser sickly.

They did some overtime that night. It was five o'clock then. The doctors said they could talk to both of them in a couple of hours. Mendoza called Alison, and of course Alison always knew what to say and what not to say; all she said was, "I'll be waiting up for you, *amado, Hasta más tarde.*"

Palliser and Higgins called home, and they went out to the London Grill, but none of them wanted much, and there was no point in speculating. At seven o'clock they were back at the hospital.

Hoffman was under moderately heavy sedation. He lay on the bed and looked at the ceiling. When movement caught his eye he turned his head very slowly and saw Higgins and then Palliser. There wasn't any expression in his eyes, but evidently he recognized them. After a while he said, with no emotion at all in his voice, "Something to think about. Not at first. Kind of grew—nasty little idea—back of my mind. Fantastic. A *green* bicycle. No good—I had to look. Ashamed to have—little idea." And after another while he said, "Gun to have fun with, you know—teach the boys." And a while later he said, "Judas. Why? Why? No rhyme or reason. You have to write a report on it, Palliser. Have to talk to him. Tell him something from me, Palliser. After they give him life—and he's loose in seven years on P.A.—tell him never to come near me, to call me Dad again." And then he just lay and looked at the ceiling.

The boy wasn't so heavily sedated. He had bandages on his face and arms, a puffed-up black eye. Where he'd suffered more was in the sudden, shattering shock to his own absorbed sense of egotistic Self: he'd had a naked look out of the teenager's little world of Self, and it had shaken him to his foundation. So he'd retreated again into that world, absorbed only with his desires and reasons. He had no defense against the men looking at him, but he scowled at them rebelliously.

He was seventeen, a big, lithe boy with longish blond hair, a rather girlish mouth, a too-long chin.

Higgins gave him just one word. "Why?"

Larry Hoffman's eyes moved away sullenly. "It wasn't any of his damn business. Argue Dad out of building that big pool. Damn it, it'd have been just great—wouldn't have to ride all the way up to school every day— You got to keep in form for the team! I thought about it ever since—*him*, it was all his fault I couldn't have that big pool. And I saw Tom Robsen at the pool at school that day, his mother was out—and I knew old Robsen'd be at home alone, his damn day off— Oh, what's the damn use?" He rolled over on his side.

They went out to the corridor.

"*¡Què lástima!*" said Mendoza very quietly. "There are two families ruined and split. What's going to happen to them?"

"Nothing good," said Higgins. "My God, Luis—" he took a breath. "It scares you. It scares you. They thought they'd raised him right. What would any of us feel—what would I do, God—Steve going wrong? What would you—"

"But it could never happen to us," said Mendoza. They just stood there smoking.

"They'll probably try him as an adult," said Palliser. "Murder One. Because he went home to get the gun. And I feel as if I'd done that to Hoffman, you know— it's senseless, because it had to come out—but I'm the one told him about the new evidence. I was so damn pleased about it."

"The truth," said Mendoza, "however bad it may be, is always better than ignorance, John."

"Don't be so damn sententious," said Higgins. "You know what the man means."

"Oh, yes, I know. And there'll be all the paper work on this, and the statements to get, and the long, drawn-out ritual in court—" He flicked his cigarette into a sand tub. "By the way, John, did we ever find out about the verdict in Steve Smith's trial?"

"I called to find out. He got life."

"Well, the paper work can wait until tomorrow. Let's go home," said Mendoza, and headed for the elevator.

Piggott was telling Schenke about the end of that funny little affair—Brock had been flatteringly grateful, but Piggott felt he'd just followed his nose the way a good detective should—about nine o'clock on Thursday night. They hadn't had a call yet. Schenke said that was the queerest one he'd heard about in a while. "It's funny too," he said after a minute, "but isn't it quiet, Matt? You remember how we used to cuss E. M. and that damned transistor radio?"

It was quiet in the big office, just the two of them sitting there, but five minutes later they got a call. It was on Sixth, a bar. They got there expecting a heist or a brawl of some kind.

One beat man was trying to mold on to two men at once, and one man had a grim hold on the other. The second patrolman greeted the Robbery-Homicide men with relief.

"I guess it was a heist of some kind. Bartender called in a 415—said this fellow all of a sudden started to yell 'robber' and glommed onto this guy—"

"Aha!" The booming, triumphant voice belonged to Mr. Baumgartner. "Now you see! For you the robber I have caught! I said I would know if I see! Here he is!" He shook the other man in his powerful grip as a dog shakes a kitten. "A little glass of beer I am drinking when—hah!—I see him come in! Now you will in jail put, *nein?*"

"I'll be damned," said Schenke. "All right, sir, you can let go of him now."

The other man was long and thin, and he was wearing a stained white jumpsuit with *Dick's Garage* embroidered on the breast pocket. As Baumgartner let go of his collar, he resettled it calmly. "All right, what's your name?" asked Schenke. The man didn't say a word. Schenke took him by the shoulder. "Speak up—what's your name?"

The man reached into his breast pocket and handed him a card. It said, *I am a deaf mute.*

"Now I *will* be damned," said Schenke. "This is a twist. You're sure it's him? The one held you up?"

Baumgartner nodded vigorously. "It is him who robbed me. He is dummy? That is funny."

"Listen," said Piggott, and caught himself. He got out his notebook and wrote in it. *This man says you held him up. Did you?*

"We still don't know his name," said Schenke, and bent and added the question.

The man promptly produced I.D. He was Joseph Bentley, an address on Third. He looked at the notebook, took Piggott's ball-point and wrote under the questions, *Sorry you caught me.*

"Well," said Schenke. He wrote, *Work at garage?*

Bentley borrowed the pen again. *Good job, I was bored with life.*

This time Piggott almost said he'd be damned too.

They took him in.

Mendoza sat at his desk on Friday morning thinking about Hoffman and those two ruined families. It was in a way worse than sudden ruin: it was forever ruin. For never again would Bill or Muriel Hoffman, or Cathy Robsen, be able to believe all the way, without question, in a friend, in any firm emotional foundation in life. Would Hoffman see Muriel, now, as the mother of his friend's killer? The two women—what sort of friendship was left?

He shook off the gloom impatiently. Palliser and Higgins had started the paper work on it, and he had been talking to the D.A.'s office. He had a very good notion what the men at Hollenbeck precinct were saying and feeling.

At least Joseph Bentley had given him a little laugh, as he read the night report.

It was eleven o'clock when Macinnes from Questioned Documents came in and said, "Well, we finally got round to this." He laid the two pages on Mendoza's desk: the recipe for lemon cake, the other with a single line scrawled: *Too much trouble to keep on, nobody to miss me.* "There's absolutely no resemblance at all, even superficial. Not even an attempt at imitating the genuine writing."

"*¡Media vuelta!*" said Mendoza. "So now we know. Definitely. And a very peculiar picture it does create. Thank you so much. I wonder, for what?" He stared at the two dissimilar documents, swept them into his pocket; he got up and went out. The office was empty.

He drove up to the quiet, little backwater, parked the Ferrari and sat for the length of a cigarette looking at the street, the houses, wondering what more to ask these people, where to start looking for what on this. It wasn't a shapeless thing—as he had said the other day, it was the wrong shape. Someone behind the scenes manipulating things, creating a picture to his own specifications. And the picture was flawed. But why had it been drawn at all? For what conceivable reason had someone wanted these aged, harmless, poverty-ridden people dead? There wasn't any property involved, or not much: the houses. Scarely prime property down here. They hadn't had any family. They'd just been quietly moldering away here, content in their own ways, and in the course of nature none of them could have lived many more years anyway.

"¡Ca!" he said to himself. They hadn't even, when he thought about it, known many people. Their lives had narrowed down at this end, as transporation became a problem; very likely none of them had been out of the immediate neighborhood in years.

The immediate neighborhood— Well, that was something, of course. The woman who had been away: they had never talked to her. Mrs. Babcock, whose daughter had just had a baby, who had left the very day Pearl Davidson was murdered to stay with her daughter in Arcadia. Who was now presumably back.

You never knew where a lead would turn up. Mendoza got out of the car, stepped on his cigarette and walked across the street to the little frame house next to Mrs. Davidson's house. It was conventionally painted white with green trim.

Down here in the central city, it must have been nearly a hundred degrees. The blacktop street was sticky, as though it sweated.

He pushed the doorbell, waited. The woman who appeared on the other side of the screen door was matronly without being fat; she'd be much younger than most of her immediate neighbors, in the fifties. Her eyes brightened with interest on the badge, and she held the screen door open hospitably.

"It'll be about Mrs. Davidson—you're still looking for the one killed her. That was a terrible thing, I couldn't believe it when Mrs. Hallam called to tell me. Mercy, I thought, it could be I had a narrow escape— he could just as well have picked my house right next door! But I can tell you, I'd have put up a better fight than poor old Mrs. Davidson. That's a wicked shame—poor, harmless old soul like that. But I couldn't tell you anything about it, you know—I wasn't here."

"Well, that's one thing we wanted to ask you," said Mendoza. "When exactly did you leave?" Garrulous

178

females were often useful: set them talking, they went from one thing to another.

"Well, let me see," said Mrs. Babcock. "Jim was late—my son-in-law—picking me up, because he had some car trouble. I'd expected him about seven-thirty, and then he phoned to say he'd be late but he'd be here, so I just sat waiting. I had my bag all packed. It was awful hot that night, and there's some holes in that screen, so I just sat in the dark, no light to bring the bugs in. Made it seem a little bit cooler, anyway." She shook her head. "I suppose that criminal didn't come till way late at night, way they do. It's a scary thing, so many criminals around—and I've heard they go for the old folk who can't fight back. Well, I know it was just nine-thirty when Jim came—"

So much, thought Mendoza, for the people who had said, no car down here that night. But some of them would have been sitting in backyards, and they hadn't heard Jim's car.

"You're sure of that?" he got in. The autopsy report had said between nine and midnight.

"Oh, yes. Jim said it was. So you see," said Mrs. Babcock, "she was all right then, if you weren't sure when it happened, because Mr. Purdy was there then."

"Mr. Purdy?" said Mendoza.

"Why, yes. I saw him go up on the porch about ten minutes before. He doesn't usually go out visiting so late, but of course Mrs. Davidson was a night owl, up all hours, and he'd know that. Such a hot night— I saw her let him in," said Mrs. Babcock, "and about five minutes later Jim came, all in a hurry because we were late. But you see, she was all right then, it must have been a lot later that that terrible criminal came."

10

"OH, I SEE," SAID RONALD PURDY. "HOW VERY DIS-concerting. Of course, I had no idea she was still at home." He gave Mendoza a rather wintry smile. "So we needn't waste time on what's called cross-questions and crooked answers."

Mendoza had found him at home in the little stucco house on the corner. Purdy was sitting in an old Boston rocker, facing him in the airless, stuffy little living room, looking at him calmly and quite sanely; his sunken dark eyes were intelligent and serene.

"Martha Fogel's handwriting was quite different from the suicide note," said Mendoza. "We know from the autopsy report that Pearl Davidson died rather soon after Mrs. Babcock saw you go in there."

"Waste of time," repeated Purdy. He took off his rimless glasses, pinched the bridge of his nose between forefinger and thumb.

"Why?" asked Mendoza. "Just why in the name of all that's holy did you do it? Your old friends and neighbors—for God's sake, why?"

"Because they were—just that," said Purdy quietly. "I had worried about it for some time, of course. I had hoped that all of us would be peacefully dead and gone before it came. But the inflation moving at such an accelerated pace, it can't be very far off now. I do not think. You may not believe me, but I am a student of economics and I know. There is an economic holocaust before us. There is only one classic end to the fiat paper money with no backing of intrinsic value. Soon or late, it will come down in one overnight crash, and of course it will be beyond anything called a depression. The classic example is Germany of 1923."

He dangled his glasses in the air; his tone was

precisely academic. "It may be hard for us to imagine, but of course the effects are easily predictable. Within a few hours, after a course of runaway inflation, currency will lose all value. Everything will come to a screeching stop—services, supplies, trade, transportation. The banks will be closed. The food markets will be cleaned out by looters within hours, and no more supplies will come in. There will be no medium of exchange—for a while at least any existing trade will be in the form of barter, and those without much of value to exchange will soon be reduced to starvation. Particularly in the cities, crime will run rampant as desperate people plunder and loot for bare necessities. It is, of course, probable that when any semblance of order is restored, it will take the form of an oppressive dictatorship. That is the classic historical pattern."

He looked at Mendoza thoughtfully. "If you think I am insane, you have only to wait a little while to find out. But in any crisis, it's our own we have to think of, isn't it?" He smiled. "Pearl—and Guy and June—and poor Martha. You see, the Hallams and the Millets have large families here who would undoubtedly do their best to care for them as they could. The others had no one. There could be nothing ahead for them but misery and fear and starvation and bitter, painful deaths. I wanted—most desperately—to prevent that. They were old friends, dear good people, Meg's friends—they'd led useful, productive lives, and they deserved peaceful and dignified deaths—before this madness of the twentieth century caught up to them."

"Yes, I see," said Mendoza softly. "It was because they were old friends and neighbors."

"Exactly. I—it was a terrible decision for me to make," said Purdy, and there was a sudden tremor in his voice. "A terrible responsibility. I've never been a man of action, much less violence. But as the indications worsened, the crisis so much nearer, I—I saw I must take the responsibility—it had to be done. If I was going to save them—if they were to be gone and at rest before it happened."

Mendoza regarded him, fascinated. "I'd like to hear about the mechanics, you know."

"Certainly. As I say, it was all very repugnant to me, but it had to be done. I thought it out as carefully as I could. I saw there was no possible way, for Pearl, but some measure of violence. She wasn't taking any regular medication except aspirin, for the arthritis. But I did some research into the matter, and it seems that garroting is nearly instantaneous and relatively painless. I was very sorry—to do it that way, but it seemed to be the most effective—and of course I saw how it would, er, pave the way—for the others. The young couple who live on one side of the house would be out, and of course I thought Mrs. Babcock had left. I simply came up and rang the doorbell, and she let me in. She was always up late. She offered me a glass of lemonade, and it was when she turned to the refrigerator to get it that I—used the garrote. I had cut a length off the clothesline that morning."

"After she'd got out two glasses," said Mendoza.

"I—I don't remember," said Purdy. "I disliked it *very much*. But it had to be done, just as I'd planned. I hope she didn't know—I think she died very quickly. I went around pulling out drawers, all the rest, to make it look like a burglary. That was—the very worst one— of them, you know. The very worst. And yet, perhaps, even worse than that is not knowing—whether they would understand, if they knew. That it was to save them such terrible suffering. I don't know whether you can understand it. I can only say, I—I felt it was a thing Meg would have understood.

"You can see how that—paved the way. The others were quite easy. I knew June Burdine had a prescription for Nembutal, for her sinus headaches. It was quite easy for me to get a prescription, by telling the doctor it seemed to give me the best relief for migraine. I hadn't gone to that doctor before, he didn't know me from Adam, and he didn't ask many questions. You understand, I knew the Burdines must go on a Saturday night, for they never missed church, and the minister would come and find them. That, you know, was why I left Pearl's door open—to give myself an excuse to find her body. I couldn't bear to think of her lying there long. Of course Guy and June were right next door. I knew they'd be sitting in the backyard. I simply went over, with my own opened package of lemonade mix—I'd already mixed in the crushed Nembutal tablets. They were pleased—June went to mix it up—and we sat there in the dark, so they couldn't see that I wasn't drinking mine. I just waited until they had both dozed off, and went into the house, washed my glass and put it away, and took all the Nembutal tablets out of June's bottle. Then I typed the note on Guy's typewriter."

"And Martha Fogel?" said Mendoza.

"Oh, that was easiest of all, in a way. Both of us were taking digitalis. I made a little excuse to have my prescription refilled—I told the pharmacist I'd had a stupid accident, dropped the open bottle into the toilet. I just crushed up all the tablets into some more lemonade mix, and went across to Martha's after dark. She was surprised—it was a little out of character for me to go visiting her that late—but of course she didn't think much about it."

"And you waited until she was dead, and washed your glass again, and stole her digitalis."

"That note," said Purdy. "I had to take a chance that it'd be taken at face value—I'd never seen a sample of her writing at all." He sighed. "It was all—I disliked doing all that very much. But they were all dear, good people, and they were old and tired, they didn't deserve to suffer through all this holocaust that's due to descend. I felt—it was a thing Meg would want me to do. A sort of last gift I could give them." He looked gray and very tired. "I don't suppose you'll understand that."

"Oh, yes," said Mendoza. "In a way, Mr. Purdy. Your economics are quite sound. I suppose you know you'll have to come with me now. We'll get all this down in a formal statement."

Purdy drew a long breath. "At the jail," he said with a faint smile. "Oh, yes, of course. Should I take some clothes?"

"Not necessary."

"Well, I would like——" Purdy looked apologetically at the threadbare old cloth slippers he wore——"to put on a pair of shoes."

Mendoza followed him into the bedroom; Purdy bent to the floor of the closet, emerged wearing shabby old oxfords. He was silent all the way down to Alameda Street: on request he courteously emptied his pockets for the desk sergeant, and was given back his handkerchief, keys, a ballpoint pen. He smiled gravely at Mendoza.

"When it comes, Lieutenant, perhaps you'll understand better that I was only trying to do my level best to prevent my old friends dying——much, much worse deaths than they died."

Snyder had been arraigned that morning; Galeano had covered that, and then gone back to the never-ending routine. He had ended up with Hackett on the Woods case, Higgins and Palliser busy on the clean-up work on Robsen. And there had been inevitable delay in getting on with the routine while they hashed that over, a thing that hit them all deeply.

They were discussing what had shown up on Woods, desultorily, when Mendoza came in about two-thirty and told them about Purdy. He sat in Higgins' desk chair and smoked lazily, and they recognized with inward amusement that the thing in him forever seeking the neat patterns, the final answer, was at rest for the moment. The wrong shape had resolved itself into tidiness, and he was satisfied.

"Is he legally over the line?" asked Hackett.

There was a flash of cynical amusement in Mendoza's eyes. "Very far from it, Arturo. He knows his economics, at least. Wait and see. What have you been accomplishing, on what?"

Hackett didn't pursue it; normally, that offbeat a thing would have provided meat for discussion and argument, but like most of the men he had the Hoffman thing uneasily at the back of his mind, was mechanically going through the motions of routine. He said absently, "We kind of like this Lee Strang, on Woods. There are a few young punks living around there with little records—shoplifting, purse-snatching—she might have opened the door to one of them, having known them since they were kids. The Strangs live three doors down, and she knew his mother. Strang's a known user. If he rang the bell and said he had a message from mama, Mrs. Woods might have let him in."

"I don't suppose you've got anything from the lab yet."

"Nor on the D.O.A. in the drugstore, except that it was a .32 Colt. They always take their time."

Mendoza was still sitting there when Rachel Holly came in to make the formal statement, and sat somnolently listening to her. She was calmer today, and read the statement Wanda typed and signed it, but she was still talking. "If only Mr. Smith had been home—just bad luck he happens to be away. If it'd been last week—well, and then of course he had his nephew staying with him up to then, if even he'd been there—a man to hear Mother scream—it was just bad luck—"

Hackett asked her about the nephew; it was the first they'd heard of him. "Oh, he was here just a couple of weeks—Mr. Smith's sister's boy from Arizona. Mother said he seemed a nice-enough young fellow, only saw him a few times. He was staying with Mr. Smith while he looked for a job here."

"What's his name, do you know?"

"Oh, Joe Frame. I think Mother said he found a job and moved to some place of his own a few days ago, when Mr. Smith went to San Diego. To think, if either of them had been there—it's just like fate, like it was meant to happen. Mother, that never harmed a soul, good Christian woman, has to end up like that—it just don't seem right. You have any idea who did it?"

"We'll hope to have sometime, Mrs. Holly," said Hackett.

Mendoza got home a little early. The twins, in very abbreviated bathing suits, were splashing in the wading pool, with Cedric circling it barking. He watched them for a minute with a smile, his hostages to fortune, before they discovered him and came running. "*¡No*

185

tocar!" said Mendoza. "This is a reasonably new suit."

"Daddy, Luisa knows how to laugh, I tickled her toes an' she laughed—*Mamacíta* let us watch—" Terry.

"But Mama let me put the powder on when she washed Luisa," announced Johnny importantly. "How soon can she play with us?"

"Next week," said Terry with nonchalant confidence. "Next week Luisa can play hide-'n'-seek."

Mendoza laughed. "Maybe week after next, *niños*. No, you don't have to come in yet—Máiri'll call you." With daylight saving, the sun was still high, and the temperature still in the nineties. He went gratefully into air conditioning, and greeted Máiri in the kitchen, and strolled down to the living room to find Alison just gathering up the baby from a blanket on the floor.

"Oh—hello, darling, you're early. Reasonably good day?"

"Mmh," said Mendoza. "You could say reasonably." He bent to kiss her, and lifted the baby out of her arms. "You know, what with this and that, and these two females so assiduous about naps and bottles, I haven't got acquainted with you yet, *Señorita* Live Wire." He joggled her experimentally, and she gave him a gurgle, and then screwed her face up and began to yell. He joggled her harder. "Why on earth have you got her all bundled up in blankets in weather like this?"

"Oh—there's a little draft from the air conditioning," said Alison rather vaguely. "You'd better let me take her, it's time for her next bottle—"

"Aye," said Máiri briskly, coming in from the kitchen, "and here we are, my wee lamb. I'll take her, then—you might just have a look at the potatoes, *achara*—"

He drifted after Alison back to the kitchen, and poured himself a jigger of rye, jumping convulsively as El Señor landed on the counter beside the bottle. "*¡Señor Barracho!*" He poured him half an ounce and El Señor lapped appreciatively.

"Now he'll go and cuff Sheba," said Alison. "It

always turns him belligerent. I'll have some sherry, please." She carried it back to the living room. "I'm dying to get up there to see how much progress they've made—I'm feeling fine, Máiri fussing over me like an old hen. I will, on Monday. You know, Luis, I rather got cold feet there for a while, there's so much to be done and it's costing such a lot—but after I found the Kearneys I felt it was all meant, somehow. They're going to be such a help—and it's going to be such a beautiful house. The house it used to be—and with the old name too, the house of happy people."

La Casa de la Gente Feliz, thought Mendoza, and suddenly something walked over his grave and he shuddered, thinking about Hoffman. He finished the rest of the rye quickly.

They still hadn't had a lab report on Woods or the drugstore shooting, and they were rather stymied on Woods at least until they got one. They'd done a little legwork in the neighborhood without turning up anything suggestive but Lee Strang. Mendoza came in on Saturday morning while Hackett was arguing with Galeano that they ought to bring Strang in and lean on him.

"Not worth the trouble," said Galeano. "The lab may give us something definite."

"And they might not too," said Hackett.

"And he might have a definite alibi, which would put you that much further," said Mendoza. "The routine usually pays off in the end—" He stopped abruptly, and they looked around.

Higgins had just come in with Muriel Hoffman. "This won't take long, it's just a formality we have to—"

"Yes, I know," she said. "It's all right." She was neatly dressed, and her voice was steady. Higgins looked at Wanda Larsen, who came over with her pencil and pad. Mendoza vacated Higgins' chair, moved over to Hackett's desk.

Higgins took her through the bare facts quickly, trying to keep it impersonal, on the surface. Wanda went back to her typewriter and began to type the statement, and aside from the typewriter's discreet clicking a silence fell because there was really nothing to say to her. None of them was normally inarticulate, but there wasn't anything at all to say to Muriel Hoffman.

She said, "Bill's still in the hospital. They say he's gone into a sort of depression and he ought not to be—unsupervised. You know, what frightens me so— the men come to see him, try to talk to him—and he won't even look at them. He can't look at them— because he's so ashamed. I never saw him so ashamed." And she didn't say anything else until Wanda brought the statement over, and she signed it with a fairly legible signature.

"I'll take you home again," said Higgins.

"You needn't have driven me, I could have—" She went out with him. They felt relief to see her go. They sat for a minute thinking of what was ahead for the Hoffmans. There had already been the stories on the front page; news was news, and reporters had to make a living too, but they didn't seem much given to restraint.

Into the silence Scarne came with a manila envelope. "Occasionally we do you some good," he said, sounding pleased with himself. "There were four dandy latents on the handle of that knife. Nice, dull, wood surface, and of course it was hot, his hands were sweaty. Anyway, they weren't in our files so we wired 'em to Washington and they had him—I just got the word."

"And who is he?" asked Hackett without much interest.

"One Joseph Daniel Frame. The Feds had him listed because he was picked up for robbing a post office." Scarne passed over a Xeroxed sheet.

"The Feds," said Galeano, "are getting sloppy." It was an incomplete record. Joseph Daniel Frame, five ten, one-sixty, Negro, black and brown, twenty-eight now, arrest record on that one count from Phoenix, Arizona—he'd got one-to-three and served a year— and that was all.

"Hell," said Hackett, "and we know he's here. But

where? At least he was here. And this Clarence Smith probably knows where."

"Little rigmarole," said Galeano. "Take another day to get anything out of Washington. Have we got Mrs. Holly's number?" He found it, dialed, got her and asked whether she knew where Smith was in San Diego. She didn't. She'd never heard what his brother's name was.

"Also," said Hackett, "he'd just got here, and if he's driving anything it'll have Arizona plates and Sacramento won't know a thing about it."

Galeano was still on the phone to Mrs. Holly. "Do you by any chance know where in Arizona Frame came from?" She said she was pretty sure it was Scottsdale, and why did he want to know? Galeano thanked her and hung up. He was just getting connected with the Scottsdale police department when Pat Callaghan came in, looming even over Hackett, and politely stayed quiet while Galeano wrestled with a bad connection.

Scottsdale said they'd look in their records and get back to him, and Galeano abandoned the phone. "Conway or Landers in?" asked Callaghan.

"It's Tom's day off," said Hackett. "Grace is filling in—they're back there leaning on a suspect, I think." He heaved himself up and went down the hall to the one interrogation room in use, tapped on the door. Conway and Grace came out to the communal office.

"I just thought you'd be interested to know," said Callaghan, "that the bomb squad finally—and the doctors—came to the conclusion that there were three bodies represented in all the debris. One of them female. Oh, and that other address in Lockwood's notebook was a wholesale pharmaceutical supply place."

"Is that all you wanted?" said Conway. "Well, for God's sake, we'd guessed about the bodies. So what? Oh, well, we weren't doing any good anyway, I don't really think he's the one on the drugstore heist." He lit a philosophical cigarette. "We might as well let him go, Jase. Is anybody doing any good?"

"Oh, we just dropped on one," said Hackett. "Only we haven't got a leash on him."

"That's nothing new," said Conway.

Scottsdale called back after a while. They had a pedigree on Joe Frame: narco, burglary, assault. The address they had for him was in a suburb, where he lived with his mother, Mrs. Cora Frame. "That's fine, thanks," said Galeano. "Could you let me have her phone number?" He scribbled it down. "Run up the phone bill, but we don't want to rock the boat. She'll know about his record, but what Mrs. Holly said about Smith, I might doubt he does."

"That's who it turned out to be?" asked Grace.

"Some nice prints on the knife." Galeano hung on the phone patiently, and it was finally answered. "Mrs. Frame? You won't know my name, but I've been trying to get in touch with your brother, Mr. Clarence Smith. It's a business matter. He's visiting your other brother in San Diego, and I'm afraid I don't know his name. Oh. Oh, I see. Thank you so much." He put the phone down. "His name," he said, "is Lorenzo. Lorenzo Smith on Fourteenth Street."

"Nice going," said Hackett. Callaghan had wandered out. Galeano took up the phone again, but his luck had run out. Lorenzo Smith wasn't answering his phone.

At five o'clock Conway and Grace had just brought in another possible on the drugstore heist-killing when Horder came in with the first lab report they'd had on that. "Better late than never," said Conway sarcastically.

"Listen, we've been busy, stuff coming at us hot and heavy. Anyway, we may have something for you," said Horder. "A little clue. While we were crawling around the floor behind the counter there, we came up with this. It's been printed—smudges." He laid it on Grace's desk; it was a Visa credit card made out to John Ferrystone of Fallbrook, California. "It was on the floor half under the counter where the cash register was."

"Now isn't that pretty." Grace brushed his moustache back and forth. "You know, Rich, this could say something for sure. We read it that that clerk put up a fight to a heister, and that was why he got shot. Does this maybe make it read another way?"

"Oh," said Conway. "Oh. Like maybe, he questioned the card, started to check on it— It wasn't a heist at all?"

"Little idea," said Grace. They went down to Communications and fired the information on the card at NCIC. Computers were helpful; in short order information came back to them. Ferrystone's credit card had been among the proceeds of a burglary at his home in Fallbrook; credit had been stopped on that card. There was a want out on the identified burglar, one Carlos Montoya.

"A want out in Fallbrook and environs," said Grace. They had put the query to the D.M.V. in Sacramento, got the make on what he was driving, and put out the A.P.B. "Sit back and wait," said Conway. "It looks as if we've halfway cleared one up, anyway."

Mendoza came in late on Sunday morning and looked over the night report. Two more heists, and an unidentified body in a public parking lot—male Caucasian about twenty, possible O.D. It had been a quiet night for Saturday. At the moment only Glasser was in, over an inevitable report; it was Wanda's day off, and everybody else was evidently out on something. Galeano, said Glasser, still hadn't contacted Lorenzo Smith.

He opened the top drawer and reached for the cards, and saw the rosary lying there coiled around on itself. Joyce McCauley's rosary. Damn, he'd meant to see it got back to McCauley. Remembering his little supersitious feeling about it, he smiled grimly and picked it up.

Carey wasn't in his office today. He could mail the thing—Not exactly the cordial image of your friendly, sympathetic LAPD officer they liked to build. Mendoza hadn't the smallest desire to seek out McCauley, summon up words of sympathy; he didn't know whether man was still in the hospital, he didn't know where he lived.

It was getting on toward eleven o'clock. He sat there

a minute without making up his mind, finally dropped the rosary into his pocket and went out past Sergeant Lake, sitting there over a paperback.

Sometimes in August they had a slight respite from heat, in preparation for the worst heat to arrive in September; this year it hadn't let up at all. The parking lot, open to the sun, was like one vast, glaring desert, the sunlight reflecting from all the cars, the blacktop sticky underfoot. At least Hackett was somewhere in the building—or more likely chasing suspects in George's car; the Monte Carlo was sitting there in all its screaming iridescent lime-green-and-saffron glory. Mendoza got into the Ferrari and switched on the air conditioning.

When he got out to Brentwood Estates and parked in front of the iron gates, the air was slightly fresher, being that much nearer the beach. He hesitated, wondering if they held late mass; but it was unlikely, and he wouldn't be here five minutes. He pulled the bell.

After about five minutes a different novitiate came to the gate. He said, "I'd like to see Sister Mary Katharine or Sister Mary Constance, please." She let him in, and this time he was left in the tiled entrance lobby of the building past the little chapel. He waited another five minutes, and Sister Mary Katharine came to him.

"Oh, Lieutenant—have you found out anything more?"

"I'm afraid not," said Mendoza. "I'm afraid we may never find out." He wasn't about to tell her about Clyde Moore. He reached into his pocket. "I just came to return this. I thought Joyce's father might want it—" He let his voice trail off.

She took the rosary. "Where—did you find this?"

"It was with the body, practically under it. It was probably in the pocket of her dress, and fell out—"

"But it's not Joyce's" said Sister Mary Katharine. "Joyce had a very pretty crystal rosary her father sent her from Rome. We've just finished packing all her things—to send back to him. It was there, on her dresser." She was staring at the rosary.

Mendoza was faintly surprised. "Perhaps she'd got a new one—"

"Oh, no," said Sister Mary Katharine. "No. This belongs to Paula. She's never without it—it was a present from Mother Superior. I don't believe she actually knows the inner meaning of a rosary, but she can recite it by rote very well." And she raised her eyes to his, and suddenly turned and hurried away, her slippers pattering on the bare tile.

A small, cold finger moved up his spine. He heard Clyde Moore saying passionately, *"No kid ever came out there—"* And he thought, that great dim cavern of a hall, the little crowd of children wandering around—

When further steps approached, the Mother Superior came to him. She held the rosary in both hands. She looked, most uncharacteristically, frightened. She said without preamble, "This was—with Joyce? Paula could have dropped it—"

"I think we ask her, don't we?" said Mendoza gently. She nodded stiffly, and led him down a hall to a small music room. A large grand piano occupied most of it, and Sister Mary Katharine and Paula stood beside the piano.

The girl was dressed in plain white, her smooth brown hair neatly confined; her expression was vacant. A little interest came into her eyes on Mendoza. He took the rosary from the Mother Superior and cut across her voice on the girl's name. "This is yours, Paula, isn't it?"

"It used to be mine," she said. She spoke as simply as a child of five, but she was a big girl for fifteen, big-boned and heavy. "I gave it to Joyce."

There was a relieved gasp from both women, but Paula added, "I thought it would be nice if she took it to heaven with her."

"You knew Joyce was going to heaven?" asked Mendoza.

She nodded. "She wanted to go, she said. She was scared of the needles and all the medicine tasted bad. She said she'd like to go to heaven right away. And the eagles looked like they were flying right up there so I thought it was a good place."

"The eagles," said Mendoza. "Paula, do you remember—that day in the museum, with Joyce? Can you tell me about it? I'd like to hear—about Joyce going to heaven."

"All right," said Paula shyly. "I can remember. I love Joyce, you know, she's so pretty. She said that a lot, she wanted to go right away and not have any more needles, just be with Jesus and Our Lady. The museum—that day—" she gave a tiny giggle—"she found a secret. A big secret. She came and told me, and showed me the eagles. You went under a big curtain and there they were. Right up close to heaven, oh, they were pretty. Pretty. Joyce loved the eagles and so did I, and they were so close to heaven, I—" She faltered and slow tears came down her cheeks. "I didn't want to hurt Joyce, but you've got to die to get to heaven. And I did see the gardener make that bird die, it was easy—the bird's neck—it *was* easy, I didn't hurt Joyce. Joyce just laid down and went to sleep. So I put her with the eagles so they could take her to heaven."

The Mother Superior collapsed rather suddenly onto the piano bench. Sister Mary Katharine was on her knees.

"It isn't time for prayers yet," said Paula. "Do you think Joyce is got to heaven yet, Mother? How long does it take to get there?"

"I am quite sure," said the Mother Superior steadily, "that Joyce will soon be safe in heaven, child."

"Then that's good." She looked back at Mendoza, at the Mother Superior. "I am playing jacks with Peggy, can I go back now?"

The Mother Superior nodded, and Paula ran lumpishly out.

"Mother of God, have mercy on us," whispered Sister Mary Katharine. "Always such an obedient child—so gentle—never the slightest—"

Mendoza said quietly, *"Por mi vida.* The last thing anybody would have—" He looked at the two of them. "You understand, she can't stay here."

"She's been with us since she was five," said the Mother Superior numbly. "She will be lost—so bewildered—anywhere else."

"The other children, you know," he said. "When she's done this once— You could never be sure."

"No—no—I do see. But—what will happen to her?"

"It's not a perfect system." He wondered what would happen to Paula. She would probably end up at Camarillo. "There'll be a couple of policewomen will come to take her. We'll make it as easy as we can."

They nodded at him blindly. "A—a trial?" asked Sister Mary Katharine.

"Just a hearing." He put out his hand, and the Mother Superior let him take the rosary. It was evidence—and the only concrete evidence he had.

When he came into the office nearly everybody was back, and they all stopped what they were doing to hear about that, make the appropriate comments. "My good God, Luis," said Hackett, "if you hadn't just happened to have taken that thing back there— That girl! And what Bainbridge said—it wouldn't have needed much strength—"

"*Exactamente.* And just accidental that the body was hidden so well, until the quake— At least we know, if unexpectedly." Mendoza went up to Juvenile to talk it over with somebody there, dispatch the policewomen.

Galeano still hadn't reached Clarence Smith. The A.P.B. hadn't turned up Montoya.

Mendoza came back to the office at four-thirty, and Lake said, "The Alameda jail's been after you. And a Dr. Windrow."

"*¿Cómo?* So get me the jail." Presently he was talking to a chief warden who told him he was damned sorry to have to tell him, but they'd lost a prisoner. "What?" said Mendoza. "Who?"

"Well, you'd better talk to the doctor. You're going to say it was careless, and I guess it was, but— That Purdy. He was found dead in his cell about two hours ago."

"*¡Caray!* Of what?"

"Well, I'll put you through to the doctor."

Dr. Windrow said promptly, "Digitalin poisoning."

"Don't tell me you've already performed an autopsy."

"Hardly," said Windrow dryly. "I recognized the one tablet left."

"Are you telling me he smuggled in— *¡Imposible!* His pockets were gone through, he hadn't a chance—I was watching him, I booked him in myself—"

Windrow chuckled. "He must have been a wily old bird. They didn't issue him jail clothes until this morning, which gave him time to fish all the tablets out of the cuff of his pants. Old-fashioned suit with turnup cuffs, you know. He missed just one. Must have been nearly a full bottle—plenty to do the trick."

"I will be damned!" said Mendoza. He remembered Purdy fumbling in the closet for his shoes—maybe just chance he had the bottle on him, or had he planned ahead in case the worst happened? They'd never know now. But Ronald Purdy had at least had the courage of his convictions. More power to him. Sit back and wait for his prognostication of doom to come true.

At ten o'clock on Monday morning Galeano finally got Lorenzo Smith to answer his phone, and talked to Clarence Smith. From a hundred and fifty miles away he could feel the shock and grief and remorse through the line.

"Sir," said Clarence Smith, "I never knew the boy'd ever been in trouble. Cora never told me. Just, he wanted to come over here to work. If I'd known anything about that—I thought just the world and all of Mrs. Woods."

"Do you know where Frame moved to?" They had just got the make on the Arizona plates.

"He told me he got a job at the Goodyear plant. I helped him move his gear—it's a place in Compton, Palmer Street. If I'd known—"

At one o'clock on Monday, instead of going back to the office after lunch, Mendoza headed for Burbank and the house of happy people. It was his intention, if Alison was still there skipping around the piles of lumber and loose tiles, to send her firmly home. But Hardpenny told him she was gone. She *had* been there, he said— "And looking just fine too, I might say—but all of a sudden she remembered she wanted some piece of statuary for that forecourt, and off she went in that sports car of hers."

"*¡Caray!*" said Mendoza.

"And Mr. Kearney's here somewhere. We got all the new grilles and balconies on, and them fence people finally came back—they're on the other edge of the hill just starting to dig postholes. Here!" shouted Hardpenny suddenly. "What are you doing here? This is private property—"

A large pickup truck was bumping up the rough path. Out of it there came a man Mendoza recognized instantly. He'd never seen him before, but Alison had sketched him in a few words. He was a short stocky man with bulging muscles and shy brown eyes.

He said simply, "I have the lady's gates. The gates for the happy house."

"But she said it'd take months—"

"Oh, *señor,* the lady was very anyious to have the gates. She is a very gracious, lovely lady, I wished to oblige her. I work day and night. She has said the house is so old, Spanish times, historical? I am proud to have made the gates. Could I perhaps see the house?"

Mendoza burst out laughing. "Oh, by all means! I am the lady's husband—for all the sins on my head— and she will be pleased about the gates."

"*Bien,*" said Ricardo Rodriguez. "Now you must see the gates. They are good work." He insisted on hauling them out of the truck at once, and they were indeed fine ironwork, intricately scrolled, the name of the house spelled out in a border at the top. "I am pleased that you are pleased," said Rodriguez formally.

He trotted away to look at the house as Hardpenny was asking where in hell he was going to store these things until the locks were on, they'd be damn valuable. Ken Kearney came strolling over the hilltop and greeted Mendoza warmly. Kearney was a nice fellow, and Mendoza liked his plump robin of a wife, Kate, too. But before he knew it, he reflected, he'd be presiding over a feudal household of retainers.

"I've been thinking, Lieutenant," said Kearney. "Your wife says, leave a lot of that hill, wild, natural—just some landscaping up near the house. Well, that sounds all right, but in this climate you're going to get nothing but a lot of unsightly weeds coming up all down the hill there to the gate. And you know, a pretty good answer would be some sheep."

"Sheep!" said Mendoza.

"That's right. I went in for sheep some, first had my own spread. Nice critters and not much trouble. Shear 'em once a year, feed 'em a bit off season, get some permanent pasture seeded, couple of acres down there, and you'd have a pretty sight all year round. Like a big lawn, and the sheep'll keep it mowed down even. Say four–five head of Suffolks."

"Sheep, *por Dios*," said Mendoza. That girl—a household of humans *and* animals. And there was also the Kearneys' black cat Nicodemus, and how he and El Señor were going to share even four and a half acres—

When he got back to the office Hackett and Galeano had just picked up Joe Frame and were starting to question him. He was a decent-looking young fellow, and nobody who didn't know his record would hesitate to open a door to him; he was neat and clean, short-haired.

"I never done anything like that," he said.

"Oh, come on," said Hackett. "Let's not waste time, Joe. Your prints were all over that knife."

"They were?" said Frame, surprised. "Oh. That's a real bummer. I sure never thought about that. I just haven't had no luck in California at all." He said it sadly. "Everything goin' wrong since I come over here. I got that job, but what's it pay—lowest minimum, and the boss yellin' at me so I yell back an' get fired. And I needed some bread to get started again, I thought that old lady might have a wad, owning the house and all, but there was only twelve bucks in her purse." He was aggrieved at fate.

"Get started again at what?" asked Hackett.

"Well, hell," said Frame reasonably. "I didn't have a gun. I needed bread to get a gun so I could pull some heists for real money, see."

Galeano was pretty familiar with the menu of the place where Marta Fleming worked, now. It was all right—as a bachelor he wasn't fussy about food. Tonight was one of her split shifts, she'd been off in the afternoon. Tomorrow night was one of her school nights; she was taking typing and shorthand, hoping to get a better job. Galeano hoped she wouldn't have to.

He smiled at her, Marta pretty and feminine even with her tawny-blonde hair in a severe net, and said, "You can bring me the T-bone. Well. And a baked potato with sour cream."

"But no," said Marta. "It is too many calories, Nick. You must keep—" she smiled at him—"nice and thin to chase the crooks. Your mother and I agree that you must lose at least fifteen pounds."

"Listen, I've got to keep up my strength, you know. A steak—"

"The beef stroganoff is quite good. Over rice. And a nice salad with oil only."

"Oh, all right," said Galeano.

He thought it would be all right. The way she was starting to boss him—in the little things. But she was pretty conventional. Her husband had been dead for seven months; he guessed he'd have to be patient that conventional year. But he hoped in the end it would be all right—though why she'd want to take on an unromantic cop ten years too old for her—

She came back with his salad and asked him, "Did you attend mass yesterday?"

He supposed she'd prod him back to church again too. Well, it probably wouldn't do any harm.

Mendoza got home a little late. He kissed Alison,

199

duly admired the efforts of the twins at their newest coloring books, and left them in Terry's room squabbling happily over what they were going to name the ponies. Ponies! he thought. He'd forgotten the ponies momentarily. He wandered out to the kitchen where Máiri was sliding a batch of scones into the oven, and opened the cupboard to get down the bottle of rye. El Señor was equipped with a dark ESP of his own, and immediately appeared at the back door, rattling the screen to be let in for his share. Mendoza poured it for him—"That cat!" said Máiri—and carried his rye down to the living room, where Bast, Nefertite and Sheba drowsed in a feline pile on the sectional and Alison was unaccountably absent.

He swallowed the rye absently. Cedric came in, leaving large muddy footprints on the carpet; he'd been in the wading pool again, and Máiri would have a fit.

Alison came in with the baby. "We've decided," she said, "that the time has come to break a piece of news to you about the latest addition to the family."

Mendoza regarded her with vague, growing alarm; her tone was solemn. "What? Is there something wrong with her?"

"Well," said Alison, "not from my point of view exactly. But her hair's started to come in—it's funny, how it started at the back—" She handed Luisa Mary to him, bundled in blankets. "And I'm afraid, you know—" Mendoza began to laugh—"yes, it's even redder than mine."

"¡Por el amor de Dios!" said Mendoza. "Wasn't I just thinking it again today—the things you get me into, mi corazón! One thing after another—es el colmo!" Luisa Mary cooed at him. "Lo que no se puede remediar, se ha de aguantar—that which can't be cured must be endured."

And then he thought about those ponies, and then the sheep, and he shut his eyes and said, "Por Dios—one thing after another, say it twice. I think I need another drink."

ABOUT THE AUTHOR

DELL SHANNON is the author of over thirty books including *Felony File, Streets of Death, Appearances of Death*
and *Felony at Random*. Meticulous in her research of the
Los Angeles Police Department, she has a firsthand
knowledge of police procedures and criminal laboratory
techniques. This acounts in large part for the vivid
realism and strong characterizations in the Lieutenant
Mendoza mystery series. Dell Shannon lives in Southern
California with a menagerie that includes several cats,
two sheep and a dog.

MEET THREE TOP-NOTCH MISTRESSES OF MYSTERY

They all write under pseudonyms. They all have created favorite detective characters. They all are highly praised for their spellbinding novels of murder and detection. Catherine Aird (British, born Kinn Hamilton McIntosh); Dell Shannon (American, born Elizabeth Linington, also writing as Lesley Egan and Anne Blaisdell); and Patricia Wentworth (British, known as Dora Amy Elles Dillon Turnbull).

CATHERINE AIRD
Ms. Aird, whose novels are now being introduced in paperback for the first time, began writing in 1966 with THE RELIGIOUS BODY (to be published in July). Other books include THE STATELY HOME MURDER (July), and HIS BURIAL TOO (Oct.). All feature CID Inspector Sloan. *The New Yorker* calls Ms. Aird, "a shining new star . . . a most ingenious lady."

DELL SHANNON
Under the Dell Shannon name her more than forty books feature Detective Lieutenant Luis Mendoza of the Los Angeles Police Department, who himself has gained thousands of fans interested in his fictional private life. He appears in STREETS OF DEATH (July), FELONY AT RANDOM (July), and APPEARANCES OF DEATH (Nov.). Ms. Shannon-Linington-Egan-Blaisdell has been called the "Queen of Procedurals."

PATRICIA WENTWORTH
The late Ms. Wentworth is best known for her series of thirty-two novels featuring private enquiry agent Maud Silver, a stubborn spinster who has great English common sense and an iron will to succeed. Ms. Wentworth has received critical acclaim for THE FINGERPRINT (July), THE LISTENING EYE (July) and POISON IN THE PEN (Sept.).